Love Finds You

North Pole
in

ALASKA

Love Finds You

in North Pole

ALASKA

BY LOREE LOUGH

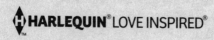

H HARLEQUIN® LOVE INSPIRED®

 LOVE INSPIRED BOOKS

Recycling programs
for this product may
not exist in your area.

ISBN-13: 978-0-373-78789-0

LOVE FINDS YOU IN NORTH POLE, ALASKA

Love Inspired Books/October 2013

First Published by Summerside Press, Inc.

Copyright © 2009 by Loree Lough

Back cover photo and interior photos of North Pole, Alaska, taken by Kevin McCarthy, www.northpolegallery.com.

Cover and interior design by Müllerhaus Publishing Group, www.mullerhaus.net.

Scripture references are from the Holy Bible, King James Version (KJV).

www.Harlequin.com

Printed in U.S.A.

Dedication

To Larry, my knight in shining armor,
and my daughters, grandkids, and sons-in-law,
for it's their love and joy that feeds my muse.
To everyone at Summerside for adopting me
into their publishing family. Heartfelt thanks
to Kevin McCarthy, talented photographer and
mayor of North Pole, and Paul Brown, manager
of the Santa Claus House, for their advice
and guidance. To every man and woman in
uniform who, like the hero in this story, makes
daily sacrifices that give my readers and me the
freedom to choose any book on the shelves.
Most importantly, to the Lord my God, whose
steady guidance enabled me to craft a story that
promises a few laughs, some cleansing tears,
and the knowledge that every reader—like the
characters who live within these pages—can find
shelter from life's storms in His loving arms.

In April 1944, Bon and Bernice Davis rented a car in Fairbanks and headed south in search of a homestead. Upon spying an abandoned section of the original Richardson Trail, they parked and hiked until the wild vista stopped them. Breathless, they drank in the beauty of towering blue spruce and squatty scrub tree forests, home to moose, deer, wolves, fox, and snowshoe rabbits. Bald eagles screeched overhead, and in the bubbling streams, grayling and beaver thrived. It was decided: "This is it!" Locals claim the region's frigid winter temperatures—typically ten degrees colder than the rest of the Interior—inspired folks to say, "It's as cold as the North Pole!" And in January 1953, the cognomen became the town's official name. Known as the town "Where the Spirit of Christmas Lives Year Round," North Pole's friendly residents annually welcome thousands of visitors from around the world who come to see its candy-cane-striped lampposts and fire hydrants, colorful lights, street names like Donner Drive and Santa Claus Lane, and holiday-themed shops. North Pole is home to the Santa Claus House (where letters from Santa himself are mailed from the post office), a Christmas museum, and breathtaking displays of aurora borealis. Does another town exist where, despite occasional shoulder-deep snow, you can encounter some of the warmest-hearted people on the planet? Only one, I think: North Pole, Alaska.

Loree Lough

Chapter One

Curt gave the ancient chair a half-spin and then held it steady as Bryce dropped onto its well-worn leather seat.

"Don't tell me," the barber said, flapping a white cape in the air. "Just a little off the top. And the back. And the sides."

Bryce jammed both forefingers under the cape's collar, the only foolproof way to ensure his Adam's apple would still function after Curt snugged it up. "Good to know you remember that I like it high and tight," he said, chuckling.

"And I wish *you'd* remember that I don't speak 'marine.'"

"Short," Bryce explained. "It means I like it short."

"Short? Short is what *my* hair is!" Whistling through his teeth, Curt added, "Yours borders on *bald.*" His smile faded as he shook his white-haired head. "So how long do you have to wear that thing?" he asked, pointing dagger-sharp scissors at the ex-soldier's black eye patch.

Bryce's uncovered eye widened with feigned shock. "Whoa," he said, hands up in mock surrender, "you tryin' to poke out my *good* eye with that thing?"

"That'll be the day. Why, I've been…"

"…cutting hair my whole adult life," Bryce recited, finishing the quote that, as a kid, he'd heard dozens of times. "So how many years *has* it been, anyway?"

Curt traded the scissors for an electric razor. "Forty, come July." Holding a narrow, slant-toothed comb near its teeth, he shaved a quarter inch from Bryce's already short hair. "You were in here for a trim less than a week ago," he said over the tool's drone. "I won't even need to sweep up when I'm done."

Even Bryce knew his attention to detail sometimes bordered on the obsessive, but he explained it away by quoting one of his favorite mottos. *"Good enough never is."*

"Far be it for me to argue," Curt said as minuscule hair bits floated onto Bryce's shoulders. "But four bucks for this? Y'make me feel like a snake oil salesman."

"That'll be the day," Bryce said, echoing Curt. If only his elderly friend's jokes could block the tune wafting from a boom box near the cash register. Mel Tormé's dulcet tones should've made it easier to bear "The Christmas Song." But it didn't. Because Bryce had only just turned over the June page on his calendar!

Bryce loved the majestic vistas and small-town atmosphere of his birthplace. Loved the hale-and-hearty people who called North Pole, Alaska, "home." What he didn't love was that, in addition to their ambition to improve what could easily have remained a barren wasteland and turn it into a thriving tourist attraction, they'd turned what should be a holy, pious day into a commercial year-round free-for-all.

He'd hoped going away to college would dull the

keen edge of his distaste. But it hadn't. Ten years with the Marine Corps, including four grueling tours of duty in war-torn Afghanistan, hadn't, either. If not for his injury—and the fact that Aunt Olive had decided to become a snowbird—he'd have signed up for a fifth go-round. So here he was, back in what the travel brochures called the city "Where the Spirit of Christmas Lives Year Round," feeling more like Scrooge than gnarly old Ebenezer himself.

It amazed Bryce that none of the town's residents shared his attitude, considering how every shop and storefront glittered with multi-colored lights. Weren't they tired of looking at fire hydrants and lampposts painted to look like candy canes? Tired of watching mechanical snowmen and elves—some wood, some painted plastic—as they waved to passersby *all year long*? And that infernal holiday music, blaring from well-positioned speakers, made him long to hear a good old-fashioned ballad, an upbeat hoe-down, *anything* that wasn't—

"Any idea when you can shed that thing?" Curt asked again.

Bryce shrugged, remembering that the original purpose of his eye patch had been to help keep the wound clean and dry. Now, its primary function was to hide the ropelike scar snaking from his right eyebrow to his cheek. The first time he'd gone without it, a child seated in front of him on a plane had shrieked, "Mommy, Mommy…it's the Bogey Man!" The mother's *shame on you for terrifying a child*! glare prompted him to replace the patch, and he hadn't taken it off in public since.

Until the week before last, when he'd worked up a sweat hot-footing it through the Fairbanks airport. From out of nowhere, a pint-sized kid of six or seven had tugged at Bryce's sleeve, then hiked up his own pants leg. "Got *my* scar falling through a plate glass door," he'd boasted. "Wish it was on my face, like yours. *That* would keep those girls and their cooties away, for sure!"

Bryce frowned at the memory as Curt asked for permission to peek under the patch, his white-bearded face reminding Bryce of the forty-two-foot Santa that welcomed visitors to North Pole. He might've obliged his old friend—if a mother hadn't chosen that moment to enter the barber shop, leading two small boys by the hand.

"Maybe some other time," he said, nodding toward the door.

Curt followed his line of vision and gave a "gotcha" nod. "And when you do, maybe you can tell me how it happened. You've never said…."

With good reason, Bryce thought as his mind flashed on the rugged Afghan terrain, with its narrow rutted roads and mere handful of scrubby shrubs dotting the bomb-pocked landscape. Ordinarily, a captain like himself wouldn't have led a small band of men on patrol. But that day, with his lieutenant out of commission, he'd taken up the gauntlet, determined to locate and detonate land mines hidden in the gritty soil in preparation for the arrival of new troops. One cautious boot step at a time, he'd picked his way around rocks and debris, cautioning the soldiers to follow in his footsteps. Sadly, one had lost his balance and—

"Look, Mommy," shouted the youngest boy, "a pirate!" And pointing at Bryce's eye patch, he narrowed his own eyes and asked, "Are you a *real* pirate?"

His brother, who outranked him by a year or two, groaned and rolled his eyes. "Of course he isn't, dopey. There's no such thing as real pirates." Chin up and shoulders back, the older boy ignored the whining protests his comment inspired and plopped onto one of six red chairs against the mirrored wall. "You should get some *Ranger Rick*s in here, Curt," he said, leafing through a tattered issue of *Newsweek*. "'Cause these things you call magazines are *borrr-ing*."

Curt opened his mouth to respond, but the kid was a beat faster. "So, what happened to your eye, mister?"

Grinning, Bryce was tempted to say it had been poked out when, as a boy, he had asked one too many questions. As he tried to conjure a story that would satisfy a curious youngster, Curt said, "Son, I'll have you know this man's a war hero. He got that fighting for the good old U.S. of A."

"Steven," came the mother's harsh whisper, "mind your own business, please."

Bryce loved kids and had once prayed to have a house full of his own. But that was before shrapnel had turned him into a weird rendition of Al Pacino's *Scarface*. Odd, he thought, that he'd braved a thousand battle horrors without flinching, yet the inquisitive stares of two young boys set his teeth on edge.

Suddenly, he wanted out of the barber chair. Out of the shop. Out of North Pole and away from *Christmas*. "You finished?" he asked Curt.

"Yeah…not so a body could notice." He pointed at

the tiny bits of hair scattered on the white tiles. "See? Won't even need my broom."

Standing, Bryce peeled off the cape and reached for his wallet.

But the barber held up a hand to stall him. "No, no...put that away. I'd feel guilty, charging full price," he said, pointing at the floor again, "especially from a war hero. Give me two bucks, and we'll call it a day."

Bryce handed him a five, headed for the door, and, with a quick wave over his shoulder, stepped into the bright late-June sunshine. Slapping his Baltimore Orioles' cap onto his head, he thought of the unexpected turns his life had taken. He'd turned thirty-two in a barracks overseas, surrounded by his men—all married with children, except for the very youngest recruits. Oh, how he'd envied the guys with families! Back in college, he'd mapped out his life. "The Plan" had him married by twenty-seven, a dad by thirty. He could almost hear his aunt Olive saying, "Tough to become a husband and father when you're off fighting in foreign countries year after year...."

He glanced up and down Mistletoe Drive, where tour buses and RVs lined the curb. Even in his present mood, Bryce couldn't help but smile at the joyous laughter of children, harmonizing with Brenda Lee's rendition of "Jingle Bell Rock" emanating from the loudspeakers. He took a deep breath of clean Alaska air and shook his head, thinking of the To Do list he'd scribbled that morning. Except for "haircut," not a single item had been checked off. But since it wouldn't turn dark for nearly nineteen hours yet, he'd have more than enough daylight to get everything done.

Shoving both hands into the front pocket of his sweatshirt, he hiked toward Snowman Lane. Despite the bright day, the air held a dry chill, making him wish he'd grabbed a jacket before leaving his apartment above Rudolph's.

His parents' shop came into view, and it was more than enough to raise his hackles. His dad had tinkered and fiddled with the hideous two-story white structure until it became a flat-faced replica of Santa's sleigh, and above the door stood the biggest, ugliest reindeer ever crafted from wood and metal. The deer grinned stupidly around a thick chain that supported a crimson sign, where softball-sized lightbulbs spelled out Rudolph's Christmas Emporium. As if all that wasn't high enough on the tacky scale, Rudolph's nose—a gigantic, red-glowing ball—blinked to the beat of whatever tune blared from the store's speakers.

Today, "Jingle Bells" twittered from above, and Bryce gritted his teeth as he yanked open the shiny green door, upsetting a dozen strands of tinkling gold bells hanging from the doorknob.

"Well, looky what the wind blew in."

Bryce's face softened. "'Mornin'," he answered. His mood had brightened instantly, because as much as he hated Christmas, he loved his aunt Olive ten times more.

"I thought you were gonna get a haircut," she teased when he whipped off his cap.

Running a hand along the short, flat surface of his hairdo, Bryce laughed. "I did!"

Olive harrumphed and went back to labeling snow globes covering the glass-and-stainless counter. "Coulda fooled me."

Since his parents' tragic deaths, Aunt Olive had been his only family. But if the truth be told, she'd filled that role long before they died. As he'd winged his way from the Afghan village where he'd been stationed, it had been Olive who'd arranged the memorial service, and by the time he arrived in North Pole, she'd put in her resignation at the elementary school. "I need a change," she'd said when the last of the mourners left the church basement. "Soon as you head back overseas, I'll manage Rudolph's. By the time you retire, I'll have the place running like a top...and paying for itself." As his parents' only child, Bryce had inherited the shop—along with a hefty mortgage and a stack of unpaid bills. He knew Olive had done her level best to keep that promise. It wasn't her fault that a dozen other stores in North Pole sold similar merchandise.

Bryce leaned on the counter and covered her hands with his. "Wish I could change your mind about retiring."

Olive winked. "If wishes were fishes..."

"I'll be lost without you," he said, meaning it.

"Pish posh," she said and, waving his admission away, began counting on her fingers. "You've jumped out of airplanes into enemy territory, slept in foxholes, gotten shot at, dodged land mines—except for *one*—and escaped from a POW camp, yet dealing with a few Christmas shoppers scares you?" She laughed. "You're *weird*, nephew!"

"Well, when you put it that way..." Bryce shrugged. "Besides, I suppose it is time you did something for Olive for a change." To his knowledge, her plan for an extended vacation in sunny Florida marked the second thing she'd ever done for herself. Decades of caring for her aging parents had freed her brother to play shop-keeper. It didn't seem to matter to anybody, least of all Bryce's dad, that he was a horrible businessman. Bryce often wondered if his parents even realized that Olive's "do the right thing" mind-set had required her to sacrifice any hope of having a life of her own.

"I couldn't agree more," she said, slapping a price label onto another snow globe. Setting it aside, Olive began humming along with Bing Crosby as he crooned the words to "White Christmas."

Bryce wondered how she'd react when he confessed that he'd been talking to a real estate agent with ties to a national chain about selling the place. And that once it sold, he'd use the proceeds to turn his lifelong dream of opening a carpentry shop into reality. His dad hadn't left him a dime, but he did leave a few decent tools. If they hadn't rusted from lack of use and storage in the cold, damp garage, Bryce might just get a jump-start on crafting sample pieces that would show buyers what he was capable of. Over the years, during weeklong furloughs, he'd designed and built an armoire, a rolltop desk, a dresser, and a kids' rocking chair. But he'd need more than that if he hoped to eke out a modest living from the trade…especially in a town where *Christmas* was the main draw.

"All right," Olive said, one fist propped on a chubby hip, "out with it."

He felt the eye patch rise as his brow rose. "Out with what?"

"Oh, don't give me that. I taught school too long

not to recognize when somebody's got something up his sleeve."

Chuckling, he met her dark eyes. "Never could fool you, could I?"

"Main question I've always had is…why do you even *try*?"

She had a good point. So why not just spit it out? Might ease her mind, knowing that while she sunned herself on warm sandy beaches, he'd be happy, doing what he'd always wanted to do. Elbows between two snow globes on the counter, Bryce spelled out his plan, then held his breath and waited for her reaction.

"Honey," she said, patting his cheek, "that's the best idea you've had since…well, it's your best idea yet." She walked around the counter and threw her arms around his neck. "Now I won't have to worry about you while I'm dipping my toes in the warm blue waters of the Atlantic. And let me tell you, I am *so* ready for that!"

A nice picture, he acknowledged…for Olive. But he bit back the sadness roused by mere thoughts of her leaving.

"Of course, with me gone, you're gonna need to hire somebody to run the store…until it sells."

Bryce heard the unspoken warning in her gravelly voice. The North Pole real estate business hadn't exactly been brisk. The fact was, Olive probably made more selling snow globes than anyone in town had earned selling property.

"I've been trying to find help for nearly three months. Hope you'll have better luck than I did."

"Me, too, 'cause the idea of sitting inside all day, every day, makes my hair stand on end."

"What hair?" she teased.

Bryce laughed, savoring the bittersweet moment. He sure was going to miss her! "Maybe while you're in Florida, you can get work in one of the beachfront comedy clubs."

She ignored his feeble attempt at humor. "I know you've never been the 'stay indoors' type, but it might be good to try it on for size. Maybe it'll knock that chip off your shoulder."

"Chip? What chip?"

"Oh, please." Olive began moving snow globes from the counter to a shelf along the side wall. "You haven't been yourself since you walked through that door a couple weeks ago, wearing that patch and a Captain Hook attitude." She shook her head. "I know it hasn't been easy, dealing with the fact that you'll never see out of that eye again, but even *you* have to admit, things could have turned out worse."

Lots worse, he admitted, remembering all the soldiers who had fallen while defending their country. And some of those who'd made it home would spend the rest of their lives in wheelchairs or struggling to adjust to prostheses that replaced lost limbs. Bryce felt the heat of shame creep into his cheeks. "I didn't realize I was behaving like…I never meant…" Had his demeanor really made others think he felt sorry for himself? Bryce sure hoped not. "It isn't the blindness that bothers me," he said dully.

Olive turned, a snow globe in each hand. "Oh? Then what?"

How could he admit how much he disliked being back here, where every man, woman, and child—

whether born in North Pole or visiting by choice—*loved* the town where it was Christmas, twenty-four-seven, three-sixty-five? He didn't bother voicing his hearty objection to the sell-sell-sell attitude surrounding the day on which the Lord was born, because on a practical level, even he had to admit how much the whole Christmas thing had pumped up North Pole's economy. Besides, his attitude toward God and religion had taken a big hit during the past few years, so it seemed hypocritical, even to him, to use the over-commercialization of a holy day as his excuse.

Bryce took a deep breath and decided to follow her example of doing the right thing, simply because it needed to be done. "So, what can I do to help?" Might as well dive in headfirst. He'd been home nearly two weeks and hadn't done a real lick of work to help her out. If he hoped to sell the place and make a profit, he'd better learn the ropes while she was still around to teach him, because the lessons he'd learned as a kid, working beside his parents, had long ago retreated to the dark recesses of his memory.

On the heels of a muffled yawn, she said, "A shipment arrived this morning, and I haven't had a chance to unpack it."

He paid little attention to the dark circles under her eyes. His aunt often spent all-nighters reading novels by her favorite authors. He'd tried the "Even a powerhouse like you needs a good night's sleep" speech, but since it had always fallen on deaf ears, Bryce didn't bother now. Instead, he stood at attention and snapped off a smart salute. "Captain Stone, reporting for duty, ma'am!"

Olive snickered. "There's the clipboard," she said,

nodding toward a peg on the wall, "and a pen. Now get crackin', soldier!"

He hung his baseball cap on the hook behind the door as she added, "And when you're finished with that, get busy writing a want ad." Almost as an afterthought, she tacked on, "'Cause I'm leavin' next week whether you have help or not. Got it?"

"If anybody answers it, will you do the interviews?"

Olive harrumphed. "'If,' the biggest little word in the English language."

As Bryce headed for the back room, he envisioned the first line of the ad: Wanted: Part-Time Manager. *Just don't send me a* woman, *Lord*, he prayed, because of all the things Bryce didn't need right now, yet another heartache topped the list.

Chapter Two

Squinting, Sam adjusted the visor to cut the sun's glare. If only her rowdy brothers could see her now, steering a twenty-five-foot RV down a major highway with the skill of a professional semi driver.

They'd given her a hard time on Easter Sunday, when the family had gathered at her parents' house for dinner. Scott, the eldest, had dropped his fork when she announced her plans.

"Are you crazy?" he'd asked. Then right on down the table it went, with Seth, Shane, Steve, Spence, and Stu nodding like a row of bobbleheads. Only her youngest brother—named Bill when her mom had run out of S names—had given Sam a thumbs-up.

"Dad," Scott had implored, "talk some sense into her!"

"Don't look at me," the family patriarch had said. "She's more stubborn than your mother. When she makes up her mind to do something…"

Sam had read all about the candy-cane-striped lampposts and fire hydrants that decorated North Pole, but seeing them in person as she rolled into town nearly took her breath away. An excited giggle escaped her throat as she slowed to gaze at the gigantic Santa statue. In Sam's mind, this was the perfect place to settle down.

From the day in second grade art class when she'd created her very first Nativity card, Sam had always felt an intense passion for Christmas. It had been Sam who'd roused the Sinclair family's holiday spirit every year by decorating the house. She'd have started the day school began in August, if her mom would have allowed it, but she curbed her enthusiasm by beginning on Thanksgiving night. By the time she'd turned twelve, her dad had put the brakes on the ornaments and garlands Sam bought with her babysitting money.

"You've filled every nook and cranny in the house with doodads and knickknacks," he'd told her. "If this keeps up, we'll become known as 'That Crazy Christmas Family'!"

When she got a place of her own, Sam quickly filled the basement of her town house with snowflake-decorated boxes of Christmas adornments. Selling them to make the move to Alaska had been one of the hardest things she'd ever done.

The whole mess surrounding her move faded from memory as she drank in the sights. She'd have more than enough time to muse about it once she settled in at her new job.

Thoughts of running her own kitchen energized her despite the dozen hours she'd spent behind the wheel. She had worked long and hard, earning her bachelor's degree in culinary arts, and growing up the only girl among seven siblings had helped her develop traits her classmates envied, such as leadership skills and a natural ability to make and maintain peace.

Two years as the assistant chef at a popular Baltimore eatery whetted her appetite for bigger, better things, and after much thought and prayer, Sam began a serious search for a kitchen of her own. When she found nothing in the area to suit her background or her dreams, she paid a visit to church and fired a heartfelt plea heavenward, asking God to lead her to the place and the work He thought best fit His plans for her life.

As it turned out, the Lord made His will known in the dentist's office, as Sam watched a home and garden show on the fuzzy screen of the TV affixed to the reception room's ceiling. When the program featured an annual ice sculpture festival in North Pole, Alaska, it was all she could do to tear her eyes from the glittering pictures when the hygienist called her name. Then, while waiting for the doctor to give his final approval to her newly shined molars and bicuspids, Sam paged through a travel magazine and nearly squealed out loud when colorful photos of the town leapt from its center pages.

Sam couldn't wait to get home and type "North Pole, Alaska" into her computer's search engine. Item after item popped up, each making her more certain that God wanted her there. She didn't question *why* the Lord would invite a girl who'd never been a fan of cold weather to a place like this. But if He wanted her in North Pole, then her new motto would be "Alaska, here I come!"

And now, as she turned off the motor, the excitement that had been building during the long trip to her new home threatened to flag her as a wet-behind-the-ears youngster—the last image Sam wanted to project when meeting her boss for the first time! So she darted into the back end of the RV for a quick change of clothes and some fresh makeup, praying the entire time that Mr. Edmunds would recognize, as they talked, that she only *looked* younger than her twenty-six years. Grinning as she fluffed her curls, Sam told her reflection, "Doesn't matter what he thinks *today*, because tomorrow—and every day after that—you'll show him what you're capable of!"

Donning a beige suede blazer, Sam grabbed her purse and headed for the lobby, whistling "Zip-a-Dee-Doo-Dah" as she marched up to the counter. She was greeted by a freckle-faced young man who matched her smile, tooth for tooth. "Do you have a reservation, miss?"

"No, but I do have an appointment with Mr. Edmunds." She glanced at her watch. "Ten o'clock." And she was right on time.

As the boy left to announce her arrival, Sam gave the lobby a quick once-over. From where she stood, she could see the sandwich board inviting hotel guests, tourists, and North Pole residents into the Silver Bells Restaurant. No doubt Mr. Edmunds would give her a tour of the kitchen, to ensure that tomorrow, she'd be familiar with—

"Miss Sinclair, I presume?"

Sam spun around and met the bespectacled eyes of a tall, gray-haired gentleman. "And you must be Mr. Edmunds," she said, extending a hand.

After giving it a hearty shake, he invited her to sit in one of the wingback chairs near the huge stone fireplace. "Can I get you something to drink while we talk? Coffee? Tea? Hot chocolate?"

"No, I'm fine, thanks." Sam would much rather just get down to business, so that when she called her family later, there'd be plenty of good news to report.

"I don't quite know how to tell you this," Edmunds said as she took a seat. "There seems to have been a terrible misunderstanding." He rubbed his chin then adjusted his eyeglasses. And on the heels of a heavy sigh, he said, "I'm afraid the chef's position has been filled."

Sam's heart pounded. Surely he was mistaken. Or maybe she'd misunderstood. Or *he'd* misunderstood. Sam opened her purse and withdrew the letter he'd sent weeks ago to accompany their employment contract. Why, he'd even gone to the trouble of writing out directions to help her get from the Alaska border to North Pole!

He nodded sheepishly at the document in her trembling hands. "I…I'm terribly sorry, Miss Sinclair, but it seems my authority as manager here has been, shall we say, *usurped.*" A stern frown sketched a furrow between his eyebrows. "Dan Brooks, the hotel's owner, gave the job to his nephew."

"B-but…but I've come all the way from *Maryland* for this job!" She tapped the letter. "We…we have an agreement!"

Edmunds leaned forward, as if that alone could make up for what he was about to say. "No one feels worse about that than I do."

"I can think of one person who's sorrier," she muttered. Then brightening, Sam sat up straighter. "Surely if we remind Mr. Brooks that you wrote this letter as his representative..."

Again, Edmunds' pained expression silenced her. So Sam shook the letter. "I can't believe a successful businessman such as Mr. Brooks would think his nepotism outranks a written commitment. I'm all for people helping family members, but..."

The expression on Edmunds' face silenced her and told Sam what words needn't: "Dan Brooks is a powerful and stubborn man. Once he's made up his mind..." A one-shouldered shrug punctuated his statement.

Ordinarily, Sam was calm and even-tempered. Everybody said so. But these were hardly ordinary circumstances. "I considered this a binding contract, Mr. Edmunds. I took you at your written word, sold my town house—and everything in it—gave up my car, spent weeks on the road making my way here in time for this meeting." Suddenly, she was on her feet, pacing the plush carpeting between her chair and his. "This is highly unprofessional and...and dishonest!" she steamed. "And if you don't mind my saying so, it's downright *mean*, to boot!"

"You'll get no argument from me, Miss Sinclair. Jobs here are hard to come by. Still, I hope you'll understand when I say my hands are tied."

For a reason she couldn't explain, the adage "You can catch more flies with honey than with vinegar" popped into Sam's head, followed quickly by "Never burn your bridges." Maybe God was trying to tell her that, somewhere down the road, Mr. Edmunds—or even Mr. Brooks—could help her secure other employment in North Pole. And she would do her level best to get a job here and make things work out. Because the idea of calling her parents and brothers, telling them she'd fallen flat on her face, *on the very day she arrived...*

Sam shivered involuntarily at the thought and squared her shoulders. "Mr. Edmunds, do you see that RV in the parking lot?"

He followed her gaze then nodded.

"That'll have to be my home until I can find another job." *Flies and honey*, she reminded herself, and sweetened her tone. "So, is it all right if I run an extension cord to an exterior outlet, just until I get on my feet?"

On his own feet now, he grabbed her hands. "So, you intend to stay in North Pole?"

Lifting her chin, Sam crossed her arms over her chest. "Yes, sir. I most certainly do."

He drove a hand through his hair. "Well then, of *course* it's all right! Anything I can do to make you more comfortable, just say the word."

She considered asking him if he knew a good lawyer in town but shot him a half grin instead. "Maybe you can vouch for me if I need a personal reference."

"But of *course* I will!" He turned her hands loose as the freckle-faced kid signaled to him. Reaching into his suit coat pocket, Edmunds withdrew a dinner coupon and scribbled something on the back. "This will entitle you to free meals for as long as you need them." Pressing it into her hand, he added, "And if anyone in the restaurant questions you, send them to *me*."

Oh, right, Sam thought, *send them to the guy with no power*. Besides, why would she want to eat in the place where the new chef was eighteen, if that? "Thanks," she said as the threat of tears prickled behind her eyelids.

Before they could spill down her cheeks, she headed for the door, wondering how in the world she could have misread God's signals so badly.

"Miss Sinclair," called Edmunds, "wait, please…"

She held her breath and willed the tears to subside as he caught up with her.

The hotel manager handed her a copy of *The North Pole Daily Star*. "Perhaps you'll find something to your liking in the want ads."

Sam murmured a less than enthusiastic "Thanks" and tucked it under her arm before shoving through the big glass doors. *Please, Lord*, she prayed, *just let me make it to the RV before the waterworks start.*

Bryce paced the well-worn hardwood floor at Rudolph's, hoping a qualified assistant would soon materialize. Because if he had to spend one more ten-hour day cooped up in this cramped, cluttered gift shop, frustration might just drive him out the door, where he'd bellow like a wounded bull moose. And in a town like North Pole, that just might invite trouble…of the four-hoofed kind.

He'd placed the want ad in the paper just as Olive had suggested. So far, his poor aunt had suffered through four dead-end interviews. The first was a housewife who spoke so softly, Olive found herself nodding even though he couldn't make out a word the woman said. And while the arthritic man with the cane spoke more than loudly enough, Olive admitted it wasn't likely the poor fellow had the stamina to last even one hour, let alone six hours, five days a week.

The high school kid who showed up fifteen minutes late for the scheduled appointment showed some promise, and Olive said she might just have hired him… if his mom hadn't tagged along and recited her son's long list of extracurricular activities. Then Buster, the town drunk, came in to say, "I might-could squeeze in a couple-few hours a day…if the li'l woman approves." As it turned out, Olive hadn't needed to turn Buster down, because the little woman *didn't* approve.

By the end of the second week of interviews, Bryce gave some serious thought to boarding up the place and heading for Quantico. Last he heard, the Communications Specialist position the marines had dangled like a carrot was still available. Not his favorite option, but better than no options. Hard as it was to admit, working Rudolph's beat sitting in a windowless office eight hours a day. Still, if he could figure out how to cope with the confinement of a desk in a windowless Quantico office for a couple of months, maybe he could pull in a favor from his buddy the lieutenant general and snag a choice reassignment that didn't involve florescent lighting….

Bryce's email program pinged, announcing an incoming message. As he spun his desk chair around to face the computer, he prepared himself for yet another disappointing want ad response. Instead, he grinned at the brief letter of introduction.

Dear Mr. Stone, it began, *I have read with interest your listing in* The North Pole Daily Star *and would appreciate an opportunity to speak with you at your earliest convenience about the advertised management position. If, after reviewing my résumé (attached), you feel I'm qualified for the job, feel free to contact me at this email address to schedule an interview. I am avail-*

able to begin work immediately and look forward to hearing from you soon. And it was signed, *Sam Sinclair.*

"Hot dog!" Bryce exclaimed. He hastily pecked out a reply message inviting Sam to come in for an interview with Olive that very afternoon at three. If that was too last-minute, he typed, Sam could suggest a better time tomorrow. Hopefully, he thought as his forefinger mashed the Send button, good ol' Sam was still at his computer and would confirm the appointment. Soon.

"Hot dog!" he repeated when, a moment later, the machine alerted him to Sam's response: *I look forward to meeting with you today at three.* He printed out the attached pages, left a phone message for Olive that spelled out the details, and headed for his garage workshop. Though he hadn't read Sam's résumé, something told him the guy would be perfect for the job.

Bryce passed the time by checking every power tool on the shelves. Miraculously, none were beyond repair. A little sharpening here, a little sanding and oil there, and he could get down to the business of building one-of-a-kind furniture.

It wasn't easy, but he made a point of staying away from Rudolph's. At least until four o'clock. By then, Olive would have had more than enough time to review Sam Sinclair's résumé and finish up the interview. When he couldn't stand the suspense a minute longer, he tidied the workbench and headed for Rudolph's.

"So, how'd it go?" he asked, even before the shop's door banged closed behind him.

Wearing her usual happy grin, Olive winked. "You'll be happy to know we've got a brand-new full-time manager."

"Full-time? I though we advertised for part-time."

"Sam was able to work a full schedule, and I thought it best. Frees you up to spend as much time as possible in your shop."

"Starting when?"

"Eight tomorrow morning."

He heaved a deep sigh. "That's a relief. Thanks for handling the interview. It's been so long since I did any real work around here that I doubt I'd know what to tell—or ask—a job candidate."

"Well, you're not off the hook, nephew. Not by a long shot! You're the owner of this establishment, and that means *you're* the one who'll have to check on h—"

"No problem. At least you've spared me the monotony of being here all day, every day."

"You'll get your freedom *after* you've opened the shop tomorrow and spent the day giving Sam the nickel tour."

"No problem," he said again, because how long could that take? An hour? Two at most before he could return to the garage and start sketching the plans for the highboy he intended to make.

He popped a kiss to Olive's cheek. "Thanks, old girl. You're the best."

"Who're you callin' old?" she asked, feigning a frown.

Bryce headed up the stairs to his apartment, whistling the tune to "From the Halls of Montezuma." Something told him that tonight, he'd get the best night's sleep he'd had in ages.

Bryce woke half an hour before the alarm was set to chime, feeling refreshed and rested. Two cups of coffee and a bowl of cereal later, he decided to pass the time before Sam was scheduled to arrive by unpacking the shipment of Santa's elf ornaments that had been delivered yesterday. As soon as he gave the guy a quick tour of the place, he'd head for the hardware store to make a copy of the keys to the front and rear doors. And from Bryce's point of view, that couldn't happen fast enough.

Half an hour and four unpacked boxes later, as the clocks lining Rudolph's shelves chimed eight times in off-key succession, a young woman entered the shop. *Whoa, is she ever easy on the eye*, Bryce thought, watching as she shook the wind damage from her mass of ebony curls. He doubted she weighed a hundred pounds, even if she hopped onto the scale carrying that enormous leather purse. For a moment, he found himself picturing the tiny waist that was sure to go with her shapely legs. He watched her glance right, then left, and when she finally spotted him behind the counter, a smile lit up her face. "We're not officially open for another hour yet," he said. "Can I help you?"

When she moved closer, he marveled that she did it without sounding like a horse clip-clopping across the floor, despite the heels on her tiny red shoes.

Smiling, she glanced left and right then met his eyes. "What an absolutely adorable shop!"

The music of her voice sang into his ears like a gentle lullaby, and Bryce found himself hoping Sam Sinclair wouldn't show up on time for work. Because right now, all he wanted to do was find out more about this beauty who hadn't even seemed to notice his eye patch.

"I'm here to see Mr. Stone?"

Grinning stupidly, Bryce wondered how she knew

his name, but before he could phrase the question, she plopped her bag onto the counter with a loud *thud* and folded creamy white hands, one atop the other, over its handles.

"I'm Sam. Samantha Sinclair? Ms. Stone told me to meet her nephew here at eight...."

Chapter Three

Bryce didn't know how to feel. Part of him was furious with Olive for hiring a woman. If anybody knew how he felt about working so closely with a female, it should have been his aunt. Mostly, though, he was frustrated with himself, because if he'd taken time to open the attached résumé, as suggested in her cover letter, he might've known Sam was short for Samantha. But he'd been so eager to find somebody—anybody—to save him from working indoors that he hadn't bothered.

Having stammered his way through an awkward introduction, Bryce was now trying his best to be polite to the ridiculously youthful-looking girl as he explained what her duties would be. But after casting a few furtive glances her way, Bryce's appraisal confirmed his suspicions. Sam didn't look nearly strong enough to heft cartons and boxes of Christmas stuff, let alone unpack them for display on the shelves. Even if she *could* handle the physical demands of the job, how much energy would she have left to deal with customers, order merchandise, and balance the books?

If she could balance the books!

Olive had made her choice, and he had little choice but to respect that.

For now.

But the very first time this…this elflike creature messed up, he'd be on her like white on rice. And Olive would have to respect *that*.

"So, aren't you at all curious to know why someone with my background is interested in a job in sales?"

Bryce frowned as her voice—which he'd found so musical and appealing just minutes before—interrupted his thoughts. "Your background?"

She raised one eyebrow. "You didn't read my résumé?"

"Nope."

"Your aunt warned me you probably hadn't." Then, "I came to town to run Silver Bells. My degree is in culinary arts."

He watched as her smile faded, as her long-lashed eyes flashed with something akin to anger.

"Seems the owner decided to give the job to his *nephew*, despite the fact that his manager sent me a detailed letter confirming the job." She shook her head. "I take it Mr. Stubborn-and-Powerful has a lot of control here in North Pole?"

"Only in his own mind," Bryce said, picturing Dan Brooks, his rival for as long as he could remember. With Dan's reputation as a womanizer, it was clear the man hadn't interviewed Sam in person. One look at her, and no way he'd have given the job to his nephew. "How long did you say you'd been in town?"

"Day before yesterday. I can't tell you what a relief it was when you responded to my email so quickly."

Sam rolled her eyes. "My brothers gave me a month before I ran back to pick up my former—to quote them—'East Coast pampered lifestyle.'" Giggling, she added, "Can you imagine what they'd have said if I told them I couldn't last even a *day*?"

Yeah, well, we'll see if you last a week. Out loud he asked, "Where's 'home'?"

"Baltimore. Which you'd know if you'd read my résumé."

Bryce didn't quite know how to react to her teasing grin, so he pointed to the baseball cap hanging on the peg behind the door. "Orioles and Ravens, my two favorite teams."

"Is that so."

A statement, he noted, not a question. Did it mean she wasn't a fan, or that she wasn't interested in the fact that *he* was a fan? Not that it mattered. Bryce didn't intend to spend any more time with this girl than was necessary. "Let me show you around before the customers start pouring in."

"How many people come through here in a day?"

"Depends. A couple hundred during the height of the tourist season, a couple dozen when it isn't, hardly a soul in the dead of winter."

Sam brushed her hair back, exposing tiny ears, each with the faintest hit of a point on top. Maybe he'd suggest a uniform to attract more shoppers: green-and-white striped socks and pointy-toed shoes.

"So," she said, "is there a formal job description that describes my duties as manager of Rudolph's?"

"Nah. We don't stand on formality around here."

Chief Elf, perhaps? he thought with a grin. *That elf costume sure would look cute on her....*

As a marine captain, Bryce had always taken the safety of the men and women under his charge very seriously, and he'd learned early on that the most efficient way to accomplish this was to separate the hard chargers from the jokers. When Sam stood toe to toe with the hard labor required to run the place, which category would she fall into?

As he tucked her purse under the counter with a quiet *oomph*, Bryce realized that if she could drag the thing around wherever she went, she just might be able to handle the rigors of the job! And he fervently hoped she would. Because the last thing he needed was to waste time introducing her to the stock and the store, only to have her turn tail and run when the going got tough... and at the height of tourist season, the going *would* get tough. The question was, did Sam have the courage to handle it? She had basically admitted that she didn't have the guts to tell her family about the mix-up over her job at the hotel. Which made no sense, since Dan's decision had nothing to do with her.

Or did it?

"So, why haven't you told your family about your change of plans?" he asked, leading the way into the storeroom.

When she breezed past, he caught a whiff of white orchids, his mother's favorite scent. He hadn't thought about that in—in—

"Because as the youngest of eight kids—and the only girl—they think I need protecting, like I'm some sort of empty-headed little weakling who's made of spun glass."

Were her brothers just being guys? he wondered. Or had her behavior inspired their attitude? Obviously, they'd never lifted that suitcase she called a purse.

Sam ran her fingertips along a shelf edge and then pulled a tissue from her jacket pocket and wiped dust from her fingertips. She looked around the room, nodding and muttering "Mmm-hmm" and "Ah" as her gaze traveled the wall-to-wall, floor-to-ceiling shelves. "Soon as I get the lay of the land around here, I'll get busy on this place. Whipping it into shape shouldn't be all that different from organizing a professional kitchen." And then, as if on cue, her stomach growled.

"Sorry," she said, grinning as she patted it, "but I didn't make time for breakfast this morning."

Bryce was about to point out she'd skipped the most important meal of the day when she gave him a quick once-over, starting with his well-buffed loafers and ending at the collar of his polo shirt. He braced himself for the "poor baby" comment that would surely follow when those blue eyes of hers made their way to his patch.

"And here I thought *I* was the only person in America who ironed creases into her jeans. Better keep your distance, boss," she teased, "'cause those pants of yours are sharp enough to draw blood!"

Chuckling, he leaned on the doorjamb as she continued her inspection. No doubt he'd rack up his share of frustration teaching her the ropes. Might even feel annoyance from time to time. But something told him that the one thing he *wouldn't* feel while working with Samantha Sinclair was boredom.

After three hours of tossing and turning, Sam gave up trying to put her handsome boss out of her mind. Climbing out of bed, she wrapped herself in a thick pink robe and flicked on the lamp behind her driver's seat. Plopping down at the tiny table, she tried to read her Bible. But not even her usual favorites from scripture could keep her from thinking about Bryce Stone.

All during his tour of Rudolph's, she'd hoped he would explain why he wore the mysterious black patch over his left eye. His stance, close-cropped haircut, and occasional use of military terms told her he'd probably been a soldier. Plus, he reminded her of her youngest brother, who'd served a long harrowing year in Iraq. Bill hated talking about his time over there, unless, of course, *he* brought it up. So Sam hadn't asked Bryce about the patch or the angry scar visible beneath it.

It hadn't been easy, as he described North Pole's weather and explained how daylight lasted twenty-one hours a day this time of year, to tamp down an overwhelming desire to comfort him…though she didn't know from *what*. Bryce's demeanor hinted at a past fraught with physical and emotional pain, and despite his polite smile, no joy glittered in his beautiful brown eye.

Was it her fault that something in her DNA made her want to *fix* things for people? Maybe she'd have been better off taking her mother's advice to study nursing or become some sort of therapist. "Put all that empathy of yours to good and sensible use!" her dad had tacked on.

Suddenly, a weird thought crossed her mind, and it got her heart to beating double-time....

What if Bryce hadn't been a soldier after all? What if he'd earned that stiff-backed posture *in jail*? She'd seen more than enough old black-and-white movies to know that marching around the exercise yard for hours on end wasn't just a way for wardens and guards to keep control of wayward convicts. It was also how the cons built iron-strong muscles to defend themselves…from one another. So what if the injury had been the result of a prison yard battle?

Sam jumped up and checked the RV's front and rear doors. Assured that both were securely locked, she returned to the table where her Bible lay open to the book of Psalms. Catching sight of her worried expression in the reflection of the window, she laughed out loud. Because really, what crime could a man like that have committed to earn a prison sentence? Besides, his aunt seemed like a really sweet woman. Surely she wouldn't have exposed Sam to danger, even to protect her nephew.

Right?

"Oh, grow up, Sam," she scolded herself. And yawning, she stretched and thanked the Lord for the sleepy feeling that finally began to settle over her. Lights out, she padded back to her narrow bedroom and climbed under the covers, smiling as she pictured the town. From the thatched roof of the log cabin Welcome Center to streets with names like Mistletoe Drive, Snowman Lane, and Kris Kringle Turnaround, there didn't seem to be a single drawback to living in North Pole, Alaska!

So why, she wondered as drowsiness deepened and the image of Bryce Stone floated in her mind, did it seem that her new boss didn't like his hometown?

Chapter Four

Of all the days to oversleep, why *this* one? Sam wondered, rushing through her morning routine. The only upside to forgetting to set her alarm was that in her rush to meet Bryce at the shop at eight sharp, she'd all but forgotten why she'd had to take the job in the first place. Besides, it was impossible to dwell on negative stuff when at every turn, she was faced with colorful decorations reminiscent of Baltimore's 33rd Street Christmas display. Candy canes, elves and reindeer, Santas and Mrs. Clauses adorned just about every free space in town, and the pleasant expressions of shopkeepers were matched only by the bright faces of tourists.

Wearing khaki pants and a long-sleeved white shirt, she scrunched her hair into a high ponytail and laced up her sneakers before setting out on the four-block walk from the hotel parking lot to Snowman Lane. In no time, she found herself at Rudolph's Christmas Emporium.

Her joy at the prospect of working here was dampened by thoughts of what her father would think about her new job. "So let me get this straight," he'd no doubt say, "I helped fund your degree in culinary arts so you could work *in a Christmas gift shop*?" She looked up at the huge reindeer overhead and grinned. "It's okay, Rudolph. Dad doesn't mean any disrespect."

"Are you planning to stand out here and talk to that big ugly deer all day?"

She'd have recognized that voice anywhere. "Have you ever thought of becoming a DJ?" she asked, grabbing the silver handle on the big green door and looking over her shoulder to where Bryce stood on the sidewalk behind her.

"A DJ?" His brow furrowed. "No. Why would I?"

With a voice like that? Was he *kidding*? Shrugging, Sam marched into the shop. "Or you might consider a career in espionage," she said, stepping into the shop, "since you seem to have a talent for sneaking up on—"

"Sam!" Olive hollered. "You look even prettier today than you did yesterday."

Sam would have thanked Olive for the compliment but found herself smothered in an enormous motherly hug instead.

"I can't tell you what a pleasure it's gonna be, having somebody to talk to while I work!" Grabbing Sam's hand, Olive led the way to the counter and relieved her of the big purse. "My goodness, how does a tiny thing like you lug this big satchel around all day?"

"Careful planning," Sam said with a giggle. "It helps that I only need to lug it short distances."

Olive's merry laughter led the way into the storeroom, where she stowed Sam's purse on a shelf behind the door. "We have virtually no crime here in North Pole," she said in a loud whisper, "but I see no point in leaving temptation out in plain sight." Then she clapped her hands. "So, what has that nephew of mine told you about me?"

"Only that you've run Rudolph's single-handedly for the past five years."

"Accent on *single-handedly*." And narrowing eyes the same shade of brown as Bryce's, Olive jerked her head in his direction. "Even when he's here, he isn't. Doesn't like being cooped up inside, doesn't like handling what he calls 'dainty little knickknacks,' doesn't like—" Olive stopped talking long enough to aim a phonily stern expression in Bryce's direction. "Why are you still here?" she teased.

One broad shoulder lifted in a slight shrug. "Guess I thought I could mind the register while you show Sam here what's what."

"I think we can handle both." She gave Bryce a gentle shove toward the door. "This place ain't big enough for the three of us, so why don't you see about cleaning up that nasty garage." To Sam, she said, "He's been threatening to turn it into a woodworking shop for years." Eyes on her nephew again, she added, "You're gonna need something to put food in your belly once this place sells."

Once it sells? Sam thought, gasping audibly as Olive gave Bryce another nudge that put him on the sidewalk. "Come back at noon," she said as he grinned and backpedaled toward the curb, "and maybe we'll let you buy us lunch at The Coffee Cart." After flipping the Closed sign to Open, she faced Sam. "I take it he didn't tell you the job is short-term."

It was all Sam could do to squeak a quiet "no" past her lips. The hotel was out of the question—unless they had an opening for a maid—and now this news? She'd promised to call home tonight. What would she tell her family? "Just *how* short-term?"

Olive waved the question away. "Don't you worry your pretty head about it, Sammie-girl. Bryce *thinks* he's gonna sell this place, but no way that's gonna happen. He *can't* sell it, not only because it's the only tie he has to his mom and dad, but because the real estate market just plain stinks right now. And we won't even begin to list the mountain of bills my brother and his addle-brained wife saddled the poor boy with." She winked. "You'll see. In no time, he'll come to his senses and stop pretending he wants to put a 'For Sale' sign in the window."

If Sam could believe that, maybe the lump in her throat would dissolve. "How can you be so sure?"

"Honey, that boy's the closest thing to a son this ol' gal will ever have. My brother and sister-in-law were nothing but a couple of silly hippies, I don't mind telling you. Always on the lookout for the next get-rich-quick scheme. No wonder they died poor as church mice." Olive cocked her head and grinned. "Church mice, indeed," she echoed. "One of these days, I'm going to look up that phrase and find out what it *really* means." Dusting chubby hands together, Olive said, "Follow me, sweetie." And with that, she led the way into the back room again.

Oh, Lord, Sam prayed, *please don't let this be a temporary assignment.* Or else her brothers would never let her live it down!

"Samantha Sinclair, I want you to stop looking so

worried," Olive said, shaking a finger under Sam's nose. "You're as safe as a baby in her mama's arms."

Sam shot Olive a half grin. "Baby, eh? Maybe that's why I feel like crying."

"Bryce doesn't know it yet, but you're the one who's going to teach him that he loves North Pole and that he doesn't hate Christmas, either."

"What! Hate Christmas? How can anyone hate Christmas? It's my all-time favorite holiday!"

"News flash," Olive said. "He doesn't like chocolate, either."

"Good grief. Are you sure he's *human*?"

Laughing, Olive explained how everything was falling into place just in time for her trip.

"By the way, I haven't told that jarhead nephew of mine the *real* reason I'm leaving town.

"Jarhead? So I was right," Sam said, mostly to herself. "I *thought* he had a soldier look about him...."

Olive's pride was evident when she said, "Nearly ten years of 'soldiering,' I'll have you know."

"What happened to his eye?"

"One of his men stepped on a land mine, and Bryce put himself between it and the other guys."

Sam gasped again as the image of a fiery explosion flashed in her mind. "Oh, my. How awful for him."

"He saved nearly twenty men, but all he remembers is the one he *couldn't* save." Shaking her head, Olive sighed. "Shrapnel carved up his face but good and left him blind in that eye."

"Poor guy. I feel so bad for him."

"Me, too. But don't make the mistake of letting *Bryce* hear you say that. He firmly disapproves of self-pity."

Sam pictured the strong, manly face with its open, honest smile…and the ragged scar that crossed from his eyebrow to his cheek. "How long ago did it happen?"

"Just over a year, now. I've never had the heart to ask if it's the reason he didn't re-enlist—or if Debbie had something to do with it."

"Debbie?"

Nodding, Olive handed Sam a clipboard and a pen. "I'll read what's on the bill of lading, you count how many of these ornaments we have on the shelves." Then, "Debbie was his fiancée. It nearly broke his heart when she called things off."

"It's a good thing I didn't pry, then."

"Knowing Bryce, he would have danced all around the question, even if you had. Most of what I know about the 'wounded in battle' part of his life, I learned by telephone from the doctors at the Walter Reed in D.C."

So he was the strong silent type, was he? Well, nothing wrong with that, especially compared to Joey's never-ending whiny need to be the center of attention.

"So what's it like growing up in a houseful of kids?" Olive wanted to know. "I just had the one brother, myself."

"Never a dull moment. Never a quiet one, either."

"I imagine it was tough, finding any privacy."

"Oh, once in a while the boys plucked my nerves," she admitted, "but mostly it was a wonderful, loving experience."

Sam told Olive about Bill, who'd been more a best friend than a brother, and how just one year in Iraq had changed him in every conceivable way. And during the next two hours, as the women unpacked shipments, logged merchandise into the computer, and gave each article its own price tag, Sam had told Olive about the rest of her brothers, her parents, and her grandparents.

"You know what?" Olive asked. "I believe it's our good fortune that Dan Brooks has a giant dollar sign where his heart oughta be. Everybody in town knows what a skinflint that boy can be, but I'd stake my reputation he hired his nephew for no reason other than it would save him money. So his loss is Rudolph's gain."

Sam grinned. "Think he's the type to admit he's wrong when his nephew messes up?" That sure would solve the problem of where she'd work if *Olive* was wrong and Bryce really did intend to sell the place.

"No question in my mind he'll come to you, hat in hand, if the boy messes up." Olive gave Sam a playful elbow to the ribs. "But he'll sing every sad song ever written to convince you to work for next to nothing." Bending at the waist, she leaned both palms on her knees and laughed, long and hard. "I just got a picture of him getting his first look at you. Oh my," she added, fingers fanning her face. "Then he'll have *two* reasons to be sorry!"

Straightening, Olive winced and patted her growling tummy. "Gotta quit skippin' breakfast." And in the next blink, she was smiling again. "Hopefully by the time that pinchpenny Brooks realizes he passed over the prettiest girl in North Pole for that li'l whippersnapper, my hardheaded nephew will have fallen baseball cap over loafers in love with you."

Love? Sam repeated mentally. She'd only met Bryce yesterday, for heaven's sake! And he was her *boss*, after all. Besides, she'd barely put the Joey fiasco behind her. No way she intended to go down Romance Row again. At least, not this soon. "No offense," she began, "but I'm not in the least bit interested in a relationship right now." Sam paused. "In fact, I may never be interested in a man again."

"Aww, some cad broke your heart, eh?"

Just as Bryce preferred not to discuss his battle scars, Sam didn't like talking about her most recent failure with the opposite sex. Especially not Joey Michaels, who'd led her to believe that "happily ever after" could happen in real life and not just in fairy tales. She'd devoted herself to helping him build his construction company. When she wasn't at work or school, Sam could be found in his basement office drumming up business, finding innovative ways to get him a little free publicity, designing mailers and brochures, business cards and letterhead, furnishing and decorating his office, and taking great pains to ensure he'd look presentable and professional on every possible level. Sam had refused to accept a salary, too, even though she usually clocked twenty hours weekly on top of her other job and college schedule…believing that someday, the company they'd built together would support their growing family. Their hard work paid off, too, and before long, Michaels Construction had more work than she and Joey could handle. It had been Sam who'd placed an ad and interviewed candidates to take over her duties when graduation and final exams loomed, so didn't *she* feel like the little ninny when, three months later, Joey announced he'd fallen in love with her replacement.

"Cat got your tongue?" Olive asked.

"No. Sorry. My mind's just wandering, I guess."

Sam's brothers had often teased her, saying, "Whatever's in your head is written all over your face!" But she'd managed to balance work and daydreaming before. Hopefully, Olive wouldn't see what her brothers had.

"What's his name?"

"Joey," she said, forcing a grin. She didn't even need to close her eyes to remember how he'd blamed her for the breakup, saying that if she'd spent less time at school and more time with him…

"Take it from a gal who knows, sweetie. When the man God has chosen for you comes along, you'll forget all about this *Joey* character."

"Yeah, and I guess I've come to the right place," she said, laughing. "I read there are five men to every woman in Alaska."

"Hmpf," Olive snorted. "Just another one of those crazy rumors that goes around so many times it *sounds* authentic. Way out there in the boonies, that might be true, but then isn't the same thing true for every other state in the U.S.?" Softening her tone, she patted Sam's hand. "All you need is one man, Sammie-girl. The *right* one."

Sam wondered where Olive had picked up such wisdom when it came to relationships, because hadn't Bryce mentioned that she'd never married? As if to answer Sam's unspoken question, Olive continued.

"Just because no man has put a ring on my finger doesn't mean I haven't come close a time or three," she said, winking again. And handing Sam the last of the

Christmas music boxes they'd been cataloguing, she whispered, "Can you keep a secret?"

Sam's mood brightened. "I love secrets, especially when they don't involve me!"

Olive glanced right and left to assure herself the coast was clear. "When I leave for Florida in a couple weeks, it'll be for my honeymoon."

Though Sam barely knew this woman, her heart overflowed with joy on Olive's behalf, mostly because of the happiness radiating from Olive's dark eyes. "Oh, that's wonderful news! But…why keep it so hush-hush?"

Smile fading, Olive shook her head. "Bryce has been through a lot these past half-dozen years or so. First, he lost his best friend in Iraq, then his parents, then came the awful breakup with Debbie and the injury…."

"Oh, poor Bryce!" No doubt misplaced guilt was responsible for his sad-eyed look, because he blamed himself for not saving the soldier who'd died the day he lost his sight.

"Right, and that, too," Olive said.

"What, too?"

When Olive repeated what Sam had been thinking, almost word for word, she said, "I hope you won't take this the wrong way, but you're one spooky lady, Olive Stone. That isn't the first time you've read my mind!"

"Pish posh," she said, waving Sam's comment away. "I did no such thing. I just pay attention is all."

"Very close attention, obviously!"

But Olive didn't seem to have heard her. "People think I can read minds because I notice nuances, subtle little things that most folks miss. Like the way you looked just now when I mentioned what Bryce went through. I don't suppose you even realized that you touched *your* left eye when I made that short list of what he survived, did you?"

"No," Sam admitted, "I didn't."

"So tell me, sweetie, where are you living now that you're a fully employed North Pole resident?"

Talk about an abrupt conversation turn! "In my RV." Sam explained how she'd sold her town house, her furniture, and her car to buy the RV and fund her trip West. "I have permission to park behind the hotel, at least until I find other arrangements. I saw in the paper that there's a campground not far from here."

"I can top that." Olive paused. "There's an apartment right upstairs."

That captured Sam's full attention. "How much is the rent?"

"There isn't any. It's there for the sole purpose of housing the manager of Rudolph's."

"But…you don't live there?"

"Heavens no! I moved into the apartment over the garage years ago, and I've got it all fixed up, just the way I like it." She gave Sam another gentle nudge. "Besides, soon I'll be living in a pretty little house on the edge of town." Grabbing a key ring from the cash register drawer, she said, "C'mon. I'll show you the apartment."

In minutes, Sam found herself in the middle of a cozy one-bedroom apartment that included a fully stocked kitchen and an old-fashioned claw-foot bathtub. "It's… it's just *adorable*," she said, peering out the window at the brightly decorated street below. Then, pointing at the opposite end of the kitchen, "What's through that door?"

"Bryce's apartment. These units share the kitchen, but otherwise, you'll have complete privacy." She put an arm around Sam's shoulders. "I sure hope knowing your boss is just a hop, skip, and a jump away won't be a deal breaker…."

Sam didn't know what to say. She loved the place and everything about it, right down to the braided rugs on the polished hardwood floors and the overstuffed plaid chair across from the TV. But sharing a room as important as the kitchen with her…with her *boss*? "I—I don't know…."

"If it's any consolation, the boy never cooks. Only time he'll be in there is to make himself a cup of coffee in the morning. And if I know him, once he gets his workshop all set up, he'll put a pot out there and he won't use this one at all." Olive chuckled. "Unless of course you *want* him to. I'm sure he wouldn't turn down a home-cooked meal now and then." She shrugged. "If you get bored and feel like cooking, that is."

The place couldn't be more perfect. "I suppose I could try it out, at least for a while, see how things work out." She shrugged. "Worst-case scenario, I can always move back into the RV. According to the ad in the *North Pole News,* the campground is fully equipped."

"True…but then you'd need to buy a car. You're hale and hearty, but it's still a long hike. And walking will be near impossible once the bad weather sets in. Besides," she tacked on, "have you ever tried to heat one of those tin cans when it's thirty below and the winds are blowing at forty miles an hour?"

No, Sam admitted to herself, she hadn't. In fact, she hadn't even given it a thought. Her plan had involved moving into the room provided by the hotel as part of her salary and selling the RV so she could buy a used car and open a bank account. But Dan Brooks had completely rearranged all that.

Olive dangled the keys in front of Sam's nose and let out a merry giggle. "Seriously, Sam. Just think how nice it'll be, living just steps from your place of employment, when Old Man Winter takes control of this town."

As though hypnotized, Sam stared at the reindeer-shaped key ring that held two shiny keys. "It's tempting, I'll give you that." It would take no time to pack the few articles of clothing she'd boxed up for her trip. If she could find a safe, out-of-the-way place to park her RV—

"Why not park the big ugly thing beside the garage?" Olive answered Sam's thoughts again. "Nobody ever goes back there, so there's plenty of room. And that way you'll be nice and close to give tours when prospective buyers stop by to see it."

Had recent events turned her into a suspicious woman, or had Olive actually thought of every possible detail that would keep Sam closer to Bryce?

"You can hardly blame me," Olive said, "for wanting to make sure the boy's happy and settled before I start *my* new life." She aimed her pointer finger at Sam. "I'm counting on you to keep *that* little tidbit of information to yourself, don't forget...."

Sam pretended to zip her lip. "When will you tell him?"

"Soon."

"Has he met your fiancé?"

"No one has. Yet." She giggled like a schoolgirl. "I had to close the store this past winter so Miranda

Electric could replace the ancient wiring, so I booked a cruise to pass the time. Turned out, Duke was assigned to my dining table." Blushing, Olive clasped both hands at her waist. "We've met a couple dozen times since—long weekends when I convinced Sally Mae to run the place for me—so I could visit him at his ranch. And we talk on the phone, couple times a day. And of course, there's email…"

"So he's a cowboy, is he?"

Another giggle. "Can you believe it? Until a few weeks ago, he owned one of the biggest cattle ranches near Amarillo." Olive shook her head as if unable to believe it herself. "He sold it to his son and daughter-in-law for a song, said he'd much rather spend his golden years here, with me." Another glance toward the door seemed to assure Olive that she and Sam were alone. "We bought an old house at the end of Santa Claus Lane, and we've already picked out a name for the place: Duke and Duchess Bed and Breakfast. That's what he calls me," she said, her blush deepening, "that silly wonderful romantic man." She giggled yet again. "Duke says with my cooking skills and his people skills, we'll make out like bandits."

"Oh, Olive," Sam gushed, hugging her. "I'm so happy for you!"

"He's the answer to all my prayers, Sam. I've waited a lifetime for a man like him."

Suddenly, what Olive had said earlier made perfect sense now. Maybe the day *would* come when Sam would forget all about Joey and everything he'd done to hurt her.

"Just put your faith in the Lord, sweetie. I'm living proof He won't let you down." Olive mussed Sam's thick curls. "But I'll pray He won't make you wait till you're in your fifties to find Mr. Right, like He did me!"

The bells above the big green door jingled and a rich baritone called out, "You ladies ready for lunch?"

"Well," Sam said with a glance at the clock, "I don't know yet if he's Mr. Right, but he's surely Mr. Right-on-Time!"

The look of confusion that crossed Bryce's face when he walked into the storeroom and found his aunt and future manager doubled over with laughter made them giggle all the harder.

"Women," was all he said as they wiped tears of hilarity from their eyes.

Chapter Five

As neighbors went, Sam had been a good one. Quiet and courteous, she wasn't one to play loud music or turn the TV up full blast, and she'd never run the vacuum or garbage disposal after supper. Several times, while retrieving her own mail, she'd grabbed his, too, and left it on the kitchen table where he was sure to find it, propped against the Mr. and Mrs. Claus salt and pepper shakers.

Once, Bryce found a plate of homemade chocolate chip cookies beside his daily delivery with a note taped to the plastic wrap that read, *"I'm supposed to be on a diet, so do me a favor and take a few of these off my... hips!"* In place of a signature, she'd drawn a smiley face—wearing an eye patch.

Olive had told him with words and gestures what a good choice they'd made, hiring Sam. His aunt also made it clear that their new manager was starting to press for details: how long he planned to keep the shop before putting it on the market, how much notice he'd give her once he did, and whether there was any chance at all he might change his mind.

In truth, Bryce didn't know the answers. But as the days passed and Sam forged order from clutter and organization from chaos, he began to believe that maybe he could hold on to the shop *and* eke a meager living out of furniture making.

As his only real link to his parents, Rudolph's had at least as many good memories as bad. And besides, Sam had, in just a few weeks on the job, turned the place into a selling machine by stocking merchandise that would appeal to younger shoppers. She'd crafted artsy flyers to guide tour buses to the store and designed a website where customers from around the globe could order gifts and collectibles "Straight from Santa's hometown!"

If only he hadn't discovered a "minus" to balance every "plus" of her personality…

Bryce had let it slide when she left the milk to spoil on the counter. Hadn't said a word when he found a stale, half-eaten sandwich on the table. He'd held his tongue when she left the front door standing wide open—not once but four times—*and* when she forgot to turn off a four-hundred-degree oven. The ancient refrigerator they shared might not have the appeal of a newfangled stainless steel model, but it kept the food cold and the ice cubes frozen. How long would it take Sam to figure out that an appliance that old naturally came with a few quirks—such as the need for a good kick to the front vent to quiet its rumbling and a hearty slam to secure the door's latch?

Yeah, he'd overlooked all those things and more, but it had been the butter knife, left standing in the peanut butter, that broke the proverbial camel's back—and the fact that though he'd hunted for half an hour, he still hadn't found the jar's lid. If he didn't have it out with her soon, he might just come home from the workshop one day to find a moose in the entryway...or the North Pole Fire Department rushing up the stairs.

She'd been nothing but rational and levelheaded in the shop, even when dealing with difficult customers, so Bryce expected she'd behave just as reasonably when he asked her to try and be a little more careful in their shared kitchen.

He brewed a pot of coffee and, after placing two mugs on the counter, dropped four slices of bread into the toaster. Maybe if he buttered her up first with some crispy cinnamon toast—one of his breakfast favorites— it would make his words easier to deliver *and* bear.

When she padded into the room on tiny bare feet, the sight of her nearly shook his resolve. Looking pretty in a blue sweater just a few shades lighter than her eyes, she'd secured her thick dark curls with one of those clawlike things that looked more to Bryce like a torture device than a hair accessory. If she could take pain like that, he thought, grinning to himself, what he had to say shouldn't faze her in the least. "Hey, Sam," he began, "can I ask you a question?"

She tilted her head and smiled. "Sure!"

Hopefully, his gentle admonition wouldn't darken her sunny mood. "I was just wondering if maybe you were born on the side of a hill or something."

"I haven't had any coffee yet," she said, laughing, "so I apologize if I seem obtuse..."

He pointed at the open cupboard doors. "You think

they'll drift closed all by themselves, thanks to gravity?"

Sam pressed them shut. "Oops," she said, shrugging. "I would've sworn I'd—"

"Like you'd have sworn you put the top back on the peanut butter jar? And locked the front door? And turned off the oven that was set to *four hundred degrees*? And I guess you think that since we're in Alaska, everybody's kitchen stays cool enough to keep milk from spoiling on the counter...."

One perfectly arched brow rose as she narrowed her eyes. "Silly me, thinking you'd been spending all your time away from the shop creating one-of-a-kind furniture."

It was his turn to look confused.

"Seems you've clocked quite a few hours making lists of my...transgressions."

"I wouldn't call them transgressions. Exactly." He needed to try a new tack, because it was clear he'd upset her. "Look, I don't mean to sound petty, but—"

She stopped him cold with an icy stare that made him clear his throat. "It's just...I...well, leaving the oven on...something like that could start a fire. And I know this is a low-crime town, but you can't just walk off and leave the wide door open like that. Anybody—or any*thing*—could wander in and—"

"Duly noted," she huffed. "But last I checked," she continued, pouring herself a cup of coffee, "while all of those things were careless, none are against the law." Wriggling her shoulders, Sam added, "But then, I've never been a soldier, so what do *I* know about rules and laws and such?" Lifting her chin, she sniffed. "I'll replace the milk today, soon as I close up the shop. So can you ratchet it down a notch or two, *sir*?"

"Now, now," Bryce said, "no need for sarcasm. I've been a marine too long *not* to notice when things are... when they're out of place." Why did he suddenly feel like the transgressor here? Sam had been the one who'd put them at risk of...who knows what! "And unsafe," he tacked on for good measure.

She had more to say and would have said it...if the music of her cell phone hadn't interrupted them. Mug in hand, Sam walked out of the room and made a point of closing the door between her apartment and the kitchen. Last thing he saw before she disappeared behind it was the quirk of her left eyebrow. He'd never been a betting man, but if he had been, Bryce would have bet she had a fiery temper to go along with that dynamic personality of hers.

Frowning, he ran a palm across his flattop, wondering how he might have handled that better. He hadn't shouted, and he'd chosen his words carefully. At least, he thought he had. But by her reaction, it was pretty clear Sam saw him as Captain Hook, sans the hook. She'd grown up in a house full of rowdy boys, after all, and more than likely, they never missed an opportunity to rub her face in every little mistake.

And maybe he'd been a marine so long that he'd lost all sense of how to talk to anyone not dressed head to toe in camo. Last thing he'd wanted to do was hurt her feelings. Bryce didn't like thinking his mini-lecture might have alienated her.

Then he caught sight of the coffee she'd spilled while filling her mug moments ago, and every other infraction reappeared on his mental list. What did she expect him to do, follow her around twenty-four-seven, making sure she didn't do something to put them—and Rudolph's—in danger?

His experience with women was slim to none. Not counting his mom and Aunt Olive, the few female encounters he'd survived had been with soldiers. And because every one of those could dish it out as well as she could take it, he'd never felt like he had to walk on eggshells. Sam might not have a military background, but she was a grown-up, for the love of Pete. If she could handle the trip from Maryland to Alaska and the disappointment of being passed over for a wet-behind-the-ears *nephew,* why couldn't she take a little constructive criticism? Especially if the criticism might prevent a fire—or worse!

He'd been right to bring her to task. So why did he feel like such a heel? Might be best—for both of them, he decided—if he steered clear of her for the next couple of days. And in the interim, he'd try to come up with some sort of peace offering that wouldn't make him appear too namby-pamby. Because wouldn't it be a rotten shame if he'd alienated the first woman to turn his head since the breakup with Debbie?

Chapter Six

In fewer than five minutes, Sam had been scolded by her boss and invited to breakfast by the man who'd almost become her boss. She doubted any other woman in Alaska could say that.

Okay, so Bryce's list of grievances hadn't been pleasant, but she could hardly blame him for bringing them to her attention. Leaving the oven on and the front door open *had* been stupid. Careless. And dangerous! Forgetting to put the milk away or replace the cap on the peanut butter, well, that had been downright wasteful. For the life of her, Sam couldn't remember what she'd been doing to preoccupy her mind so badly that she'd—

Inhaling a sharp gasp, Sam slapped her forehead. "What if he thinks you're this addle-brained in the shop?" she asked the decades-old fridge. Olive had made no secret of the fact that all Bryce's parents had left him was Rudolph's—and a sizeable mortgage to go with it that forced him to drop most of the shop's insurance coverage. So naturally it would make him nervous, wondering what her next airhead mistake might cost him. She wouldn't blame him one bit if he decided to follow her around like a puppy, watching her every move to protect his major asset.

You'll just have to be a lot more careful from now on, she decided, locking the door behind her, *and prove to him that he didn't make a major mistake by hiring you.* Not an easy feat, considering it was her tendency to behave even *more* like a klutz when she knew somebody was watching her.

Hopefully, meeting with Dan Brooks would take her mind off things and calm her enough to keep her from providing Bryce with still more evidence that she couldn't be trusted to run Rudolph's. As an added perk, maybe getting together with the guy would pave a path to a new job in the event her present boss decided she wasn't worth the risk.

A glance at the clock told her she had nearly an hour to tidy up a few things in the shop before heading off for her appointment with Mr. Brooks. Strange, she thought, that he'd refused to say *why* he wanted to see her....

Olive's voice interrupted her thoughts. "You look too serious to work in Christmas City. Why the long face?"

Sam blew a stream of air through her lips. "Had a little run-in with your nephew this morning."

"Oh?" Olive's brows drew together.

Sam recited Bryce's list of grievances. "So now he's no doubt wondering if I'm harebrained enough to burn the place down someday."

"Oh, don't let it ruin your day. Bryce has never been one to hold a grudge."

"But he's thinking of selling this place. What's to keep him from doing that sooner, just to save himself the anguish of whatever catastrophe this featherhead he hired might cause?" She growled under her breath. "I hate that the whole scene put me in this silly, self-pitying mood. But I need this job, Olive. My family is just *waiting* for me to goof up so they can join in a harmonious 'we told you so!' song."

Olive gave her a motherly hug. "Where's your faith, girl?" She held Sam at arm's length. "God sent you here for a reason, and He didn't do it just to watch you fail. Besides," she added, winking, "I'm convinced that *one* of the reasons you're here is Bryce."

Sam couldn't help snickering at the notion. "Please," she said, waving the idea away. "He barely tolerates me. The man is way too *marine* to go for the likes of me."

Bryce's aunt went back to stacking one-dollar bills in the cash drawer. "What makes you say that?"

"Oh, you know...he's Mr. By-the-Book. A real straight arrow. And me?" A giggle escaped her as she drew quotation marks in the air. "I've never even seen 'The Book.'" Sam sighed.

"Let me get this straight...are you implying you—you're *interested* in Bryce?"

The question caught Sam by surprise. She hadn't given any thought to how she felt about him. At least, not consciously. *Oh, who are you kidding?* she asked herself.

Olive stood quietly, waiting for an answer. But Sam couldn't very well admit that the thought of seeing Bryce in the shop was the reason she'd started wearing mascara again, the reason she started every day with a smile, now could she? Or that images of him, flitting through her head all night, were responsible for each of a hundred romantic dreams? "What eligible woman *wouldn't* be interested?" she said, hoping to throw Olive off course, at least a little. "I mean, what's not to like? He's tall and handsome, intelligent, and…and he can be downright funny, when he puts his mind to it…which, admittedly, isn't nearly often enough, because he's positively *gor*geous when he smiles." Sam was rambling and knew it, but she seemed powerless to stop now that she'd started. "Believe it or not," she continued, "I admire his 'do the right thing' attitude. But that's the very reason *he'll* never be interested in *me*."

The woman shook her head. "Give an old lady her due, will ya? I've known that boy since before he was born. Believe you me, girl, he's interested, all right."

Sam's heartbeat doubled at the possibility. "Y'think?" She didn't even try to hide her delight, which no doubt was already painted all over her hot-cheeked face.

"I don't *think*," Olive said. "I *know*." She waved Sam closer then said in hushed tones, "I've seen him in love before—or when he thought he was in love, anyway. The way he looks at you?" Olive laughed. "Oh, honey child, if he looked at any of the so-called eligible females you just referred to the way he looks at you? He'd have to beat them off with a giant candy cane!"

The clocks in the shop chose that moment to announce the nine o'clock hour. "Oh my goodness, I have to run or I'll be late. Will you be okay here by yourself for an hour or so?"

"'Course I will. I've spent the past half-dozen years here all by myself." Olive narrowed one eye. "But… where are *you* off to in such a hurry?"

"Got a call from Dan Brooks this morning," Sam explained, grabbing her purse. "Didn't say why he wanted to see me, just that I should meet him at Dalman's Restaurant at nine fifteen."

"You watch your p's and q's with that one, Sammie-girl. He never does anything nice without a self-serving motive."

Olive had said something similar not long ago, and the repeated warning set Sam's teeth on edge. "Oh, he probably just wants to apologize for reneging on our employment agreement."

"After all these weeks?" Olive harrumphed. "No way. He's got something up his crooked sleeve."

She made a good point. "Don't worry, I'll be careful. Besides, it's only breakfast." Sam opened the door a crack. "Need anything while I'm out?"

"Just your promise that you won't fall for any of his tricks." The hard glint in Olive's eyes made it clear just how serious she was.

"I'm not as naive as I look, you know," Sam said, smiling. "I'll be fine, just fine."

"From your lips to God's ears."

Heart hammering, Sam stepped outside, and as the bells above the door jingled, she prayed, *Lord, don't let me do or say anything stupid with this guy, okay?*

She repeated the prayer all the way from Rudolph's to Dalman's, echoing *please, please, please* with every step. Sam had been so focused on the toes of her shoes that a deep voice made her leap six inches into the air.

"I sure hope you're Sam Sinclair," it said.

One hand to her chest, she took a deep breath. "Yes, I am." Extending a hand, she added, "And you must be Mr. Brooks."

"Dan, please," he corrected. "Mr. Brooks is my father."

Built like a linebacker, Dan cast a huge shadow. Sunlight shimmered from his shining blond locks as he took her hand in his. "I'm so glad that slave driver you work for let you take time to meet me."

"Olive? Oh, she's a sweetheart. Very easy to work with," Sam said, smiling.

Slanting green eyes narrowed. "I think you know that I was referring to Bryce Stone." Then, "He hasn't sold that miserable excuse for a gift shop, has he?"

Sam tugged to free her hand. Though she already had a bad feeling about this guy, she decided to be fair. It was way too soon to make a judgment call about his character. "It's a wonderful store," she said, lifting her chin. "We're doing a very robust business."

A wide smile threatened to split his face in two. "Once you get to know me, Sam, you'll realize I have a very wacky sense of humor." He held up a hand, traffic cop style. "I meant no offense, honest." He held open the door then bowed low, and with a grand sweep of his arm, invited Sam into the restaurant. "After you, m'lady."

Once inside, Dan took charge as if he owned the place. "We'll take that table by the windows," he told the hostess. "And we'd like to order right away." Without waiting to hear if that was acceptable or not, he placed his hand on the small of Sam's back and gently guided her forward.

When the waitress showed him the menu, Dan waved it away. "We'll each have two eggs over easy, with a side of hash browns and biscuits with country gravy.

Wheat toast, too, lightly buttered, a small tomato juice, and coffee." He stretched his neck to peer at her tablet. "Got all that?"

The girl tucked her pencil behind her ear and said, "Yes, sir, Mr. Brooks," before hurrying away. Sam stared in amazement, trying to remember the last time anyone had ordered a meal for her. Joey had tried it on one of their first dates, and she would have liked nothing better than to tell Dan what she'd told Joey that day: "I have a mind—and tastes—of my own, thank you." Sam didn't know whether it was a good thing or a bad omen that he'd asked the waitress to bring all of her breakfast favorites.

"So tell me," he said, leaning forward, "how do you like North Pole so far?"

Finally, she thought, something pleasant to talk about! "I love it! Almost from the start, it felt like home."

"Almost?"

Sam leaned back and crossed both arms over her chest. "Well, I had a very bad experience on my first day here...when I showed up, employment contract in hand, only to discover the job I'd been promised had been given to someone else."

Dan lifted both shoulders in a silent shrug. She sat quietly, fully expecting him to explain that his poor nephew needed the job for any one of a dozen excellent reasons. But no such explanation came. Instead, he slid his cell phone from his shirt pocket and squinted as he punched numbers on its minuscule keyboard. Holding one finger aloft, he winked. "This'll only take a minute, hon," he whispered.

Hon? The word made her a little homesick for Baltimore. But how had *Dan* known that the term was as commonplace in Charm City as "Christmas" was in North Pole?

"Sorry about that," he said, grinning as he snapped the phone shut. "Didn't want anything to interrupt our meal, so I've left instructions with my secretary that we not be disturbed."

They'd been here ten minutes already, and so far all they'd shared was small talk. "So, Dan, why are we here?"

"Whoa," he said, laughing, "you don't believe in beating around the bush, do you?"

"As my father is so fond of saying, 'It's a waste of time and unnecessarily hard on the shrubbery.'" It was all Sam could do to keep from holding her breath as she hoped her father's *other* favorite saying, "Curiosity kills the cat," wasn't true.

"The truth?"

"That'd be nice…."

"Edmunds said you were a looker. I wanted to see for myself."

Sam could hardly believe her ears. "For real?"

Another shrug.

"You could have done that without the price of breakfast," she pointed out, "if you'd just walked past Rudolph's and peeked into the window."

He leaned forward and clasped his hands on the table. "I never do anything from a distance that I can do up close and personal." His smile warmed the space between them. "And I'd pay a hundred times the cost of this meal to get up close and personal to *you*. You're not just a looker. You're positively stunning."

Sam wished the waitress would arrive with coffee or juice or water. Anything to occupy her hands so she'd have something to focus on besides Dan's bright green eyes.

"I hear you're from the Baltimore suburbs?"

Nodding, she said, "Ellicott City, to be exact."

"Never been, but if all the girls there are as pretty as you, maybe I should book a trip to Maryland."

Oh, he was a charmer, all right. But Sam refused to allow his flattery to distract her. "Surely there was a better reason for a busy and important man like yourself to arrange this meeting than merely looking at me."

"Samantha," he said, slowly pronouncing every syllable, "there's nothing *mere* about you."

Years ago, one of her college roommates had dated her brother Bill and said afterward, "Oh, he's smooth, that brother of yours. *Smooth*." At the time, Sam hadn't understood what Anna meant and, unwilling to admit her naiveté, had kept the question to herself. She understood now, though, and couldn't help feeling a bit surprised that her silly, roughhousing brother had developed a talent for putting Dan's type of move on unsuspecting girls. No wonder he'd never had a steady girlfriend, she thought, smiling to herself.

Dan must have misread her amusement and thought she'd fallen like a tree in the woods for his line, because he reached for her hand. "Have you ever been to Paris?"

She retrieved her hand. "As a matter of fact, I have." Though she'd only known him a few minutes, Sam could see that her answer had surprised him, as evidenced by his slightly parted lips, big staring eyes… and uncharacteristic silence. "I spent a year there during college, earning my BA in culinary arts." Would he remember, she wondered, that she'd included that bit of information on her résumé? Had he even bothered to *read* her résumé?

"I'd love to see you in the City of Light," Dan said. "We could be there in six hours, you know, on my private jet."

"Whoa," she said, borrowing his earlier quote, "you don't believe in beating around the bush, either, do you?"

The waitress showed up before he could respond and began doling out their breakfasts. "Cream for your coffee?" she asked.

"None for me," Dan said as Sam replied, "Yes, please."

He flapped a napkin across his lap. "Seems we've finally found something we don't have in common."

"Oh," said a deep resonant voice, "I'm sure in time you'll find there are hundreds, even thousands of things you two *don't* have in common."

"Well, as I live and breathe," Dan said. "If it isn't Bryce Stone, in the flesh." He got to his feet and held out his hand.

Sam noticed that Bryce hesitated before taking it and then remembered something Olive had said about these two being rivals since high school. At the time, she hadn't felt it was her place to ask why, but now Sam wished that she *had*. "Won't you join us?" she said, scooting over to make room for Bryce. "There's more here than I could possibly eat all by myself. I hate wasting food, so you'd be doing me a favor, helping me—"

"Don't mind if I do." He slid her coffee cup over as he sat down. Bryce was smiling, but the edgy expression on his face didn't escape Sam's notice.

"I had no idea you guys were an item," Bryce said, signaling the waitress.

Sam gasped. "We're *not* an item!" she corrected. "I only just met him ten minutes ago. He's the one who called this morning when we were in the kitchen, remember? You left before I could tell you who it was."

One brow rose on Dan's forehead. "In the kitchen this morning, eh?" Chuckling, he added, "Maybe it's *you* two who are the item."

I wish, Sam thought as Bryce said, "She manages Rudolph's for me." He met her gaze. "And she's doing a great job." Facing Dan, he said, "Big mistake, my friend, choosing your nephew over this one. She's a real go-getter."

"Actually, Dan arranged this little meeting to apologize for that very snafu," Sam said. "Isn't that right, *Dan*?"

Frowning, he buttered his toast. "I'm hoping to make it up to her by flying her to France for dinner at *Le Ciel de Paris*."

Bryce turned toward Sam. "Is that the one way up on some building, where you can see the Eiffel Tower and stuff…?"

Nodding, she said, "I've never eaten there, but I hear the view *is* spectacular. They say you can see for miles."

"So you're going then?" Bryce asked.

Sam giggled. "Of course not!"

"Your breakfast is getting cold," he said, using her fork to spear a bite of hash browns and holding it near her lips.

Like an obedient child, Sam opened her mouth and ate it, though she didn't know what in the world had inspired Bryce to do such a thing. *Was* he interested in her, as Olive had suggested? Or did he just want Dan to *think* that he was, as part of their age-old rivalry?

Dan took a call on his cell phone and, forefinger in the air, mouthed, "I'll just be a minute," before walking toward the lobby.

"I wouldn't put it past him to duck outta here," Bryce said, grinning, "and stick us with the tab."

Sam didn't intend to let him off the hook that easily. "I don't appreciate being a pawn in your 'Get Even with Dan Brooks' game," she whispered.

Bryce turned slightly on the bench seat. *"What?"*

But Dan returned before she could explain. A very good thing, Sam decided, judging by the irritation on Bryce's face.

Dan didn't sit down but remained standing beside the table. "Sorry to eat and run," he said, "but something's come up, and I need to go." He laid a hand on Bryce's shoulder. "It's good knowing you survived Afghanistan."

Bryce poked two beefy fingers through the handle of his mug and said a gruff, "Thanks."

"I've already taken care of the check, so take your time. Enjoy."

Sam sat up straighter. "But what about…whatever it was you wanted to tell me?"

Dan fished a business card from his shirt pocket.

"Another time, Samantha. And really…I'm sorry for any trouble that little mix-up over the chef position caused you." One knee on the bench facing hers, he reached across the table and took her hand. After pressing the business card into her palm, he added, "I promise to make it up to you." And closing her fingers over the card, he kissed her knuckles. "I'm dead serious about that flight to Paris, so if you get a hankering for escargot, you know how to reach me."

And with that, he was gone.

Sam stared at the slick photo of his hotel and the line beneath it that read, *Daniel Garrett Brooks, President and CEO.* Despite the fancy title, she had no desire to go to Paris—or anywhere else, for that matter—with the man!

"Looks to me like you've turned Danny boy's head," Bryce said, smiling around a bite of egg.

Sam slapped Dan's card onto the table, wondering why in the world it would make any difference to Bryce, one way or the other. "Excuse me," she said, "but I need to get back to work."

He slid from the booth and stood at the end of the table as she got to her feet. Slinging her purse over one shoulder, she faced the lobby. "See you at the shop, *boss.*"

Sam could almost feel his eyes, drilling tiny holes into her back as she half-ran toward the door. A mental image of herself tripping over the restaurant's long red welcome mat slowed her pace. The last thing she wanted was to give Bryce yet another bit of evidence for his "Why Sam's too Ditzy to Manage the Shop" list.

Chapter Seven

When Bryce entered the shop shortly after closing time, the breath caught in his throat, because there stood Sam at the top of a twelve-foot stepladder, reaching for something at the back of a high shelf.

"Are you out of your ever-loving mind?" he thundered as the door slammed shut behind him. "Get down from there before you—"

Eyes wide with fright, her arms windmilled as she struggled to retain her balance. If he'd known that the sound of his voice would startle her that badly, he never would have burst into the store, roaring like an irate lion. If she fell from that height, she'd break her pretty neck. Not to mention the thousands of dollars' worth of crystal and porcelain Christmas garden houses she'd take with her.

Bryce made it from the door to the base of the wobbling ladder in three quick strides, steadying it with one hand as the other wrapped around her slender ankle. Rudolph's clocks chose that instant to announce the six o'clock hour, and he hoped the rhythmic harmony would drown out the sound of his hard-hammering heart.

"I'll get down," she said through clenched teeth, "just as soon as you let go of my ankle."

Until she mentioned it, Bryce hadn't even realized he'd grabbed it. He swallowed, hard, and released her. "You scared me half to death," he admitted as she made her way down the rickety rungs, "swinging around up there like a monkey in a zoo."

Once both feet were on steady ground, she glared up at him. "I was *fine* until you blasted in here like a bull in a china shop."

"Could've fooled me."

Hands on her hips, Sam's eyes flashed. "I'm going to go out on a limb here and assume you had only the best of intentions. But do me a favor, will you? Next time you're tempted to play the hero, make sure the person you're rescuing *needs* rescuing!"

Playing hero? Out on a limb? Bryce turned his back to her. He didn't know whether he felt embarrassed or annoyed by her attitude…or both. "Of all the ungrateful—"

She darted around and faced him head-on. "Excuse me?" It was almost comical, the way she stood glaring up at him.

Almost.

If he hadn't come into the store when he had, no telling what might have happened to her. Bryce had no intention of apologizing for saving her from certain doom. But he had no desire to stand here bickering with her about it, either. "Have you balanced the checkbook for this month?"

Sam blinked, looking a bit baffled by his sudden change of subject. "What?" She stiffened her spine and lifted her chin in defiance. "Of course I have," she snapped, "and you're more than welcome to double-check my math."

He'd heard it said that some women wore their anger well, but he'd never seen proof of it before now. Much as he hated to admit it, she *did* look gorgeous all riled up.

Bryce clapped a hand to the back of his neck and shook his head. He didn't know why, but he wanted to wrap her in a fierce hug, kiss the daylights out of her, and tell her how glad he was that she was safe and sound. And if she didn't quit looking at him that way, he might just do it. Instead, he cleared his throat and barked, "So where is it?"

"You mean the checkbook?"

He didn't trust himself to speak.

"It's in the drawer under the cash register. Right where your aunt Olive has kept it for years."

Which he'd know, her remark implied, if he'd helped out a little more around here. Somehow he found the gumption to walk away from her. Within minutes, he'd found the checkbook and made a point of focusing on its pages as she puttered in the shop.

It wasn't easy, concentrating on debits and credits, with her passing back and forth, dusting this, polishing that, and standing back to squint at her artfully balanced arrangements, but somehow Bryce managed to make a sizeable mess around the cash register. It didn't escape his notice how quickly Sam's bad mood evaporated. Debbie's snits could last hours—if not days. Not Sam! Within minutes, she was back to her usual smiling, happy self, humming along to the Christmas tunes blaring from the store's speakers as she went about her work.

He hadn't *needed* an hour to double-check her math, but because he couldn't come up with another excuse to hang around and watch her work, he'd gone over every entry a half dozen times. As much as he hated to, Bryce eventually pushed back from the counter. After their set-to earlier, she'd probably decided he was a boor and a brute, and if he sat much longer, pretending to be engrossed by addition and subtraction, she'd see him as math-challenged, too.

"Things looks good," he said, standing.

She'd been putting price stickers on mice in Santa hats and looked up to say, "Sorry."

Sorry? Bryce didn't get it, and said so.

"Well, the way you were poring over those figures, I naturally presumed you were *trying* to find a mistake." And grinning, she shrugged. "So…sorry to disappoint you."

"I'm not disappointed." He could tell by the tilt of her head and raised eyebrows that she wanted more. "Good work?" *Aw, man,* he said to himself, *why'd it come out like a question?*

"Uh, thanks," she said and went back to work.

Bryce realized she'd been at it alone for twelve straight hours, maybe more. "So, where's Olive today?" he asked.

Sam stepped up beside him to tuck the price stickers into the drawer where the checkbook was kept. "She had some errands to run, so I gave her the day off."

"*You* gave *her* the day off? But you're—"

Facing him, she narrowed her eyes. "Got a problem with my management style, Mr. Stone?"

He watched her gaze flick from his good eye to the bad one and back again, as if oblivious to the fact that the left one was blind. The thing made most people so uncomfortable, they looked anywhere *except* at the patch. "As somebody who used to order tough guys around twenty-four-seven, I can honestly say you're doing just fine." He didn't add that Sam had just herself and Olive to "manage."

In place of the "thank you" he expected, Sam groaned and then pointed at the shelf above the cash register. "Oh, for cryin' out loud, would you look at that?"

He followed her gaze but saw nothing that should inspire her obvious frustration. Even before he managed to ask, she'd dragged the stepladder behind the counter and started climbing. When it started wobbling again, she grabbed the shelf for balance.

"I declare, Sam, you'll be the death of me yet." Hands on the rails, he steadied the ladder as she tidied the colorful cookie tins. "There!" she said, making her way back to the floor. On solid ground again, she propped both hands on her hips. "So what's on your schedule tomorrow?"

He felt like a giant, standing there looking down into her pretty face. "I, uh, well, um…" *A giant idiot*, Bryce thought, and after clearing his throat, he tried again. "Why do you ask?"

"I thought maybe if you had a few minutes, you could pop over to the hardware store and buy a *new* ladder. But if you don't have time, I can probably—"

"Are you kidding? That's the—" He almost said "smartest thing" but thought better of it. "That's the best idea you've had yet. I'll *make* time."

Sam inhaled a little gasp and clasped both hands under her chin. "A fifteen-footer—aluminum, if they have one, because it'll be easier to tote around—with one of those shelf thingies on top where I can put stuff."

Bryce figured this must have been how she looked on Christmas morning, when she found doll-babies and ruffly dresses and other things under the Sinclair family tree. For a reason Bryce couldn't explain, he suddenly wanted to promise her a puppy, or a boat, or dinner in Paris if it would guarantee a repeat of that happy, eager expression. "I'll, ah…I'll see what's available," he said instead.

"Thanks," she said, giving his chest a playful jab, "you're the best!"

He was about to ask, "The best what?" when she hid an enormous yawn behind her small hand.

"Okay, that's it for me. See you in the morning, b—"

"Bryce," he interrupted, "not 'boss,' okay?"

She half-ran toward the stairs leading to their apartments and stopped in the doorway. "Whatever you say," she tossed over her shoulder, "*boss*."

He didn't know how long, exactly, he stood at the bottom of the steps, gawking up at the empty stairwell, but Bryce knew this: he liked the way he felt when she was around. Liked it *a lot*.

Chapter Eight

As a little girl, Sam had dreamed of the day a brave knight would rescue her from her prison in a high tower, but she never would have guessed he'd wear blue jeans and a black eye patch! It made her smile, despite Bryce's stern demeanor, because it wasn't likely the marines had trained him to save damsels…on high ladders.

She'd spent a fitful night reliving those moments in the shop when he'd stopped the ladder from tipping… and likely saved her from a broken bone or two. But it wasn't just the memory of his protective actions that had kept her awake. It was also the *look* she'd seen on his handsome face that told her he'd been genuinely concerned for her safety. Could his aunt have been right when she'd said God brought Sam to North Pole to teach Bryce to love Christmas, and his hometown, and the peculiar little gift shop known by all as Rudolph's?

Olive had said something else that day, and Sam wondered if it was possible that Bryce would learn to love *her*, too.

"You're crazy," she mumbled. Because she barely knew the guy, and he hardly knew her. He was still reeling from a badly ended romance, and so was she. But even if one or both of them was open to new love, what did they have in common, except for Rudolph's and a fondness for Olive?

Sam didn't like the thoughts that had been tumbling in her head all day long as she worked in the shop. Didn't like them at all. Because her tendency to fall too hard, too fast, was responsible for every one of a half dozen disappointing relationships. But she wasn't that silly high schoolgirl or naive college student anymore. No way she intended to suffer that kind of heartache again!

She'd dwell on their differences, *not* on his handsome face and pleasant baritone voice. Focus on his sometimes grouchy, standoffish behavior instead of the fact that all he had to do was smile to get her heart beating double-time. Why, the man hated Christmas, for heaven's sake. What more did she need to prove they were completely wrong for one another!

She didn't *want* to avoid him, because Sam genuinely enjoyed his company…most of the time. But what choice did she have, if she hoped to protect them both from the pain and embarrassment of—

The phone rang, putting an end to her confused thoughts, and she hurried to answer it. Olive had no sooner said a cheery "Good morning," than the bells above the door signaled the arrival of shoppers. *Lots* of shoppers.

"Make yourselves at home," she said, one hand over the mouthpiece.

"Sounds like another busload of tourists just walked

in," Olive said. "Need me to come down there and lend a hand?"

After she'd seen the older woman yawn while waiting on a group of Red Hat Society ladies, Sam had insisted that Olive go home early. "Nope," she said, "all's well here."

"Good, 'cause I'm sippin' tea and soakin' in a tub of scented bubbles." A hearty laugh punctuated her confession. "I'm just calling to ask you a favor."

"Anything!"

"Would you mind driving me to church tomorrow?"

"Not at all!"

"Even if it means getting there half an hour early, so I can get the mike and the organ ready for the service?"

"Absolutely."

Just then a little boy walked up to the counter and held out a snow globe. "How much is this?" he wanted to know. "I think my grandma would like it."

"See you in the morning, Olive," she said. Sam helped the little boy and then moved through the store, answering questions about handblown Italian ornaments, crystal Christmas trees, and the assortment of holiday houses that lined the shelves.

During her first weeks on the job, Sam had worked after hours to rearrange the merchandise, so that instead of being confronted with a jumble of mismatched items, shoppers could easily find similar things grouped together. It had made inventorying the stock easier, too, since Santas and elves, stockings and miniature sleighs were no longer scattered all over the shop. Now, when customers asked for icicles or candy canes, Sam knew exactly where to direct them.

Olive's praise of the improvements was unending. "I wish I had your organizational skills!" She'd said it a hundred times, if she'd said it once.

If her nephew had noticed the order Sam had brought to the shop, he hadn't mentioned it. Maybe like her dad, he was one of those guys who only spoke up when something *wasn't* right. Still, would it kill him to let her know if he thought she'd been earning her paycheck?

Though it was a balmy day in North Pole, the northern breezes blew strong and caused one woman's beehive 'do to tilt. "I love everything about this town," she said, patting her auburn hair, "but honestly! Is it always this windy?"

"No," Sam said, smiling as she punched the antiquated keys of the big old cash register, "but you'll be happy about it this evening."

"Why's that?" asked the next woman in line.

"Because," Sam whispered conspiratorially as she wrapped and boxed snow globes and ornaments, "it'll help blow away the black flies and mosquitoes that congregate around every puddle!"

The bells above the door tinkled again, and a white-bearded man poked his head into the store. "Is this the place where I can order letters from Santa Claus for my grandkids?"

"No, you want the Santa Claus House," Sam responded. "About five blocks east on St. Nicholas Lane."

The man tipped an imaginary hat and ducked out, his "Thanks, cutie!" leading the way.

"Letters from Santa?" echoed the woman at the register. "Oh, that's perfect for my grandkids."

"Mine, too!" said another.

"I'm sure it's on your driver's route," Sam pointed out. "It's one of North Pole's biggest attractions."

One by one, the customers paid for their holiday doodads and filed out, thanking Sam for all her help. She sent them each on their way with an early "Merry Christmas."

When the last of them had cleared out, Sam tidied the shelves her customers had rearranged, returning each item to its proper place in the store. "Now really," she told a smiling elf, "how can that boss of ours *not* love this town and everything about it?"

Chapter Nine

"Thanks for driving," Olive said. "There are a few things I hate worse than getting behind the wheel."

"I'm happy to do it. Besides, it's nice to spend time with you *outside* of work for a change." Sam turned on to Patriot Drive and a moment later signaled a left onto Refinery. Traffic loops like this were one of North Pole's claims to fame, since it was the only city in the U.S. with three roundabouts within a one-mile stretch of road. "I love these things," she said.

Olive groaned. "Not me! I get dizzy trying to figure out when it's my turn to go."

"I did, too, until my dad taught me the every-other-car rule."

"The what?"

"There's a roundabout not too far from my parents' house, and I used to take the long way there just to avoid it. Then one day when I picked up my dad from the car mechanic's shop, he taught me it's really just a matter of living by the Golden Rule."

An audible sigh escaped Olive's lips. "Best thing about 'em in my opinion is that you only have to look in one direction to blend into traffic." Then she added, "So, have you been missin' your folks?"

"You know, it's weird. I thought I'd get homesick, yet every time I talk to the family, I realize I'm anything *but*. I miss them, of course, but thanks to cell phones and computers that have cameras, I see more of them now than I did when we all lived miles apart!"

"I'm glad, Sammie-girl," Olive said, squeezing her hand, "because I'd hate to think you're spending all your nights wishing you were back in Maryland."

Truth be told, she'd had one or two nights like that, but Sam didn't admit it aloud. Running and organizing the shop kept her plenty busy during the day, and by the time she'd head upstairs in the evenings, she was too exhausted to do much more than sleep!

Sam pulled into the church parking lot and handed Olive her keys. "Think we got here in time for you to warm up before the service?"

Glancing at her watch, the older woman nodded. "Oh, definitely. We'll have a good half hour before the first congregants start showing up." Once out of the car, she said across its roof, "Guess who's joining us today, by the way?"

Her heart skipped a beat as her brain conjured the image of Olive's handsome nephew. "Bryce?"

"Maybe. Hopefully," she said. "But that is *not* the man to whom I was referring." Chuckling, she said, "Guess again…"

It took only one quick look into Olive's happy face to know the answer to that one. "Duke! Of course. How could I have been so dense?"

"Maybe because you have a crush on that one-eyed nephew of mine?"

"Of course not!"

"Methinketh thou doth protesteth too mucheth. A horrible rendition of Shakespeare, but you get the idea."

Sam decided the best way to keep from digging an even deeper hole was to sidestep it altogether. "So," she began, walking beside Olive as they climbed the sloping walk leading to the church, "are you planning to share your good news with Bryce today?"

"You bet I am! At dinner. My place. Two o'clock." She elbowed Sam's arm. "And you'd better be there, too, young lady. I need all the moral support I can get!"

"I'm sure he'll be thrilled for you. He loves you to pieces, and he only wants what's best for you."

Olive snorted. "He's more protective than my daddy ever was."

Sam had her own too-recent proof of just how protective Bryce could be! Still, Olive's reticence didn't make much sense to her. Olive, she'd learned, was a hardworking, self-sufficient woman who for decades had sacrificed her own happiness to care for others. So why was she afraid to tell her only living relative that, finally, she'd decided to take some happiness for herself? Sam held the door open, and as Olive passed into the narthex, she said, "Mind if I ask you a personal question?"

"I can't very well say no, now can I, considering all the prying into your life I've done since you rolled into town." Winking, she said, "Shoot."

"Why *have* you kept Duke such a big secret all this time?"

The twinkle in Olive's dark eyes dimmed and her shoulders sagged slightly. "You know, I haven't the foggiest notion." Grabbing Sam's hand, she added, "I think mostly I feel like a doddering old fool, falling head over heels in love as fast as I did. Maybe I'm afraid that once I let the cat out of the bag, someone will put words to my biggest fear."

"Which is…?"

"That this whole thing really *is* too good to be true."

Sam draped an arm around her friend's shoulders. "I don't know anyone who deserves this more than you do. And if I were a betting woman, I'd bet God agrees."

Shoulders up, Olive inhaled a deep breath. "We'll soon see, won't we?"

Sam watched as Olive busied herself, uncovering the organ and arranging sheet music on its stand. "Anything I can do to help?"

"You can make sure that mike is plugged in. Then you can give it a sound test."

Sam jammed the plug into the nearest outlet, flipped the switch, and tapped the microphone's mesh globe. "I've always wanted to do this," she said, grinning. "Testing, testing, one-two-three."

No sooner had her voice echoed throughout the church than Olive struck a chord on the keyboard. "Can you sing?"

"Sorta…"

"Think you can pitch hit for me, just for a song or two?" Olive patted her throat. "Need to save my voice… for the introductions, you know."

"I'll do what I can, but I have to warn you, it's been

awhile since I sang a solo." She giggled. "Unless you call what I do in the shower 'singing.'"

"Pastor Davidson!" Olive called out, waving. "Where's Carol today?"

"She'll be along shortly," he said, "soon as her cinnamon rolls are safe downstairs in the gathering room."

"I nearly forgot about the Ladies Auxiliary Tea this morning," Sam said. "I've been looking forward to this since I arrived in town!" She closed her eyes. "I can almost smell all those home-baked goodies...."

The pastor disappeared behind the altar and returned a moment later in his preacher's robe. Then he tested his own mike and placed the pages of his sermon on the pulpit, smiling as his flock began filling the pews. Quiet greetings filtered through the high-ceilinged space as friends and neighbors exchanged hellos and God bless yous and how have you beens. Soon every bench was filled with people sitting shoulder to shoulder, hymnals balanced on their laps.

Olive struck the first heart-pounding chord of "The Old Rugged Cross" then signaled Sam to take her place at the mike stand. *Dear Lord*, Sam prayed, *keep me on key and in pace*. Then she took a deep breath and launched into the first verse of the hymn.

The notes nearly stuck in her throat when she saw Bryce walk through the wide double doors at the back of the church. She hadn't seen him he'd "saved" her two days ago. Now, as he found a seat midway up the center aisle, he locked gazes with her.

Didn't know you could sing, he mouthed.

I hope I can, she thought as he settled between two

elderly women and looked for all the world like a *GQ* cover model…sporting a sexy black eye patch.

Bryce had heard the expression, "She sings like an angel," but he'd never experienced it in person. Until Sam opened her mouth up there on the altar, that is.

He'd expected a pleasant sound, since her slightly husky speaking voice rang with music whether she was placing a merchandise order over the phone or bagging a customer's purchases. But who would have thought she'd sound every bit as good as singers who'd earned recording contracts and millions of adoring fans?

He'd made a point of avoiding her yesterday, partly because he still felt bad about scaring her, and partly because he hated the idea that she probably lumped him with other guys who'd tried to control her, like one of her bossy big brothers.

It hadn't been easy staying away from the shop, especially with the memory of her sweet voice lingering in his head. That, and the flowery scent of her shampoo clinging to his nostrils. If he hadn't promised Olive that he'd come to church this morning, Bryce might have skipped the service for the very same reasons he'd used to avoid Sam yesterday. And because she made him feel like a boy in the throes of his first crush.

Sam hadn't done anything to inspire his fluttering heartbeat and sweaty palms. In fact, knowing her, if she realized her behavior was driving him crazy, she'd have done her level best to alter it.

She deserved every good thing life had to offer…a loving husband, doting kids, and a pretty little house with a rose garden out back. Bryce could not offer those things to her. Life—and war—had hardened him, and frankly, he didn't think he had it in him to change.

But when he walked into the church and saw her up there, *heard* her up there, he felt like he had on that wacky carnival ride—the one that spins you around so fast you stick to one spot as the floor drops out from under you. Her voice, her face, and the adorable curves visible under her pretty red dress...

Bryce had to remind himself to breathe!

He told himself, sitting between the Baker twins— North Pole's oldest citizens—that the instant the serviced ended, he'd hotfoot it out of the church. Then Pearl said to Blanche, "You didn't leave the blueberry muffins in the car, did you, because I baked them just for Samantha."

"Of course I remembered them," Blanche sniffed. "How could I forget our promise to share the recipe with that sweet girl?"

At the mention of food, Bryce's traitorous stomach growled.

"It isn't smart to skip breakfast, dear," Pearl said, patting his hand.

"She's right," Blanche agreed. "It's the most important meal of the day, you know."

"No biggie," said her twin. "You can eat to your heart's content after the service."

"Today's the Sunday tea, don't you know..."

No, he hadn't known. Would Sam be there? *Of course she will...to sample the Baker twins' blueberry muffin recipe.* Suddenly the idea of running out of here like a man being chased by a grizzly didn't seem any smarter than skipping breakfast.

Half an hour later, Bryce was standing near the doors to the gathering room when his aunt sidled up to him.

"Looking for someone in particular?"

Chuckling, Bryce pocketed both hands. "As if you didn't know."

"She looks pretty in that little red dress, doesn't she?"

She's an absolute doll, he thought, taking in every inch of her, from the top of her curly-haired head to the toes of her red-shoed feet. "Uh-huh," he said, watching her serve out muffins and sweet rolls to Charlie Davidson and his wife.

Why in the world wasn't a woman like her married? She had it all: looks, brains, personality…. No wonder she'd turned Dan Brooks' head.

An ugly thought ran through his mind, doubling his heartbeat and speeding his pulse so much that he heard the pounding in his ears: Had *Dan* turned *hers*? He sure hoped not.

"You could go over there, y'know," Olive said, interrupting his thoughts, "and ask her to fix you a plate of those sticky buns."

Bryce never took his gaze from Sam as he patted his flat stomach. "Trying to watch the ol' waistline."

Olive snickered. "Well, she's in charge of the coffee urn, too…."

"Honey pie!" interrupted a deep Texas drawl.

Bryce watched in amazement as his aunt was swallowed up in the arms of the biggest, broadest cowboy he'd ever seen. *Honey pie*? Hopefully Olive would come up for air soon and introduce him to this bear of a man.

"Duke," she said, "I'd like you to meet my nephew. Bryce, this is Duke."

The gray-haired fellow kept one arm around her and held out a beefy hand. "Proud to make your acquaintance, m'boy," he said, pumping Bryce's arm. "I've heard a lot about you—all of it good, I might add." He popped a quick kiss to Olive's cheek. "Told him the good news yet, honey pie?"

Was Olive…was his aunt *blushing*? Bryce tried to think of another time he'd seen her cheeks pink up that way, but he couldn't.

"I was hoping to make the announcement during supper, sweetums."

Sweetums? What in the world was going on here? He'd been home for almost two months, so why hadn't he heard about *honey pie* and *sweetums* before now? Bryce realized suddenly that Olive and Sam had been spending a lot of time together in the shop. Maybe she'd know something about it. "Coffee, anyone?"

"Don't mind if I do, son." Duke dropped a heavy hand on Bryce's shoulder. "Make mine high test— strong and black. Honey pie?"

Olive shook her head. "No, no, but thanks. Already had my quota for the day."

"Back in a minute," Bryce said, and as he ambled toward the snack table, Sam fidgeted with her apron strings. "Two coffees, caffeinated, no cream, no sugar."

"Who's the dude in the ten-gallon hat?" Sam asked, smirking.

Bryce cast a quick glance toward where he'd left his aunt. "Some guy named Duke," he said, "and I take it he and Olive are more than friends."

"So *that's* her mysterious cowboy!"

"You knew about him?"

"Sort of. Not really."

"What's that mean?"

She met his gaze. "Olive has something to tell you at supper."

Over the years he'd stared down enough stammering, guilty-faced recruits returning late from leave to recognize a flimsy excuse when he heard one. While he hadn't condoned the soldiers' behavior, Bryce had at least understood that most times, it had been rooted in inexperience. What possible reason could *Sam* have for her careful, evasive responses? "Been awhile since Olive cooked a family meal," he said, "so I have to wonder what's—"

"So," boomed the cowboy, "my sweet Olive tells me you're blind in one eye." Duke rested a palm on Bryce's shoulder. "Says you're a hero, through and through, and by all that's holy, I agree." He grabbed Bryce's hand. "Thank you, son. Thank you for your sacrifice."

Bryce felt the heat of embarrassment on his face. It hadn't been the first time he'd heard similar sentiments, and it no doubt wouldn't be the last. He'd never understood what all the fuss was about, since he hadn't done anything while in uniform that hundreds of thousands of other soldiers hadn't already done. The call to duty had been loud and demanding, and answering it had been an honor and a privilege. Bryce didn't know which was worse—people's reaction to his eye patch… or their praise.

"What this country needs," Duke continued, releasing Bryce's hand, "are more red-blooded Americans like you. So really, son, thank you," he repeated.

The last thing Bryce wanted was to appear ungrate-

ful or disrespectful. Because on one hand, it felt good
hearing that the folks back home appreciated his dedi-
cation to duty. On the other, their gratitude awakened
guilt borne in the knowledge that if he'd done something
different on one particular day in battle, the young sol-
der in his charge might have gone home to his parents.
"I was one of the lucky ones," he confessed, "able to
come home, safe and sound." Staring at his shoes, he
added, "Too many others came back in bad shape...if
they came home at all."

When he looked up, Bryce saw Sam watching
him through glittering tears. He couldn't help but be
touched—until an unpleasant thought flitted through
his head. *Oh, Lord*, he prayed silently, *don't let* pity *be
the reason she likes me....*

He was relieved when Duke changed the subject.
"Your beautiful aunt sent me over here to remind you
not to be late for supper." Duke turned to Sam and
added, "And she said to tell you that if you know what's
good for you, you'll get him there on time." He chucked
her chin. "You sing like a nightingale, by the way, young
lady." After sending her a playful wink, he faced Bryce
again. "Maybe someday you and I will sit down and talk
gerbil launchers and other pucker factors."

Only if he'd served in the military would Duke know
the nicknames for M203 grenade launchers and tight
combat situations. Bryce's mood brightened at the possibility. "Marine?" he asked.

"Ooh-rah," Duke said, standing at attention, but before Bryce could return his snappy salute, the man had
turned and headed for the rear doors, where Olive stood
giggling with two of her Ladies Auxiliary friends.

"He's quite the handsome charmer, isn't he?" Sam said when Duke was out of earshot.

Bryce chuckled. "Not bad for an old salt." He pocketed his hands. "Should I be jealous?" The instant the words were out of his mouth Bryce regretted them, because a question like that could have but one meaning: he had feelings for her. "Just kidding, of course," he said, but even Bryce knew his laugh was way too loud for a joke that small. "Maybe it's *Olive* who should be jealous."

"That man," she said, "is crazy about your aunt. She doesn't have a thing to worry about!"

Whew, Bryce thought. Maybe his enormous guffaw wasn't over the top, after all.

No sooner did he have the thought than Sam tilted her head and batted her eyes. "And neither do you."

Bryce had no idea how to respond…to her words *or* her behavior. He'd just made a mental list of all the reasons he was all wrong for her. So why had he reacted to her sweet flirtation with hot ears and damp palms? *Maybe*, he told himself, *because you're falling for her, whether it is good for her or not.*

And it most decidedly was *not*.

Like his aunt, Bryce prided himself on being a person who chose to do the right thing, even when it was tough. Admittedly, it wouldn't be easy, putting a safe distance between himself and Sam. But what choice did he have…if he hoped to do the right thing?

Chapter Ten

Sam had spent so much time serving others at the Sunday Tea snack table that she hadn't taken time to eat, herself, so by the time she got home from church, her stomach was growling like a polar bear. She popped a store-bought pizza-for-one into the oven and set the timer. As she clipped the tiny digital timer to her collar—to ensure she wouldn't forget about the pizza—she acknowledged that it hadn't been all that difficult to dot the i's and cross the t's recently…and prevent another volley of complaints from Bryce.

She headed to her bedroom to change. No sooner had she swapped her red dress for fuzzy camo pants than the phone rang. One glance at the caller ID inspired a happy squeal as she punched the Talk button.

"Billy!" she said. "What a nice surprise!"

"How're things, little sister?"

It felt good to truthfully say, "Things are great! And how are *you*?"

"My biggest gripe in life is, only a couple weeks' vacation left before school starts again."

Sam began her usual phone pace around the coffee

table. "Will you coach junior varsity basketball again next year?"

"Absolutely. I'd rather quit teaching altogether than give that up." He paused. "So you're really okay out there?"

"Sure! Why wouldn't I be?"

"No reason…"

But Sam sensed that dozens of reasons and reservations probably flitted in his head, and his doubts made her all the more determined to succeed here in Alaska. "So how's the family? Mom still pestering you to get married, give her a couple of sticky grandkids?"

Bill groaned good-naturedly. "Does the Easter Bunny hop?"

Why did she get the feeling he was keeping something from her? She'd long ago grown accustomed to her brothers and parents doling out unsolicited advice. After years of "you ought to" and "you shouldn't have," Sam learned that any attempt to defend her choices and opinions only invited more so-called guidance. Their insights occasionally roused feelings of resentment, but prayer helped her understand that every word had roots in loving concern and the best intentions for her happiness.

"All right," she said, "let me have it before you blow a gasket."

"Uh—"

"Whatever it is you're dying to say but haven't yet, just spit it out."

Another chuckle and then, "How would you feel about having some company?"

The question stopped Sam in her tracks. She'd

expected him to rattle off a how-to list for staying warm and safe in her new state. "You want to come to Alaska?"

She'd spoken to her parents a dozen times since arriving in North Pole, and most days, she sent or received e-mail messages from one or all of her brothers. But Sam hadn't yet told any of them how her job at the hotel had fallen through. Not even Bill, her closest brother and confidant. If he seriously intended to visit, she'd have to fess up....

"Think you can put up with your big oaf of a brother for a couple weeks?"

"Of course! I'd love to see you!"

"Cool. So...think you can wrangle me a discount on a room at that hotel where you work?"

Sam flopped onto the sofa and took a deep breath. Wasn't it Mark Twain who'd advised not to put off until tomorrow what you can do the day *after* tomorrow? But she'd used up her put-offs. "Billy," she began, "can you keep a secret?"

"From who?"

Sam resisted the urge to say "whom," because he was the teacher—and because she needed his support right now. "From Mom and Dad and *all* the boys."

"Uh-oh. You sure I wanna hear this?"

"It's no big deal, really. But before I tell you, you've *got* to promise you'll keep it to yourself."

"Okay. I promise."

"Are your fingers crossed behind your back?"

"Gimme a little credit!" A mischievous chuckle punctuated his remark. "I outgrew that years ago."

She heard the smile in his voice and relaxed. A little. "Remember that chef's job I came here for?"

"Of course. We all thought you were out of your everlovin' mind. Some of us *still* think that…"

Sam ignored the obvious reference to the family's belief that she'd fail. "Well, the day I showed up for work, the hotel manager informed me that the owner had given the job to his nephew."

"What? That's just crazy!" Bill hesitated then added, "And I'm pretty sure it's illegal, too. I hope you threatened to sue them for every cheap nailed-down lamp in the place!"

"How like you to get your neck hairs bristling in my defense," she said, giggling. "But honestly, everything turned out great. I found another job that pays the same salary *and* comes with a fully furnished apartment. I love this place, and I really, *really* like the work, too."

She hoped she hadn't sounded too enthused tacking on that extra "really."

"Doing what?"

Every muscle tightened as she considered what her parents would say if they heard she'd used her college degree to sell crafts in a gift shop. "You promise this is just between us, right?"

"I give you my word. If this was a video conference, you'd see me standing here with my hand raised in the Boy Scout salute."

"Which hand?" she asked, grinning.

"Sam, if you don't tell me what's going on, I'll sic Mom on—"

"I'm managing an adorable little gift shop, and it's such fun it almost doesn't seem like work at all. Everybody here is wonderful, from the people who live in North Pole to the tourists who come in, and—"

"Now I see why you made me promise to keep my big mouth shut. If Dad finds out you're a lowly sales clerk, he'll flip his lid!"

"I hate to sound disrespectful, but Dad needs to get over himself. There's no shame in working as a sales clerk. I clocked plenty of hours at Wal-Mart while I was in high school, and I didn't hear him complaining when all my other 'lowly sales clerk' jobs paid for most of my college tuition. It's an honest way to earn a living."

The silence on the other end of the phone told Sam that Bill was likely getting ready to tell her a couple of things—supposedly for her own good. Before he could, she added, "Besides, I'll have you know this job comes with a ton of responsibility. All the management stuff I learned in school is coming in handy. So when you tattle on me to Dad, you be sure to tell him *that*."

"I'm not going to tell Dad or anybody else, kiddo. You can count on me. Honest."

"Really?"

"Really. So my baby sister is the boss of things, is she?"

"You could say that." Technically, Bryce was the boss. And until Olive left, his aunt outranked Sam, too. But Bill would find that out soon enough. "So when can you be here?"

"I'll have to let you know. Soon as I can get reservations."

"Super! And I have a sofa bed in the living room, so you won't need a hotel room…"

"You're sure I'm not putting you out?"

"Are you kidding? It'll be great having you all to myself for a couple of weeks. Like the old days, when you'd take me fishing and dole out advice about boys."

"Yeah, those were the days all right," he said. "So is it true what they say about Alaska—that there are a million guys for every girl?"

"Men outnumber women, that's true," she answered, laughing, "but the odds aren't anywhere *near* that good."

"Good, 'cause if any of them come sniffin' around my little sister, they'll have me to answer to."

She thought of Dan Brooks asking her to have dinner with him...in Paris. Didn't the guy realize how inappropriate an invitation like that was, or that if word of the invitation had gotten out, every tongue in North Pole would have wagged for weeks? "Aren't we all lucky, then, that nobody is sniffin'?"

"What? Pretty little thing like you? I would've bet you're exhausted from beating 'em off with sticks. And I'm not just saying that because I'm your big brother, either."

"When you get here, I'll give you a big hug just for saying that. I hope it'll be soon…"

"I'll make some phone calls in the morning, let you know what I find out. You sure you're okay with having me underfoot for ten days?"

Of everyone in her family, Bill had always been the type who liked going places and doing things all by himself. It's what had inspired him to enlist in the army and sign up for a tour of duty in Iraq. No way she'd have to worry about how he'd entertain himself while she worked. "I'll ask around, get a list together of things you can do while I'm at the shop."

"Okey doke. Soon as I have an itinerary, I'll give you a holler."

"Good idea. That way I'll know when to pick you up at the Fairbanks airport."

"Uh, if it's all the same to you, I'd rather rent a car so I won't have to borrow yours." He chuckled. "Oh, wait. I forgot. You sold yours." Then, "What *are* you driving around town? Surely not that big clumsy RV you bought before you left home…"

"You'll be happy to know I don't need a car. My apartment is right upstairs from the shop."

"So how do you buy groceries and get to the dentist's and stuff like that?"

"Everything I need is within walking distance." A fact—for now. Once winter set in, she'd be in a pickle for sure if she couldn't find a dependable vehicle, because she'd never survive schlepping around town in subzero temperatures and knee-deep snow. But Bill didn't need to know that.

"Talk to you tomorrow, kiddo."

"Okay, and remember…let *me* be the one to tell the rest of the family about this job situation, okay?"

"When have you ever known me not to keep my word?"

She could think of dozens of instances when he'd tattled on her—after promising not to—but if Sam hoped to keep him on her side, they'd have to remain safely in the past. "I'll say a bunch of prayers that you'll get a reservation for day after tomorrow…and have a safe flight…and find the perfect car at the rental counter."

As much as she loved North Pole, it didn't feel quite like home yet, and the prospect of having her brother around for nearly two weeks took control. "I can't wait to see you, Billy!" she blurted.

"I love you, too."

The timer beeped, as if to punctuate their goodbyes, and Sam half-ran, half-skipped to take her pizza out of the oven.

After finishing her pizza, Sam rifled through her closet in search of something to wear to dinner at Olive's. Half an hour later, she decided on a denim skirt and pale pink blouse, partnered with dangly earrings. Though she'd never been into rings or bracelets, Sam more than made up for it with an extensive collection of necklaces. The silver one resembled the earrings enough to look like a set. She wondered what Bryce would wear tonight. Maybe that white, Western-styled shirt he'd had on when he joined her and Dan at breakfast…the one that showed off his big, broad shoulders and accented his trim, flat stomach…

What would he look like, she mused, if he'd let his dark hair grow out just a little? Would it be straight and shiny, like Bill's? Or thick and curly, like her own?

The question made her picture Tom Selleck, who in his fifties was even more handsome than he'd been at Bryce's age. Sam figured Bryce was the kind of man who'd age gracefully, just like Tom, and a tiny portion of her heart hoped she'd be around to see for herself.

"Oh, good grief," she said, aiming for the shower. "Where on earth did *that* notion come from?" Sam decided to distract herself with the delectable aroma of peaches and cream shampoo, because if she allowed nonsense like that to pop into her head, only the Lord knew what silly thing she might say later at Olive's!

The idea made her giggle as she adjusted the water temperature and lifted the lever that diverted water to the showerhead, because how funny would it be if she blurted, "I'd sure love to be around for your fiftieth birthday." Why, a crack like that might build enough tension inside Bryce's head to cause the strap of his eye patch to snap!

Sam felt more than a little silly harboring such thoughts about him and tried to figure out why romantic notions about him kept tickling at her heart. Maybe his ex-soldier status was to blame. Bryce had performed a truly heroic deed that day on the battlefield and had paid a hefty price. What red-blooded American woman wouldn't have a gratitude-induced crush on a guy like him? And it didn't hurt that, instead of looking scary and intimidating like the pirates in old movies, Bryce looked downright sexy in his eye patch.

Sam stepped into the tub and under the shower spray, hoping to wash away the big fat crush she'd developed—like it or not—on her tall, dark, and handsome boss. She'd jumped into a relationship with Joey without paying a bit of attention to her brothers' "Look before you leap" warning. After months of crying herself to sleep, Sam had come to terms with the fact that while her ex-fiancé had been the source of enormous heartache and disappointment, she had no one but herself to blame, because she hadn't prayed to ask what *God* had in mind for her.

If she ever got involved again, it would be after seeking the Lord's guidance. And something told her that He didn't have her too-quiet, too-serious, too-bossy *boss* in mind for the job!

Chapter Eleven

Bryce was halfway down the stairs when he saw Sam on the landing. It only took a quick glance to tell him she'd never get her door locked—not while trying to balance that huge foil-covered plate on the palm of one hand. "Hey," he said, climbing the stairs two at a time, "let me help you with that." He stopped on the third step from the top and relieved her of the tray.

"Thanks," she said, smiling. He got a whiff of something girlie, but whether it was flowery or fruity would remain her secret, because no way he intended to ask her. She turned toward the exit then, and as Sam tucked her keys into her purse, he couldn't help but notice two tiny dimples in each knee peeking out from the hem of her denim skirt. Couldn't help but notice that her pink blouse brought out the rosy glow of her cheeks, either. Bryce decided then and there it wasn't going to be easy keeping his distance from her. Not if she insisted on looking and smelling like this all the time!

He led the way into the tiny entry and changed the subject. "Weatherman said it might rain. I can wait if you want to grab a sweater or something…"

He watched her eyes widen and did his best not to react. "I know it isn't a long walk from here to Olive's," he added, hoping his practical suggestion would take his mind off those long, lush eyelashes, "but this time of year, the temps drop at night, so..."

On the heels of a sigh, she shrugged. And joining him in the entry, Sam said, "So tell me...how long does it take greenhorns like me to learn stuff like that about Alaska?"

"Greenhorn," he inserted, "is what they'd call you in Texas. Here, you're a *cheechako*, the Chinookan word for 'newcomer.'" He didn't add that it also meant "tenderfoot."

She treated him to a moment of her musical laughter. "See what I mean? Guess I oughta pray there's enough empty space in my head to store all the things I don't know!"

Grinning, he held the entry door as she added, tapping her temple, "Based on our little kitchen conversation not so long ago, you probably think there's more than enough space up here for new information." Another giggle. "Let's hope the Lord will beef up my memory, then, so that every lesson will stick!"

Obviously, she'd decided against bringing a sweater. No matter. If it was cold or raining when they headed home, he'd let her borrow his jacket.

When they headed home. Bryce repeated the phrase a time or two and smiled, liking the way it sounded. He liked it so much, in fact, that when she offered to relieve him of the tray, he shook his head and smiled wider. "I don't mind carrying it."

She gave his ribs a playful elbow jab. "You think that's funny, do you?"

The question took him by surprise. "Think what's funny?"

"You're picturing all the empty space between my ears, aren't you? Hence the Cheshire cat grin."

Any woman who could poke fun at herself deserved respect. And one who'd traveled more than four thousand miles behind the wheel of a boxy RV and had made the best of a bad situation when the job that brought her West fell through? Well, Bryce didn't think she was the least bit spacey, and he said so.

He noticed, as they followed the concrete walk connecting Rudolph's and their apartments to Olive's above-garage home, that Sam had to half-run to keep up with him, so he slowed his pace. "And I'll have you know this is anything *but* a Cheshire cat grin." To prove it, he mimicked the toothy smile of the famous feline.

If he'd known a little thing like that would invite gales of lyrical laughter, he might have worked harder to encourage it more often. *How do you expect to keep her at arm's length if you let thoughts like that into your head?* he wondered. Thankfully, Olive chose that moment to jerk open her front door. "Quit lollygaggin' like a couple of kids on their way home from school," she said, leaning over the railing, "and get up here so I can hug the stuffin' outta the both of you!"

"She's a trip!" Sam said, hurrying her pace. "You must have laughed your face off growing up around her."

Bryce admitted that, on more than one occasion,

she'd even managed to lighten the gloomy mood during somber funerals!

"I would have loved school even more if my teachers had been like her."

In no time, they'd climbed the switchback stairs leading to Olive's one-room apartment. They'd barely set foot inside before she made good on her promise to hug the "stuffin'" out of them. "Easy, woman," Bryce teased, "or you'll make me spill…whatever Sam's got hidden under this layer of foil!"

Wagging her forefinger, Olive narrowed one eye and fixed the other on Sam. "I thought I told you not to bring anything but yourself."

"It's just a fruit tray. Didn't want the stuff going moldy in the fridge."

"There's what I like," Duke thundered, "a girl who wastes not, wants not!" His hearty guffaw bounced off every wall.

"Put it on the coffee table, Bryce, while I get some paper plates so you menfolk can snack while Sam and I get supper on."

The idea of being left alone to entertain Olive's boyfriend unnerved him more than he cared to admit. "We can help," Bryce said, setting down the tray. "Everybody knows that eight hands are better than four…"

"Son," Duke said, "haven't you learned yet that men are like kids where kitchens are concerned? We're not to be seen *or* heard."

Smiling, he nodded as another rumble of Duke's boisterous laughter echoed through the apartment.

As it turned out, he needn't have worried about finding topics to fill the uncomfortable silence, because Duke had more than enough stories at the ready. Stories about his son and grandkids, his years as a marine, and his favorite horse left little more for Bryce to say except "No way" and "You're kidding!" By the time the women called them into the dining room, it was a relief to admit, "Great...I'm starving!"

No one would have used the word "gourmet" to describe Aunt Olive's cooking, but she never failed to impress dinner guests with down-home, simple foods. Tonight, a juicy pot roast, surrounded by golden onions, potatoes, and carrots, served as the centerpiece. Crusty bread and steamed green beans completed the meal.

Once they'd picked the roast to the bone, Sam suggested that Bryce help her clear the table and serve dessert. "It's the least we can do," she said to silence Olive's protests, "since you went to all this bother for us! Besides, it'll give you and Duke a little time to play footsies under the table, unnoticed...."

While everyone chuckled over her parting remark, Bryce followed Sam into the kitchen.

"Does Olive look all right to you?" she whispered, stacking plates in the sink.

"What do you mean?" he asked, standing beside her.

Sam frowned and shook her head as hot water and dish soap formed bubbles in the dishpan. "I'm not sure what I mean, exactly. She just seems...off her game or something." Looking up at him, she said, "I'm probably way off base. You know her better than I do, so if you didn't see anything—"

"I guess she does look a little tired," he admitted, taking a step closer, "but she always stays up too late, reading."

"This should be a good test of how she feels. Olive once told me that chocolate cake is her favorite."

Half an hour later, after Duke polished off three slices of the cake and two cups of decaf, he cleared his throat. "Well, darlin'," he said to Olive, "what do you think? Is it time?"

Bryce had never seen his aunt smile like that before. As he speculated an explanation for it, Duke cleared his throat again. "Son," he began, "I'd like to ask for your aunt's hand in marriage, and since you're the man of the Stone family, seems only fittin' and proper that I get your blessing first."

One look into Olive's face was all it took to convince him the big cowboy would make her happy. Very happy. Taking her hand in his, Bryce winked. "You've been mom and dad and best friend to me for more years than I can remember. It was you who taught me to thread a needle and sew up holes in my uniform pockets, and long before that, you taught me how to bait a fish hook." Giving her hand a gentle squeeze, he added, "You've spent a lifetime doing for others—mostly me—and I couldn't love you more if you were my own mother." A final squeeze and then, "So if marrying this Texan will make you happy, I'm all for it."

Bryce turned to Duke and held out his hand. "I'm sure you know what a prize you're getting," he said, smiling, "but if you ever forget it, even for a second, I'll be right here to remind you." It surprised him when his final words caught in his throat, when tears stung his eyes, and for a reason he couldn't explain, Bryce made no effort to hide them. Across the table, Sam's eyes glittered, too. That touched him almost as much as the look that passed between Olive and Duke.

The cowboy lifted his coffee cup. "To the future!" he boomed.

Olive, Sam, and Bryce clinked it with their own. "Aren't we a bunch of softies," Olive said, "all watery-eyed over the nuptials of a couple of geezers."

The comment inspired relieved laughter all around. And then Sam said, "You're the type of woman who'll never get old, Olive, so don't let me hear you calling yourself a geezer ever again!"

"Say there, young lady," Duke piped up, "what about me? Don't I get a 'you'll never be a geezer' lecture, too?"

"Duke," Sam said, patting his hand, "soon as I've had the pleasure of getting to know you better, I'll let you know."

Another gale of laughter filled the room, and Bryce felt the lump in his throat growing, because he couldn't help but realize that the thing he'd always wished for as a boy—a family—had formed itself right before his eyes tonight.

"So when's the wedding?" Sam asked.

"Two weeks from Saturday." Olive sighed. "Nothing fancy, so we should be able to pull it off before we leave for Florida."

An overwhelming sense of loss enveloped Bryce. He'd left Olive plenty of times—to attend college, when he enlisted in the marines, for every tour of duty in Iraq and Afghanistan—but he'd always known he could find her, here in North Pole, to share his good news…and to talk him through the bad. "I'm gonna miss you," Bryce choked out. "Guess I'll have to sign up for one of those stupid frequent flier cards, so I can come visit you guys in Florida every couple months."

Grinning mischievously, Olive shook her head. "Don't be silly, nephew. Florida is just our honeymoon destination. We'll only be gone ten days."

"That's right," Duke added. "When we get back here, we'll be the proud owners of The Duke and Duchess, formerly known as 'that old fire trap' down at the end of Santa Claus Lane."

It dawned on him, looking into his aunt's happy face, that she'd been keeping a lot from him lately, and while it was a relief knowing she hadn't decided to relocate, Bryce didn't understand her reasons for all the secrecy. Had he turned into such an ogre that even his sweet, self-sacrificing aunt feared a stern lecture if she shared the details of her relationship with Duke?

True to form, she seemed to have read his mind. For the next fifteen minutes, Olive and Duke explained how they'd met during the cruise, squeezed in weekend visits every chance they got, and filled the time in between with daily phone calls and emails. And all the while, it seemed to him that Sam had heard it all before. The fact that Olive had felt free to share the intimate details of her life with a virtual stranger rather than with him offered more proof that he needed to do some serious soul-searching if he hoped to zero in on the personality trait that made Olive see him as harsh and judgmental.

He felt like a first-class heel—if heels came in classes—because he hadn't been there for her the way she'd always been there for *him*. He'd told her about his every hope and shared every dream, and while she'd never been one to keep her opinions to herself, Olive made sure that he understood she loved him, unconditionally, no matter what.

She'd warned him that Debbie wasn't the girl God wanted him to spend his life with. And when things fell through, Olive hadn't said, "I told you so!" If he'd been smart enough to take her advice, he would have been spared the heartache of knowing Debbie preferred life with an M-17 and combat boots to a future with him.

If Bryce was honest with himself, "heartache" wasn't the right word for what he'd felt after Debbie called off the engagement. He'd grown accustomed to the routines they'd developed, like sharing chow in the mess tent, watching the Movie of the Week together, and swapping paperback novels by John Grisham and Tom Clancy. Doing those things alone, after she'd made her feelings known, had bothered him mostly because it changed the order of things. And it had been Olive who'd pointed that out, too. The big Texan chose that moment to walk around to Olive's side of the table. Down on one knee, he took her hand in his. "Darlin'," he said, voice trembling, "will you make me the happiest man on planet Earth and do me the honor of saying, officially, that you'll become my wife?"

Bryce watched in amazement as the woman he believed was least likely to go all damp and leaky at a time like this threw herself into the cowboy's arms and blubbered like a baby. As tears coursed down her chubby cheeks, Duke produced a tiny black velvet box that squealed when he lifted its lid.

"Remember," he said, holding it between his beefy

thumb and forefinger, "if you don't like it, we'll get a different one."

Sniffling, Olive held out her hand. "Are you kidding?" she managed between sobs. "I loved it from the start, because you chose it for me."

Sam sniffled, too, as Duke slipped the ring onto Olive's pudgy finger.

"And now, finally, it's there to stay," Duke said.

Bryce was deeply touched that Olive and Duke had orchestrated this repeat of the proposal scene for his benefit. Touched, yes—and humbled to know that his self-righteous behavior had been responsible for her secrecy in the first place.

He wanted, more than anything right then, to let her know *she* had earned his unconditional love, too. So he got to his feet and, lifting his coffee cup, said, "To Olive, who's not just my only living relative, but my best and closest friend, as well." He broke the moment of intense eye contact when tears stung his eyes. Facing the Texan, he added, "And to Duke, who managed to plaster a smile on her face like none I've seen there before…and who'd better keep it there if he doesn't want *this* marine to teach him a new drill!" When the quiet chuckles died down, Bryce concluded with, "And to our Father in heaven, for putting two people from different parts of the country on the same boat in the middle of the Pacific, at the same dinner table, at the very moment He knew was right for them."

"Amen," Sam whispered.

"Amen!" Duke bellowed.

One hand pressed to her chest, Olive nodded and mouthed a teary "Amen" through quivering lips.

Bryce noticed the slight furrow that formed between Sam's delicate brows as his aunt hid a gigantic yawn. She must have shared his thoughts, for she said, "Time for you two to head into the living room to finalize those wedding plans while Bryce and I clean up in here."

Thankfully, neither Duke nor Olive protested, and once they'd left the room, hand in hand, he followed Sam into the kitchen.

She shoved both hands into the sudsy dishwater. "Ouch," she cried almost immediately, pulling her hand out.

Bryce grabbed her wrist. "Good grief," he said, inspecting the bloody, jagged cut, "how'd you manage *that*?"

Using her free hand, Sam plucked a steak knife from the water. "I must be losing it," she said, shaking her head. "I usually save knives for last, just to prevent something like this from happening."

"Oh, man," he interrupted. "*I* dropped the knives in there!" He tore half a dozen sheets of paper towel from the roller and wrapped them around the wound. "Don't move. I'll find some ointment and bandages and have you fixed up in no time." Then he left the room before she had a chance to agree or object…or let her see how awful he felt, having been responsible for her injury.

Neither Olive nor Duke seemed to notice him dart down the hall to fetch the first-aid supplies, and they didn't quit staring into one another's eyes when he sped back toward the kitchen, either. A strange sense of hopefulness settled over him, because if Olive and Duke could find their "happily ever after," maybe he could, too.

Someday.

"It's not that big a deal," Sam said when the led her to the table. "Just a little knick, really, so—"

The instant he took hold of her hand to inspect the cut, she went utterly, completely quiet. He tried not to pay attention to the way her brows rose on her forehead and how she'd tucked in one corner of her mouth, because she looked cute enough to kiss, and that was the last thing he needed to do, considering the decision he'd made.

Uncapping the peroxide bottle, he saturated a cotton ball, saying, "This won't hurt. Much." And grinning, he stroked the antiseptic across the still-bleeding gash. Satisfied he'd sterilized the area, Bryce unwrapped a bandage and squeezed a tiny glob of ointment onto its pad then wrapped it around her finger. Turning her hand over, he gave it a gentle pat. "There. All better."

She held his gaze for a long, silent moment, making him wish he had Olive's talent for reading minds.

"Thanks, boss," she said, smiling. And before he could blink, or return her smile, or respond with a sincere, "You're welcome," she was on her feet, returning the supplies to their proper places in the first-aid kit.

"I'll finish up here," he said, taking over. "You just sit there and look pretty." He would have slapped a hand to his forehead for saying such a stupid thing if he hadn't been holding the first-aid kit.

Either she hadn't heard his comment or chose to ignore it. "I can at least dry stuff and put it away," she said matter-of-factly.

"You don't know where anything goes," he pointed out, "but I do. I'll have this place fit for a general's inspection in no time, so just park it and keep me company."

Instead of following orders, Sam stood on his left side and grabbed the dish towel. "You can put stuff away," she said.

"What's wrong with you? Don't you know how to relax?"

"I'll have you know I helped write *The Couch Potato Manual.*" Shrugging, she added, "I guess I'm too hyped to sit still right now. It isn't every day a girl gets to witness another girl getting, you know, engaged." She let out a long, wistful sigh. "Didn't Olive look happy?"

Don't you *look happy*, he thought, wishing she'd move to his right side, because in order to look into her pretty face, he had to twist his neck until his chin nearly touched his shoulder. Small price to pay, admittedly, but—

"Can you imagine how relieved she must be," she said, crossing to his other side, "to finally have this big fat secret out in the open? I can't imagine how tough it must have been, keeping all this from you for such a long time."

Bryce couldn't help but like her a little more for being sensitive enough to meet his unspoken need by moving to his right. "When did she tell you her 'big fat secret'?"

"Couple weeks ago, maybe?" A giggle, and then, "You should have seen her, Bryce. Every time the subject came up, she lit up like a Christmas tree."

All of a sudden, Sam stood up straight. "Speaking of which, what's this I hear about you hating Christmas? She was kidding, right?"

If he had a dollar for every time he'd heard this lecture, he could probably buy that top-of-the-line table sander he'd been drooling over. "I don't hate Christmas," he droned, "it's the *over-commercialization* that I hate." He focused on the roasting pan, scrubbing a little harder as he pictured gaudy decorations and flashing lights so common in North Pole. "People get so wrapped up in all the noise and glitter that they forget the real meaning of the season."

"Well, I *love* Christmas. And believe it or not, I manage to love all the noise and glitter *without* forgetting the real meaning of the season."

Bryce grunted softly then wished he hadn't, because it caused her to take a step away from him, and from this distance, he could no longer smell the delicious fragrance of her perfume. Or her shampoo. Or whatever feminine product had been responsible for the sweet aroma of peaches. "Maybe if you'd grown up around it your whole life, you'd feel differently."

"Oh, I seriously doubt that!" And to prove it, she rattled off a long list of things she and her mother did every year to commemorate the holiday, from wrapping the exterior of her house with lights to lining every interior surface with seasonal knickknacks. "We're in church on Christmas Eve *and* Christmas morning. And it's always been a family tradition to bake a birthday cake for the Baby Jesus. There are the normal prayers before the big feast, of course, and when it's time for dessert, everybody gathers around the table and sings 'Happy Birthday' to Him. And the youngest person there—usually me—gets to blow out the candle."

He tried to imagine what life might have been like

if his childhood had included such family traditions. Maybe if he'd had a few rowdy brothers of his own, his attitude about Christmas—and lots of other things— would have been different. "Might've been nice, growing up in a house like yours," he admitted, "with half a dozen brothers to wrestle with."

"I have girl cousins who would think I'm nuts to say so, but I loved it." She described how her brothers delighted in chasing her through the house, trying to scare her with worms and frogs and lizards…until her mom suggested she dig in her heels and pretend she liked the wriggling critters every bit as much as the boys did. "I thought I'd pass out the first time I put her advice to the test," she admitted, "but it worked!" Laughing, Sam said, "Guess I figured out earlier than other kids that moms really do know best. Most of the time, anyway."

"Sounds like you have a terrific family."

She nodded and then her face lit up as if she'd found a puppy under the Christmas tree. "You'll have a chance to meet one of my brothers in a day or two. Bill—he's the one closest to my age—is coming to spend a few days with me!"

"That's great. Maybe we can take a day off, show him a good time." *Idiot!* he chastised mentally. *How's spending* more *time with her gonna help you keep a safe distance?*

"I can't think of anything I'd enjoy more," she said. And if that delighted expression on her face was any indicator, she'd meant every word.

Not good, he decided. Not good at all.

Chapter Twelve

Olive had said from the start that she wanted a simple ceremony with only a few of her closest friends in attendance. So Sam, thinking it would take no time at all to make favors for the reception, the bouquets for the bride and matron of honor, and boutonnieres for the groom and best man, volunteered her time. But even if she'd known that "a few" meant nearly a hundred guests, the crafty task would still have been part of her gift to Olive and Duke.

Two days after the big announcement, Sam began assembling the favors. Two chocolate kisses, their flat sides together, were wrapped in a square of red cellophane and attached to green florists' wire. And the evening before the wedding, she got started on the bouquets and boutonnieres. The ceremony would take place at nine in the morning, and she didn't have a minute to waste.

Never a traditionalist, Olive had pooh-poohed a typical arrangement. "Can you make something like this?" she'd asked, her voice a-twitter and her eyes alight as she pointed at a glossy photo in her favorite decorating magazine.

"Shouldn't be a problem," Sam had said, admiring the collection of Texas wildflowers tied up with a wide satin bow. In Baltimore, there were half a dozen florist supply houses where she could find prairie larkspur, mountain pink, basket flowers, and surprise lilies. She'd never given it a thought that the blossoms Olive had fallen in love with while visiting Duke on his ranch would be so hard to come by in Alaska! All it had taken was one quick call to her mom, who'd pulled in a favor from a friend whose husband made weekly deliveries to Fairbanks. Sam was grinning to herself at how God provided for His children when she heard Bryce puttering in the kitchen. "Do I smell coffee?" she called through the open door.

He peeked into her living room. "You want a cup when it's— For the love of Pete, what are you *doing*?" he asked, surveying the flowery mess.

"Those," she said, pointing, "are the favors we'll give everybody at the reception. And these," she added, patting the boutonnieres, "are what you and Duke will wear for the ceremony." Sam held up the bridal bouquet. "I guess you know what this is."

"A handful of weeds, looks like to me," he teased.

"Very funny. If you knew what I went through to get them, you wouldn't say that!"

Ambling into the room, he pocketed both hands. "Haven't been in here in ages." And glancing around, he nodded. "You've done wonders with the place."

Sam didn't want him knowing that such a little compliment from him could turn her cheeks hot, so she bent down to retrieve bits of cellophane and wire that had fallen from her work table. "Just a little paint and some new curtains."

"And slipcovers, and bric-a-brac and—"

She laughed. "'Bric-a-brac'? Reminds me of something my grandmother used to say. How old *are* you, anyway?"

"Old enough to command a little more respect from a whippersnapper like you," he countered, grinning.

"I can hardly believe that in just a matter of days, my brother will be here. I'm so excited, I could pop!"

"Olive told me you have a birthday coming up, so it's good you'll have family here to help you celebrate it."

"I have no idea what we'll do—to celebrate, I mean—but you're more than welcome to join us. I'll probably make his favorite—lasagna—and my favorite, hot fudge sundaes…."

"Haven't you ever heard that three's a crowd?"

Sam waved the idea away. "Fiddlesticks. That only pertains to romantic stuff."

Bryce coughed. "Ah, the coffee should be done by now. Want a cup?"

"Only if it's high-test. Something tells me I'll need it to help me stay awake so I can finish this stuff in time for the wedding."

"Decaf has never passed these lips," he said. "At least, not to my knowledge." He glanced at the clock. "It's going on ten. You sure you want 'high-test' this late at night?"

"One sugar, two creams," she said. "And thanks!"

Sam could hear him out in the kitchen, rummaging in the cupboard for mugs and spoons. The homey sounds brought a smile to her face, because despite his effort to keep up a big bad marine image, Bryce had a domestic side, too.

"So when is this brother of yours supposed to roll into town?" he said, holding two steaming mugs of coffee.

"Day after tomorrow. Pity he'll miss the wedding, but he couldn't get here any sooner. Seems a teacher friend of his got sick, and Bill took over the guy's summer school classes."

"Is he staying at the hotel?"

"No way. Family loyalty forbids it!" She giggled. "He'll sleep right here on my sofa bed, of course." She shoved bits of ribbon and flower petals aside to make room for their coffee. "There. Take a load off."

After placing both mugs amid stem cuttings, wire, and coils of white satin ribbon, Bryce dragged the desk chair over and plopped onto its seat. "I don't know how to tell you this, but that isn't a sofa bed."

Sam held her breath. "It…it isn't?"

"Sorry," he said again.

"No problem," she told him, thinking out loud. "I'll just give Bill my room and sleep out here myself. No way he'd get any decent rest on a couch. His shoulders are almost as broad as yo—"

Sam caught herself a tick too late. If she could've stuffed the words back into her mouth, she would have done it.

Flexing his arm muscles, Bryce laughed. "Guess all those hours lifting weights and doing push-ups paid off. Thanks for noticing."

Heart hammering, Sam swallowed. *Dear Lord*, she

prayed, *help me find something even remotely intelligent to say, so he won't think I've got a big fat schoolgirl crush on him*! She sat staring into his unblinking brown eye, waiting for the witty retort God would put into her head. When nothing came, it led her to wonder whether she *did* have a big fat schoolgirl crush on him!

"So what are you wearing tomorrow?" If she hadn't been holding knife-sharp scissors in one hand and a pointy florists wire in the other, she might have thumped herself in the head. What a stupid question to ask a guy who'd spent years in military fatigues, up to his knees in grit and dust. Besides, Duke had chosen Bryce to stand in as best man, since his own son couldn't get to North Pole on such short notice, so of course he'd wear a tuxedo. The image of Bryce in one of those pleated white shirts, sporting shiny black buttons and cuff links, was enough to make her sigh out loud. Thankfully, she didn't. "Personally? I can't decide between a yellow chiffon pantsuit and a pink dress." *Good grief, Sam*, she scolded, *will you just shut up*!

"By all means, the dress. I've seen you in pink, and the color becomes you. Besides, you have great legs. Why hide 'em under pants?"

Now honestly, how did he expect her to react to *that*? There he sat, not three feet from her, looking all handsome and alluring with his black patch and confident grin, doling out compliments that would've curled her hair…if it weren't curly already. Sam reached for her coffee and took a sip, recoiling when the taste was too sweet, too creamy, and way too hot.

Bryce wrinkled his nose. "Sorry," he said for the third time. "Guess I didn't add enough fixings in, eh?"

He looked so disappointed that Sam couldn't help but say, "No, it's fine. Just a little hot is all." And to prove it, she fanned her mouth. "So you've picked up your tux?"

"Yeah, 'fraid so." Leaning back in the chair, he tilted his face toward the ceiling and groaned. "Every time I've worn one for a friend's wedding, I've ended up losing the cummerbund or one of those goofy button covers and forfeiting some of my deposit. And I just *hate* those crazy shirts."

Elbows on the table, Sam rested her chin in an upturned palm. "But I'd guess you look really snazzy in a tuxedo." *Especially with that male-model bod of yours*, she thought, grinning.

"Then it'll be my pleasure to escort you to the reception on the arm of my rented monkey suit."

She poked a fingertip into her coffee and, satisfied it had cooled enough to drink, took a gulp as the vision of the two of them, marching away from the altar in full wedding regalia, floated in her mind. The image surprised her so much that she sat up straight and slapped both hands on the table.

"What...?"

"I...this...." Sam cleared her throat and picked up the scissors. "I almost forgot the bouquet for Olive's matron of honor. Good thing they're both wearing off-white. I can't tell you how hard it was finding ribbons that wouldn't clash with these Texas wildflowers!"

He looked almost bored enough to leave and let her stew in her own thought juices. Almost...

"What color is your cummerbund and tie?"

"Black, thank the good Lord."

"Excellent. I have black ribbon, so you won't clash, either!"

Bryce leaned back in his chair and put his hands behind his head. "I remember being best man at my buddy's wedding, wearing a white tux with tails...with a white top hat and pale blue—what do you call the stuff?"

"Accessories?"

"Yeah. That." Bryce shook his head, a smile lifting one corner of his mouth. "His wife insisted that everything be..." He drew quotes in the air, his voice rising an octave when he added, "...'matchy-matchy.' So by the time we all got into our places at the front of the church, with the guys in white and the girls in puffy pink dresses, it looked like a cotton candy machine had exploded on the altar."

She pictured some of the horrible bridesmaid and maid of honor gowns she'd been forced to wear over the years. "Boy. The things we do in the name of friendship, huh?"

He inhaled a deep breath. "Boy," he echoed, "the things."

It pleased her that their conversation had erased the worry lines that were almost a fixture on his brow. She decided to share a story that might just widen his adorable grin. "I wore a gold bridesmaid gown once. I'm talkin' wedding-ring gold, mind you. The material made so much noise as we walked down the aisle that the organist had to turn up the volume so we could hear the 'Wedding March'!"

Relief surged through her at the first signs of amusement on his face. "It had puffy sleeves and—get this—

a genuine Victorian era bustle, with a gold rose the size of my head smack in the middle of it. Just between you and me," she said, leaning closer, "to this day I still giggle every time I picture the face of the poor soul who pulled *that* hideous thing out of my donations bag at the charity auction!"

There. A story that put some sparkle into his eyes.

Rather, into his *eye*. The correction made her wonder what it looked like under the patch. Had he lost the eye entirely, forcing surgeons to sew his lids shut, or was it a perfect match to his other orb…only sightless?

He laid one forearm atop the other on the table and leaned in close. "You can ask about it, you know. I'm not sensitive about the subject."

Sam blinked. Licked her lips. Swallowed, then took another sip of coffee. "I didn't mean to stare," she said at last. "I was just wondering—"

He slid off the patch, placed it on the table, and returned to his former position, one beefy forearm stacked atop the other.

The iris of his left eye appeared slightly cloudier than the right, and a minuscule ridge in the sclera followed the path of his facial scar. She wanted to trace the slightly red reminder of the wound that started at the inner bridge of his nose and follow it to where it ended at the outer edge of his left eye. Wanted to run her fingertips ever so gently over the lid that seemed to function exactly like its mate and whisper, "Thank you, Bryce, for everything your soldier's sacrifice cost you." Instead she asked, "There's no pain?"

"None," he said, "and hasn't been for months."

"Well, that's a blessed relief."

Bryce chuckled quietly. "You can say that again. There were times, right after—" He gulped his coffee. "Let's just say God took pity on this whiny marine."

She found it difficult to believe he'd ever been whiny, for any reason, and she said so. And when her words darkened his cheeks with a blush, she said, "I don't know anyone who *wouldn't* have complained about a thing like that."

Bryce only nodded.

He'd given her permission to ask about the eye, but how deeply could she probe before crossing the line between mild curiosity and blatant nosiness? "Can you… are you able to…does it—"

"Blind as a bat," he said matter-of-factly. "There's a slim chance that once all the nerves are healed, an operation could return the sight, but…." He shrugged and started fidgeting with the petals of a larkspur. "It hasn't kept me from doing everything I did before…"

"So since the doctors didn't give you any guarantees, you don't see any point in going through all that based on an *if.*"

"What are you," he asked, taking her hand, "some kind of mind reader?"

His gentle voice awakened something inside her that she'd never felt before. Not with her high school sweetheart. Certainly not with Joey. Sam didn't know what to make of the emotions that threatened to put tears in her eyes while at the same time causing her heart to beat double-time. *Get a grip, girl*, she told herself. *Last thing the poor guy needs is to think you feel sorry for him!* "Mind reading is your aunt Olive's job," she said, hoping the tremor in her voice didn't register in his ears.

The thumb of his free hand drew slow circles on the back of her hand, and now in addition to a pounding heart, she had a racing pulse to contend with.

"Yeah," he said, "she does have a knack for it, doesn't she?"

He was close enough to kiss. She only needed to lean forward an inch, maybe two, to touch her lips to his. But as much as she wanted to, Sam didn't trust herself to make more of this wonderful moment than what it was: a guy, holding a girl's hand…period.

Right?

Sam licked her lips, instantly thinking what a stupid thing that was to do, because what if he read it as a signal that she *wanted* him to kiss her? "I'm glad there's no pain," she said again, amazed that she'd found her voice. More amazed that her sentence had actually made some sense.

"Mmm-hmmm," he said, inching closer.

"It's too bad they didn't give you a better chance. To get your sight back, I mean, after an operation," she rambled. "Not that you need one…an operation that is…because like you said, you're doing just fine with one eye. Better than some of us do with two!" She giggled nervously. "Look at how clumsy I am, and I've got twenty-twenty visio—"

When Bryce bracketed her face with both hands, Sam thought surely her heart would burst with affection for this big sweet guy who'd put his life on the line— who knew how many times—for her and every citizen of the country. She couldn't explain why, suddenly, the urge to cry welled up inside her. All Sam knew was that Bryce deserved to be loved wholly and completely, and she didn't know if she was over Joey enough to give him that. At least not yet.

And just as suddenly as tears threatened to spill from her eyes, a thought flitted through her head, warning her that she should fear *giggles*, not tears, because what made her think that someone like Bryce—a gorgeous, world-traveled, brilliant war hero—wanted love from a little ninny like her!

"What's so funny?" He didn't take his hands from her face, but he pulled back a few inches as he added, "C'mon. Out with it. I can take a joke."

She tried to think of something clever to say, something witty that wouldn't lead him to believe she'd gone all googly-eyed over him, something that would make them both laugh, so they could put this moment in proper perspective. "It's…it's nothing."

Part of her wanted to protect him from pain of every kind. It didn't matter that he towered over her, that he likely outweighed her by a hundred pounds. He had vulnerabilities, sensitivities, fears…and she wanted to tell him he could share them with her without worrying that she'd leave him like his ex-fiancée had. She wondered if Debbie had been tall and gorgeous, a redhead or a brunette. Didn't matter a whit what she looked like, Sam thought. The woman didn't have a lick of sense. If she had, would she have let a terrific guy like Bryce go?

"Well," she said, getting to her feet, "guess I'd better finish this stuff or the bride will have my head tomorrow."

Bryce stood, too, and nodding, said, "Okay, I can take a hint." Hands pocketed, he walked toward the kitchen door then stopped and faced her. "You want me to shut the door, so you'll have some privacy while you work?"

"No, it'll be nice, hearing you putter around over there on your side of the kitchen." Sam didn't think she could sound sillier, even if she tried. She wiggled her fingers, embarrassed and enthralled and excited at the memory of his warm hands pressed to her cheeks—and at the thought that he just might be interested in her.

"See you in the morning, then." He was halfway across the kitchen when he added, "And please, wear the pink dress, not the pants, okay?"

Sam nodded, knowing that if he'd asked her to, she would show up wearing a burlap sack dress and a bucket hat.

Chapter Thirteen

The guy at the Fairbanks tux shop showed him how to make a proper bow tie, but Bryce opted to rent the clip-on style. Now, fastening it in place, he regretted the decision. "How could you have forgotten how uncomfortable this lousy clip feels against your Adam's apple?" he asked his reflection.

Freshly showered and shaved, he ran a palm across his buzzed head. If he and Duke hadn't stopped for lunch after the fittings the day before yesterday, they might have missed the traffic jam, leaving him time for a haircut. He couldn't remember the last time scalp wasn't visible between hair follicles. Grinning, he thought about pretending the 'do was his wedding gift to Olive, who'd good-naturedly ribbed him about his baldness ever since he'd first enlisted.

If she hadn't sprung the news of her engagement and wedding on him, he'd have built her an armoire or a replica of those antique secretaries she'd drooled over in her decorating magazines. The jewelry box he'd considered giving to Sam as a birthday gift became Olive's wedding gift, repurposed as a keepsake box. He had something else in mind for Sam, and in place of her name on top, he'd arranged the intricate inlays to spell out the initials of Olive's married name instead. Inside, on its red velvet lining, he'd tucked old black and white snapshots—pictures she'd believed his mom and dad had lost or accidentally thrown away—that he'd found while scrounging through a battered box in Rudolph's storeroom. In her capable, caring hands, they'd find homes in filigreed frames arranged on end tables and dresser tops. Maybe even on the baby grand that would soon be delivered, a surprise wedding present from Duke.

The nearly twenty-mile drive to Fairbanks gave him an opportunity to get to know Duke better, and Bryce had to admit, he liked the guy. Liked him a lot, in fact, and believed the man would mean every word of his marriage vows.

Now the alarm on his watch beeped, alerting him that it was o-seven-hundred hours. Would he ever get used to identifying each passing hour as he had when in uniform? *Maybe*, he thought. But part of him didn't want to adjust *that* well to civilian life. A big part. One good thing about a life with Debbie would have been that she'd never say "seven o'clock," either.

Though the wedding was scheduled to start at o-nine-hundred, Olive had asked him to get to the church by seven to help Sam line the altar with flowers and hang big satin bows at the end of each pew. He couldn't think of a marine who'd show up two hours early for anything, not even his own wedding, but Bryce had given his word. He'd never broken a promise to Olive in his life, and didn't intend to start today of all days.

Tugging at his starched cuffs, Bryce headed for the kitchen. He'd set up the coffeemaker the night before to ensure he wouldn't splatter anything on the white pleats of the black-buttoned shirt. Grabbing a mug from the cabinet above the pot, he saw that Sam had washed up the cups he'd filled for them last night. Then he saw the small, square envelope propped up against the salt and pepper shakers on the table. She'd written "Bryce" across the front of it, perfectly centered and underlined twice, with a dainty curlicue hanging from the bottom line. Grinning, he picked it up and held it under his nose. Perfume? he thought, his smile widening as he unsheathed the note.

Couldn't sleep last night, ran the delicate, feminine script, *so I baked you a coffee cake. It'll go great with hot black coffee, don't you think?* And like the day she'd left him homemade chocolate chip cookies, she'd drawn a smiley face. But this time, instead of covering one of its eyes, the eye patch was off to the left. Then, a *P.S. It's in the microwave. One slice = one minute on the timer. Mmmm. Enjoy!*

A strange sensation came over him, an undeniable warmth that swirled around his heart, making it tick a beat faster as his pulse pounded harder. It reminded him of the many times he'd gulped too-hot coffee in his rush to hit the road running. He'd tried hard to keep things between them professional, if not platonic, and Bryce couldn't figure out how or when he'd fallen for her.

Maybe it had something to do with the fact that Sam was forever doing kind things like this....

Sure enough, there on the microwave's turntable sat a perfectly iced, golden cake, with toothpicks sticking out of it to keep the plastic wrap from sticking to the glaze. He gathered what he'd need—a knife for slicing, a plate to put it on, a fork to eat it with—and poured himself a mug of coffee as he waited for the appliance to *ping*.

Eyes closed, he pictured the way she'd looked when he whipped off the eye patch last night. The scar didn't make her recoil, as it had a few of the women he'd dated. And knowing he'd likely never see out of that eye again hadn't fazed her in the least, either.

But it had been the look in her eyes, telling him that if she could, she would have erased the injury and everything leading up to it, that had made him grab her pretty little face in his big rough hands. She'd been close enough to kiss, and for the life of him, he didn't know what had kept him from doing just that. If she'd sensed how much restraint it had taken him to hold back, Sam gave no hint of it.

And like magic, she appeared in the doorway. Backlit by sunshine that pounded through the window behind her, she looked more like a vision than a real live girl.

"Good morning," she said, smiling. Smiling and blinking those heart-stopping eyes of hers.

She'd worn the pink dress, just as he'd asked her to, and knowing she'd had other options touched him. "I knew you'd look gorgeous in that," he said, not giving a thought to the fact that he was probably drooling icing down his chin, "and I was right."

Sam placed a tiny white purse on the table and then hung a length of sheer fabric that matched her dress over the back of the nearest chair. And standing as far from the counter as possible, she poured herself a cup of coffee. "It'd be just like me," she said, sitting across from him, "to spill something on myself before I even leave the house."

Watching her, Bryce wondered how a woman could look fresh-faced and innocent yet spellbinding at the same time. "Good cake," he said instead.

"My brothers' favorite."

"So what time are you leaving for the church?"

"Well, I kind of hoped I could ride over there with you. I know it's a nice day and not a very long walk, but in these…?" Sam held out one little foot to show him an almost-white, high-heeled shoe. "Last thing I need is to end up with my heel stuck in a grate."

He hadn't planned to drive, for the very reasons she'd outlined. Once winter set in, enjoying warm weather would be a dim memory, and he'd learned to take advantage of every opportunity to be outdoors. "I don't know about you riding in that old rattle trap wearing…" He waved his hand around, not knowing what style of dress it was. "…*that*."

"I'll throw a towel on the seat and try not to touch anything." She sipped the coffee. "Seven brothers, remember?"

He did. And he'd meet one of them in a matter of days. Now why should that make him feel nervous?

The question so stunned him that he bit down too hard on his last bite of cake, clamping his tongue between molars.

"Don't you just hate it when that happens?" she asked, one hand on his shoulder. "I can't name many things that hurt as much as…"

Sam withdrew her hand and inhaled a sharp little breath, the look on her face telling him she thought she'd committed a serious blunder by comparing something so trivial to his battle scars.

"My own dumb fault," he said, wanting to relieve her of that worry. He rose and began rinsing his plate in the sink. "Well, do you have everything ready? To prep the church, I mean?" He groaned. "Oh, shoot. I've splashed stuff all over my shirt!"

She was beside him in a heartbeat, daubing at the damp spots with a dry dishtowel. "Might just be water," she said. "If that's the case, you'll be stain-free." And then she made a thin line of her usually generous lips and emitted a tiny growl. "On second thought...this dumb thing is starched to high heaven. If they used that cheap stuff most dry cleaners prefer, you'll end up with a wavy little yellow line around every single wet spot." While Sam fussed over the shirt, blotting and patting and chattering on about the spot, the nearness of her, together with the glint of sunlight in her dark curls and the faint scent of her shampoo wafting into his nostrils, made him deaf to anything but the musical pattern of her speech.

His intent, after leaving her apartment last night, had been to go home and pray that God would give him some direction as to whether he should continue to distance himself from her or else pursue whatever was developing between them. But he'd fallen asleep instead and spent a long, peaceful night dreaming about her. The energized, upbeat mood that greeted him the instant he opened his eyes had been pleasant, but he couldn't count on it being a sign from above.

"There," she said, hanging the towel on the swing-arm rack attached to the window frame, "I think that's it." She grabbed her purse and her flimsy shawl and then hefted the canvas bags that held the satin bows. Plunking both near the door, she slid two shallow boxes from a shelf in the refrigerator.

Peering over her shoulder, Bryce admired her handiwork. "Hey, those turned out great," he said while she adjusted a bow on the biggest bouquet.

"This one's Olive's, and that's Millie's. Duke gets this boutonniere and you get that one," she said, pointing at each in turn.

But all he saw were the fingernails she'd coated with pearly pink polish. Bryce swallowed and slapped a hand to the back of his neck. "I'll, uh, pull the truck closer to the door," he said, grabbing a couple of kitchen towels from the drawer beside the sink. Tucking them under one arm, he opened the door. "For the seat," he explained, "so you won't get your dress dirty. Meet you out front."

He shot down the stairs like a bullet from a gun, knowing if he stood there a moment longer, looking into her beautiful eyes, he might be tempted to mess up her lipstick. "Lord, Lord, Lord," he muttered as he stuffed the bags behind the driver's seat, "You'd better show me a sign real soon, or I'm the one who's gonna be in a mess!"

After a heartfelt thanks to Bryce for helping her with the decorations, Sam ducked into the women's room to touch up her makeup. There she found the president and vice president of the Ladies Auxiliary leaning into the mirror above the double-bowled vanity.

"I think we should sit on the groom's side," Mabel

was saying as she patted a powder puff to each chubby cheek.

Arlene blotted her lipstick on a sheet of brown paper towel. "Oh, I don't know...Olive and I have been friends for years and years."

"Good morning, ladies!" Sam said, stepping up beside them. "Don't you both look gorgeous today!"

Mabel batted heavily mascaraed eyes. "Said the kettle to the pot. You look wonderful in that color."

"Please," Arlene injected. "Samantha is the type who'd look good in army green."

As the women shared a friendly giggle, Mabel elbowed Sam. "What do you think, dear, about helping fill out Duke's side of the church?"

"I think it's a great idea. As well loved as Olive is, the church is likely to tilt to the left if we don't do our best to balance it!"

Arlene sighed. "Do what you please," she said, snapping her makeup bag shut. "*I'm* sitting on Olive's side." Tucking it into her flowered purse, she added, "Why, I haven't even been formally introduced to the groom."

"Neither have I," Mabel admitted, tidying the black satin bow at the collar of her paisley print dress. "But really now, who in North Pole could claim to have Amy Vanderbilt's etiquette book memorized, chapter and verse?" Laughing, she turned to Sam. "Have you met him, dear?"

"I have, and he's a delight. Former marine, just like Bryce." She winked. "He's dark and handsome, with a Texas drawl and enough charm to talk the leaves from the trees."

It was Mabel's turn to sigh. "Oh, I've always *loved*

a man in uniform—and a man with a Southern accent. Guess that explains the whirlwind romance, eh?" And with a wink of her own, she added, "I'm glad I got here early."

"Why?" Arlene asked.

"So I can sit as close to the front of the church as possible and study him all during the ceremony, of course." She cupped a hand beside her mouth. "Just don't tell Ernie!"

And with that, all three women exited the ladies' room.

Naturally, Sam was looking forward to watching as Olive began the rest of her life with the man of her dreams. But she couldn't help hoping the wedding would start on time so she could watch *Bryce* up there on the altar beside Duke.

"Pity, isn't it, that the groom's son couldn't be here to be his father's best man," Mabel said.

"Oh, yes…a pity," Arlene agreed as Frank and Ernie approached, each poking out an elbow for his wife.

As the women strode down the aisle on the arms of their husbands, Sam scoped out the church. A quick peek at her watch confirmed that the ceremony wouldn't begin for another twenty minutes yet, so it surprised her that, already, so many of the pews were filled. The fact that so many North Pole residents, like Mabel and Arlene, had decided to take up residence on Duke's side of the church made her smile.

She spotted Barney, former owner of the house that was in the process of becoming The Duke and Duchess B and B, in the third row, along with his wife and teenaged sons. Curt the barber sat behind them, flanked by his assistant. Sam didn't recognize the woman and three young children up front.

She shouldn't have been surprised to see Dan Brooks, one arm draped across the shoulders of a big beautiful blond. Duke had mentioned at dinner that he hoped his temporary landlord would accept his invitation to the ceremony because, in his words, "That boy knows how to make a man feel at home!"

Sam slid into an empty pew about halfway back and moved toward the outside end of the pew. Anyone watching would assume she'd done it so that others joining her in that row wouldn't have to climb over her, but in reality, she'd done it because it would give her an unobstructed view of the altar where, in only moments, she'd get to watch Bryce fiddle with his clip-on bow tie and tug at the stiff cuffs of his starched shirt.

He'd amazed her earlier, willingly attaching gargantuan white satin bows to each pew. It had been Bryce's suggestion that she stand at the back of the church, guiding him as he positioned the flowerpots alongside the altar to assure proper balance. "Oh, the pressure!" she'd said when they finished.

"Pressure?"

"If moving mums and daisies an inch this way, a half inch that way can give me a stress headache, think what those poor guys who guide seven-forty-sevens onto the runways feel like at the end of their work days!"

His big, booming laugh had echoed throughout the church, making her wish she had a better sense of humor, because she would love to encourage more of it.

"Hey, you gonna hog this whole pew or can the lowly nephew of the bride share it with you?"

"Bryce! What are you doing here? You'd better get up *there*!" Sam pointed at the altar, then at her watch. "The wedding ceremony will start in two minutes, and I'm sure Duke is a nervous wreck back there in the groom's room, wondering where you—"

"Groom's room," he echoed, chuckling. "I thought it was called the Panic Room." Then he bent over and, leaning close, said, "Relax…Duke's son arrived first thing this morning to do the 'best man' honors. It's a surprise, so Duke won't know until he steps out of the sacristy and sees him."

Sam slid farther into the pew, understanding now the identities of the woman and children sitting in the front row. "Oh, wow, that's wonderful," she said as Bryce sat beside her. "Duke will be thrilled!"

He tugged at the too-tight collar of his shirt.

"Relax," she echoed. "You look great."

A blush crept into his cheeks as the first quiet strains of Alma Peters' prelude hymns began, and he held a finger to his lips. "Shhhh," was his teasing admonishment, "you're calling attention to yourself."

Giggling quietly, Sam shook her head. "Oh, right… this from the guy who's wearing a tuxedo to a 'casual Friday' wedding."

Suddenly, an invisible, eye-smarting fog of flowery perfume came between them as Bea Nixon leaned forward. "Honestly," she snapped, "you two are behaving like a couple of unruly children." She pointed a white-gloved finger. "If my Sunday school students behaved this way, I'd stand them in a corner, quick as a wink!"

"Sorry, Miz Nixon," he said. The woman barely had

time to slide back into place before he grabbed Sam's hand and gave it a squeeze. "Troublemaker."

Biting her lower lip, Sam stared straight ahead, unable to decide which she liked more...the fact that he hadn't let go of her hand when Alma pounded out those first rib-racking notes of "The Wedding March," or the way it made her heart feel like it had swelled to twice its normal size.

Chapter Fourteen

Sam had spent the better part of the hours after midnight covering the tables in the Moose Lodge with white tablecloths and giving extra attention to the toile drapes on the head table. It had been her idea to use snow globes as centerpieces to help clear Rudolph's shelves of the double shipment that had arrived the prior week. At Olive's suggestion, she'd hidden a big grinning Santa sticker under one chair at each table, marking the guest who'd win the snow globe.

"The place looks great," Bryce said, fingertips tucked into his trousers pockets. "If I'd known you had all this to do when I left you last night, I'd have offered to help."

"I was more than happy to do it for Olive."

Bryce turned slightly in his chair and faced his aunt and her new spouse. "Must have been a hectic day for her," he said, "because she looks kinda tired to me."

Funny, but Sam had been thinking the same thing. "Maybe it's just the reflection of her white dress."

He opened his mouth to say more but clamped it shut when their tablemates returned from the buffet. "Pastor

Davidson's blessing was pretty good," he said, spearing a chunk of chicken breast.

"You gotta love ol' Charlie," said Tim Turner.

And Bob Harris chimed in with, "You can say that again."

"Short and sweet, nice and neat," Tim added, inspiring hearty laughter all around the table.

Mrs. Harris feigned a scolding expression. "Bobby, really," she said. Flapping her napkin across her lap, she sat up straighter. "We can always count on the Ladies Auxiliary for a good meal, can't we?"

Sam thought about what she'd have prepared if Olive had asked her to cater the meal. Her famous Chicken Cordon Bleu, probably. The recipe had earned her an A in her Quantity Food Prep course and helped win monetary awards in a half dozen contests, as well. Served with rice pilaf and a steamed vegetable medley, it made a lovely presentation.

But Olive hadn't wanted to impose, explaining how much her lady friends enjoyed every opportunity to "put on the feedbag." Besides, if Sam *had* gotten all involved with food prep, she couldn't have decorated the hall and created the flower arrangements, and that would have been a shame, because she had enjoyed every finger-pricking, cuticle-cutting moment of it.

"Can't wait for a big fat slab of that cake," she said, wiggling her eyebrows. "It looks delicious." Then, "Can you believe Olive got all this done in such a short time?"

"With a little help from a friend," Bryce added. "You're the one who made all the important calls, reserved this place, gave it an upscale look, so on Olive's behalf, thanks."

Sam was about to say that she was only too happy to do it for Olive when the wedding guests began clinking forks and spoons against their water goblets. They kept up the racket until Mr. and Mrs. Duke Carter silenced them with their second kiss as man and wife. Rolling her eyes, Sam groaned. "If I ever get married, that is *not* going to be allowed at *my* reception."

Chuckling, Bryce rested an arm across the back of her chair. "Why not?"

"For one thing, it's almost as annoying as fingernails on a chalkboard. For another, well, it's just plain silly."

"You won't get an argument from me." He inclined his head slightly. "But you shouldn't say *if.* Say *when.*"

"When what?"

Before he could answer, a familiar upbeat hymn wafted from the overhead speakers, and she noticed his thumb drumming on the table as his knee bounced with the tempo. What better way to escape the discomfiting situation than to give in to a sudden, overwhelming urge to sing? "Michael, row the boat ashore, hallelujah. Michael row the boat ashore, hallelu-u-jah."

"Sister help to trim the sail," he joined in, "hallelujah. Sister help to trim the sail, hallelu-u-jah."

Their tablemates' voices blended with theirs. "The river is deep and the river is wide, hallelujah. Greener pastures on the other side, hallelu-u-jah."

Soon everyone in the hall was on their feet, swaying and clapping in time to the music. When the song ended, laughter echoed through the room as husbands embraced wives, as parents cuddled their kids, as Duke wrapped his big tuxedoed arms around Olive. The sight of so much love and jubilation, all in one place, made

Sam so grateful to be here in this amazing, friendly town that she grinned wide enough to fear her face might crack!

But when Bryce drew her to him in a warm embrace, she worried, instead, that she might cry for joy, instead.

Sam was rescued from having to respond when Duke clanged a knife handle against a plate. "Ladies and gentlemen," he began, leading Olive to a small table in the corner, "the time has come for my bride and me to cut the cake." Smiling, aproned ladies extended a white-ribboned gleaming knife, and the happy couple wrapped their fingers around its handle and made the first cut as cameras clicked and flashed all around them.

"I warn you, Duke Carter, if you get frosting up my nose," the bride teased, "I'll—"

"Too late!" he bellowed, shoving thickly iced cake into his wife's mouth.

"Give 'im as good as you got, Olive," yelled a female voice.

"That's right," called another, "don't let him get away with that!"

"Didn't you say you wanted a slice of cake?" Bryce asked.

Sam nodded.

"Then you'd better get up there," he whispered near her ear, "'cause it's going fast."

Nodding, she squared her shoulders and flashed that heart-stopping smile, then said, "I'll bring you a slice." Sam faced the table. "Can I bring anyone some cake?"

Three yeses and three "no thanks" later, Bryce watched her glide across the room on feet that seemed way too small to keep any human being upright. Everything about her, from those tiny high-heeled shoes to her pink-polished fingertips, emphasized pure femininity and grace. Which invited an ugly question: could Sam survive a harsh North Pole winter, with deep-freeze temps, snow up to her hips, and seemingly endless hours of darkness? "I sure do hope so," he said under his breath. "I sure do hope so."

Sam delivered cake to her tablemates, saving her slice and his for last. "Where'd you learn to balance that many dishes at once?" he asked, accepting his.

"One of my many jobs," she said around a mouthful of icing, "was waiting tables at the Forest Diner. I learned real quick what two things would fill my pockets with tips."

Bryce swallowed the bite he'd taken and had another one on his fork when he said, "Well…?"

"First, learn how to take diners' orders without the need for a pen or tablet, and second, never make 'em ask for refills of coffee or water or soda."

"I'm confused," he said, scratching his chin. "What do either of those have to do with an ability to balance four plates on your skinny arms while carrying another two in your tiny hand?"

"Skinny!" She extended both arms. "The politically correct term, I'll have you know, is *slender*."

"I stand corrected." Then he grabbed both "slender" wrists and turned them over in his hands.

"Practice makes perfect," she said, her voice a rumbling whisper. "Spilled my share of food before I—"

"So when are *you two* going to make the big announcement?" Bob Harris wanted to know.

"Yeah!" Tim hollered. "Another excuse for a Ladies Auxiliary feast!"

If Sam's expression was any indicator, the question had shocked her right down to her pointy-shoed toes. Jerking back, she sat up straight and adjusted the napkin on her lap. And then she completely shocked *him* when she lifted her chin and teased them right back with, "That's for us to know and you to find out."

Bryce nearly dropped his fork, giant bite of cake and all, and considered slapping a palm over his eyes. He laid the utensil beside the dish, because last thing he needed was to poke out his *good* eye.

Another question dawned on him as their tablemates asked Sam about Baltimore and her degree in culinary arts and shook their heads at the reason she'd taken the manager's job at Rudolph's instead of the chef's job at Silver Bells: why wasn't he upset about her answer to their initial question? She'd opened a proverbial Pandora's box, and no doubt he'd be the unwilling recipient of good-natured ribbing at Curt's barbershop on Monday morning. Even if she'd quieted their curiosity with a "we're just friends," he could still expect to face *some* scrutiny from the self-professed bachelors and long-married experts who gathered to swap tales as their hair cuttings fell to the tile floor.

Bryce pretended it took every bit of his concentration to unscrew the cap of the white coffee decanter and refill his cup. Pretended the coffee still tasted good and hot going down, though after three hours in the fancy thermos, it had cooled considerably. Pretended his napkin needed a re-flap and an adjustment across his knee, and that his silverware should be rearranged in a tidy row on either side of his plate.

Bryce could pretend that he was really into the Mormon Tabernacle Choir's rendition of "Amazing Grace," but none of it would distract him from the woman seated beside him. Inside of a minute, she had everybody at the table in stitches. And somehow, she'd turned the conversation away from questions about herself, leaving them no choice but to talk about North Pole, about the wedding, about *themselves*.

Every now and then, as she nodded in response to something Bob said, as she snickered at one of Tim's corny puns, she'd shoot a quick glance his way... and smile. The last grin she aimed his way resulted in sweaty palms and hot ears, making him wish he'd taken off the monkey suit jacket and grown his hair out a little *more* to hide the glowing red appendages stuck to either side of his marine-bald head.

Sam seemed to sense his discomfort and gave his knee a nurturing little *pat-pat-pat*. If anyone but Bryce noticed, they gave no sign of it.

He grabbed her hand and gently squeezed in response, might have held on, too, if Duke and Olive hadn't stepped up behind his chair. "Havin' fun, nephew?"

His palm felt cold when he turned Sam loose. "You bet," he said, standing to plant a kiss on Olive's cheek. "And you?"

"Never better," she said. Then she waved a hand, inviting Duke's family to step forward. "This is my darlin' nephew," she told them, "Bryce Stone."

After a few minutes of polite nodding and hand shaking, Bryce volunteered to borrow a friend's van and drive Duke's son and his family to the airport in the morning. "You'll come, too, won't you, Sam?" he asked, a hand in the small of her back. Any excuse, he thought, to spend time with her.

He'd already insisted on taking the newlyweds to Fairbanks to catch an early-morning flight to Miami, which meant he couldn't help Sam clean up the Moose Lodge as he'd promised. Well, he'd make it up to her tomorrow by buying her lunch at some point during the half-hour drive back to North Pole. Then he had a better idea, and it made him smile as Duke raised his big Texas voice, commanding everyone's attention.

"I just want to thank y'all for helping Olive and me celebrate this beautiful day, and I'm especially grateful for the warm welcome y'all have extended this loud-mouthed ex-marine Texan."

"You're welcome," somebody hollered.

"We love you guys!" yelled someone else.

"I know how much y'all love my darlin' wife, here, and I promise to do everything in my power to make her the happiest woman on earth." With that, he kissed her long and slow.

"Goodness!" Olive said, waving a hand in front of her face when he let her go, "he's off to a dynamite start!"

When the laughter and applause died down, Duke slid an arm round his wife's waist.

"Time for us to get into our travelin' clothes. We don't want to miss our flight!"

While Sam made sure Duke's family had proper accommodations, Bryce arranged to take Olive home so she could change and grab her suitcase before picking her husband up at the hotel. "Mrs. Duke Carter," he said as they drove toward Rudolph's, "that's gonna take some getting used to, isn't—"

The words caught in his throat as Olive grimaced and laid a hand on her stomach. "Too much rich food," she complained. "I'm going back to my down-home meat and potatoes diet the minute we get home from Florida!" Then, "Wipe that worried look off your face, nephew. You know me…tough as they come, but even I need a bit of R and R now and then. And these last few days have been crazy-busy!"

"Well, then it's good you two have ten days of vacation time ahead of you. No need to get all caught up in sightseeing. You have the rest of your lives to go back and tour Orlando and Miami and the Keys."

Olive inhaled a deep breath, her facial features finally relaxing. "Ri-i-ight," she countered, laughing, "like we'll have time for gallivanting once we open the bed-and-breakfast…"

"You'll have to *make* time, because life's too short. Mom and Dad's lives ought to be evidence enough of that."

She reached across the console to pat his hand. "Point taken. But let's not forget that your grandma Stone gave birth to *one* genius." And to emphasize the point, she aimed a pudgy forefinger at her own chest. "I hate to speak ill of the dead, but let's face it. If your daddy had been using his head for something other than to hold up his *ushanka*, he might never have started that—"

"I know, I know," Bryce said dully. He'd heard it all before, from well-meaning friends and especially from

Olive. He understood the frustration and confusion that prompted her occasional criticism of his parents—and to be honest, he shared her annoyance—but complaining about the way they'd died only added resentment to the mix. "Let's not end the happiest day of your life on *that* sour note, okay?"

She shifted in the passenger seat. "Agreed."

"Your stomach still bothering you?"

"It's just a little gas bubble."

"I'm sure it'll pass," they said in unison.

They looked at one another and burst into gales of laughter. Bryce didn't know whether to blame nervous energy or blessed relief for the tears that filled his eyes, but he knew this much: he loved Olive like a mother and wanted to go right on sharing goofy jokes with her for many years to come.

Several months after his breakup with Debbie, he'd spent two weeks' leave in North Pole, nursing his broken heart. She'd cornered him in Rudolph's the day before he headed back to Afghanistan and wagged a maternal digit under his nose.

"How are you ever gonna see the girl God has chosen for you if you spend all your days staring at the toes of your combat boots?" Jabbing the accusatory finger into his shoulder, she'd added, "Get over yourself, nephew. Debbie wasn't worth an ounce of salt even *before* she dumped you."

Good ol' Olive, he mused, grinning as he steered his pickup alongside the shop, *never one to mince words*. And he wouldn't have changed that about her, especially considering how quickly her no-nonsense lecture had roused him from self-pity, how it had given him hope that maybe someday he'd meet the girl of his dreams.

He pictured Sam's pretty, smiling face.

"Thinkin' about Sam?" she asked, unbuckling her seat belt.

Bryce nodded, then shrugged. "Yeah, I guess."

"Give her time, nephew. If a dotty old broad like me can find true love, so can a half-blind, nearly-bald ex-marine." As if to punctuate her belief, Olive gave him a gentle smack on the shoulder.

He turned off the motor and palmed his keys. "You think so?"

"Are you kidding? I've got calluses where my bony knees used to be, from praying the good Lord would send a big-hearted woman to whip you into shape!"

"And you think Sam's the answer to that prayer?"

"You never know…"

Nodding, he watched her climb the steps to her apartment. "Meet you upstairs in ten," he called to her. "If I don't soon get out of this monkey suit, I'm liable to start swinging from the trees."

He heard her laughter as he headed for his place, and he silently thanked God for the happy occasion of this day. Because if anyone had earned the chance to live a long, healthy, happy life with someone who loved her completely, it was his aunt Olive.

Chapter Fifteen

August in Alaska, Sam learned the hard way, could be unpredictable. A determined northern wind might turn seventy degrees to fifty with nothing more than a few well-timed gusts. Nearly three months in town had taught her that eighteen and twenty hours of sunshine each day didn't necessarily mean *warm* sunshine, a fact that often sent unprepared tourists into North Pole's shops in search of sweatshirts or jackets to ward off sudden chills.

She examined herself in the full-length mirror behind her bedroom door and adjusted the high collar of her tan suede blazer. She gave one last tug on the sleeves of the white flannel blouse under it and hoped her mother would be pleased to know that her only daughter had obeyed her "always be prepared" policy. But would Bryce approve, too?

Sam frowned. "What do you care what he thinks?" she asked her reflection. Maybe if she hadn't put so much emphasis on what Joey thought, he wouldn't have so easily blindsided her. She shook off the thought. If her dad saw her now, teary-eyed over a guy who broke her heart nearly a year ago, he'd shake his head and say, "Self-pity is self-defeating." And if her brothers had been around to hear the gentle scolding, they'd chime in with their usual tough-guy advice.

And they'd be right, Sam decided, chin up and shoulders back as she picked up her purse. Almost as an afterthought, she grabbed the brown tweed scarf she'd knitted to pass the time during lonely nights in campgrounds between Maryland and Alaska.

Sam had set the alarm for five-thirty to assure she'd be on time when Bryce pulled up out front in the borrowed van. "I'll pick you up at o-eight-hundred," he'd said before ducking into his apartment last night, and if her watch was correct, she'd have the satisfaction of waving hello as he parked at the curb. Hopefully, her confidence wouldn't reflect itself on her face or in her posture, because smugness certainly wasn't an attractive trait. Still, it felt good to know she'd beat the always-perfect, ever-punctual ex-marine!

As it turned out, Sam needn't have worried about appearing smug, because the unmistakable sound of a purring motor greeted her even before she locked the front door. "How long have you been here?" she asked, climbing into the front seat.

"Oh, five minutes or so." He grinned as she latched her seat belt. "You look cute today."

She didn't know which surprised her more—that he'd shown up fifteen minutes early or that she seemed powerless to control the quickening pace of her heartbeat. Then she reminded herself he'd said "cute" and not "gorgeous" or "beautiful"....

"So what's the story about that giant Santa?" she

asked, hoping to divert his attention from her flushed cheeks. "What is he, like, a hundred feet tall?"

"He seems that big to outsiders," he answered, laughing, "but he's really only forty-two feet high."

"*Only* forty-two feet?"

"And nine hundred pounds of painted fiberglass. I can't remember when they deactivated the motor and got rid of his pipe, but way back when, he puffed smoke, too."

"Guess the Politically Correct police decided Santa was setting a bad example by smoking, eh?"

"I guess."

"So, how long does a person have to live here before they aren't considered 'outsiders'?"

Laughing, he said, "Longer than four months."

Had she only been in North Pole such a short time? And since she'd loved every minute, why had it seemed longer?

"Probably only feels like you've been here forever because it's such a small town. With just a couple thousand people, it doesn't take long to find your way around and get to know everybody."

Nodding, Sam agreed. "I love the way everyone smiles and waves and asks how you're doing. Not the way they ask it back East, mind you, but as if they really care about the answer."

Bryce nodded as she continued.

"You have no idea how much I envy you, growing up in a place like this, where everybody knows everybody and—"

"There are times when all that familiarity isn't a good thing."

"Oh, c'mon," she said as he pulled into the hotel parking lot, "how can it ever be bad?"

He grinned. "When every adult knows what time your parents set for your curfew and calls to tell them why you're late. When you're home on leave and your neighbors know when you're due to report for duty as well as you do. When your fiancée dumps you to marry the marines, and you get sympathetic hugs from every old lady in town." He parked the van under the protective roof above the hotel's circular drive. "When people can tell, just by looking at your face, how much you hate listening to Christmas carols *all day long.*"

Sam giggled. "I think I get the picture." Then, "But wait…does that mean you don't like Christmas carols *either*?"

In place of an answer, Bryce tucked in one corner of his mouth.

"I don't believe it!"

He shrugged and held both hands palms up.

"That's just plain un-American! It's like saying you hate 'The Star-Spangled Banner'!"

A commotion in the hotel entry interrupted her, and Sam followed Bryce's gaze. Duke's son, daughter-in-law, and grandkids had gathered in the doorway, each tugging a rolling suitcase behind them. "Awfully nice of you to do this," Duke Junior said.

Bryce swiveled the driver's seat and stepped into the space behind it. "My pleasure," he replied, sliding open the van's side door. "Now that we're family, it'll be good having the half-hour drive to get better acquainted."

Once the family had settled in and buckled up, Bryce

aimed for the airport, pointing out landmarks along the way.

"There's the Santa Claus House," he said as they passed the red-and-white building, "home of the original 'letter from Santa.' Maybe next time you're in town, we can do some proper sightseeing."

"I want to come back when the aurora borealis are in full glow," said Duke's wife.

"Yeah, but in the meantime, you can get online and see some of the photos taken by our mayor pro tem. Kevin has won awards for his photography of the northern lights."

"And wildlife, and Alaska's gorgeous vistas, too," Sam added. "I'm looking forward to seeing all of that, live and in person, same as you guys."

"Is it true people here find moose in their yards on a regular basis?" Duke asked.

Bryce nodded, then said, "And if you leave your front door open, they'll mosey right on in." He shot her a playful grin. "Won't they, Sam."

She rolled her eyes and sighed good-naturedly. "He's referring to the time I forgot to lock up the shop during my first week in town. He scared me into never repeating the mistake by warning me that the big hairy things just love wandering into homes uninvited."

The family joined her merry laughter, and then Duke's wife said, "So how long have you two been engaged?"

Sam held her breath, watching in stunned silence as Bryce straightened his back and swallowed. Hard. Growing up around seven older brothers taught her a few lessons about men, two of the most important being:

they didn't like surprises, and they didn't like being put on the spot. So she cleared her throat and turned slightly in her seat. "Only engagement the two of us have," she said, forcing a laugh, "involves me working for him."

"Oh! I'm so sorry. I just assumed—" They didn't get to hear what she'd assumed, because their kids started to bicker about space in the cramped back seat.

"So how long was your flight from Texas to Fairbanks?" Sam asked, grateful to change the subject.

"Oh, fifteen hours or so," Duke replied, "not counting layovers."

"I sure hope Olive and your dad had a smooth flight to Miami," she said. "I remember her saying once that she isn't particularly crazy about air travel."

"Funny what we'll do for love," Duke's wife observed.

Bryce picked up where he'd left off, sounding like a professional tour guide. His voice, animated expressions, and genuine smile made her wonder why, if he disliked so many elements about this place, he sounded downright proud, sharing details about the ice festival, the Fourth of July parade, the quaint parks and a dozen other reasons to visit North Pole.

While the Carter family nodded and asked questions about the sights, Sam hoped—for Bryce's sake—that they wouldn't pass the lake where his mom and dad had drowned several years ago while on a fishing trip.

Weeks earlier, Olive had shared her disapproval of the way her brother and his wife had raised their son. Yes, she'd acknowledged, they had provided the necessities, but their come-and-go lifestyle had deprived him of pretty much everything else. Now, as Bryce and Sam delivered Duke's family to their airline terminal, she said a silent prayer of thanks that Bryce had been spared the bitter reminder of his parents' deaths.

Many hugs and well wishes later, they finally waved goodbye and headed back to North Pole.

"There's something I want to show you before we get back to town," Bryce said.

Sam chanced a peek at her wristwatch. "Okay, but just so you know…the store's been locked up tight for hours now, and it was closed all weekend because of the wedding. Wouldn't you rather I get in there, so I can—"

He reached across the console and grabbed her hand. "Humor me, will ya?"

Shrugging, she grinned. "Whatever you say, boss."

"Ironic you call me that, since I made a point of letting my folks know I had no interest in running the place."

"Is that why you decided to sell it?"

"That's why I considered it…" Then, "Did you ever see reruns of that old TV show *Sanford and Son*?"

Sam nodded.

"Realtors compared the place to Fred's garage." He shot her a lopsided grin. "If they could see it now, they'd have a change of heart, thanks to you."

So had he changed his mind about selling? Sam certainly hoped so, because she'd enjoyed every fingernail-breaking moment she'd spent fixing the place up and didn't relish the idea of leaving it in search of another job.

"If things keep up the way they have been these past few weeks," he added, "maybe I can afford to replace that eyesore of a store sign."

"You're a carpenter. Why not make a new one yourself?"

He paused before saying, "You're just full of good ideas, aren't you."

Not a question, she noticed, but a statement, and Sam didn't know how to take it. "But in all honesty, I think that old sign is cute in a kitsch sort of way."

He made a face.

"So Bryce," she said slowly, "what would it take, exactly, to get your carpentry shop up and running?"

"Money, tools, machines..." He laughed then tapped the steering wheel. "Customers...need I go on?"

"No, I think I get the picture." An idea to help him get his business off the ground began to percolate in her head as Bryce brought the van to a slow halt, pointing across the field beside the road.

"Look," he said, "a raven."

"He's so big, and...and so *beautiful*." Without taking her eyes from the bird, she whispered, "It's a male, isn't it?"

"Yeah, but...how'd you know?"

Shrugging, she said, "He's so black and shiny. Females aren't usually as bright, right, so they're better able to hide when they're nesting."

"I've got to admit, I'm amazed."

She faced him then, to see if his expression matched the tone of awe and admiration in his voice. "Why?"

"For starters, I don't know a single other woman who'd say that's a beautiful bird. And honestly? I expected an East Coaster like you would cower in her seat at the sight of a bird that has a reputation for being the deliverer of bad news."

"Believe it or not, we have ravens in Baltimore, too. But I interrupted your story. Sorry. Please. Continue. You were surprised I didn't cower at the sight of a ferocious blackbird…"

"…and you can tell a male from a female. Plus, you know *why* the good Lord made them look different. I'm impressed."

"Just goes to show," Sam said, lifting her chin a notch, "that you can't judge a book by its cover."

"Believe me, you can. Most of the time."

The tone of his voice alone would have kept her from responding to that remark, but then she caught the look on his face, all somber and serious. Sam wondered if she'd ever figure him out. "So what's this stuff about ravens being bearers of bad tidings?"

"They've sort of earned their bad reputation, historically speaking." The raven strutted in a circle, flapping its wings as Bryce continued. "Swedish folklore says they're the ghosts of people who didn't get a proper Christian burial, and there's a legend that says King Arthur disguised himself as a raven, making it seriously bad luck for the knights to kill one."

As if the bird heard and understood, it cut loose with a loud *kaw-kaw-kaw*, inspiring Sam to hum "The Twilight Zone" theme. "I much prefer the story I learned as a kid in Bible camp, of how Noah told the raven to fly away and check things out, and when it never came back, that's how he knew he'd soon be able to park the ark."

"Park the ark," Bryce repeated, chuckling. "You're a nut."

She liked making him laugh. Liked knowing that,

for the moment, anyway, he was taking some much-de-served pleasure from life. "So what's the surprise you wanted to show me?"

"It's just up ahead," he said, steering back onto the highway. As they drove, Bryce explained that Alaska got its name from the Aleut word *alyeska*, meaning "great land."

"It's the only state in the union where a man can head into the wilderness and keep going for six hundred miles without ever seeing a barbed wire fence."

"That is pretty spectacular," she agreed.

"I'll show you spectacular," he said, parking. "Better grab your jacket. Gets a little blustery up on that ridge."

After helping her shrug into it, he took her hand and led her onto a narrow, overgrown road. "This was part of the original Richardson Trail. Back in the midforties, it's what caught the attention of the Davises."

"Aren't they the couple who founded North Pole?"

When he looked down at her with a look of affection and admiration, Sam thought her heart might explode. He gave her hand a little squeeze and guided her farther down the rutted path.

"Don't know for sure what lured them to Alaska in the first place, but when I read the story of what drew them to this spot, I understood why they wanted to settle here."

Sam didn't understand why anyone would want to live on this muddy little stretch of road, miles from the highway, overgrown with weeds. But she opted to give Bryce the benefit of the doubt. Maybe this place had looked different, back then, and maybe—

They stepped into a clearing at that moment, and

what she saw stunned her into silence. Thick boughs of towering blue spruce swayed overhead as scrub pines dotted the hillside ahead. The sky was a shade of blue like none she'd seen in paintings or even in nature shows on the Discovery Channel, and it went on and on, for what seemed like an eternity.

"Olive calls this place Forever."

"I can see why." Then, "How can anyone see a thing like this and not believe in God?"

Bryce took a step forward and looked into her face. "Are you…are you *crying*?"

"Of course not," she answered, swiping the tell-tale evidence from her cheeks. "It's just…it's the wind and—"

Nothing could have surprised her more than when he took her in his arms and held her tight. "Don't be embarrassed. I had pretty much the same reaction, first time I came up here," he said. "The place has that effect on some people."

Sniffing, she rooted in her pocket for a tissue to blot her eyes. "Only some?"

"It never got to my folks that way, but Olive blubbered like a baby." He took a small step back and lifted Sam's chin on a bent forefinger. "And why do I get the feeling that if I wasn't here, you'd have done your fair share of blubbering, too?"

She stared up at him, wishing she could remove the eye patch and look into both beautiful brown eyes at the same time.

Just then a bald eagle screeched overhead, capturing their attention and making her expel a tiny gasp.

"Okay, so I've seen my fair share of ravens back East, but I have to admit, that's a first."

Bryce turned her loose so that he could point into the shallow valley ahead. "Last time I was up here, beavers had built a huge dam in that stream over there. Maybe next time we're here, I'll show it to you."

Sam realized she was beginning to understand this guy, at least a little bit. He didn't like listening to Christmas music twenty-four-seven, and he'd grown tired of candy cane lampposts and streets named after Santa's reindeer, but he did love his hometown. *This* aspect of it, anyway.

She'd been so warm, standing in the circle of his embrace, and now as the wind whistled through the pines, she shivered.

He noticed instantly and draped an arm around her shoulders, drawing her close to his side. "So what do you think, Samantha Sinclair? Can you hack it up here in the frozen North?"

"Hmpf," she teased, resting her head on his shoulder, "I'm beginning to think that's just a lot of hooey printed up by the Chamber of Commerce to encourage tourism."

"What?"

"Only ice I've seen since I pulled into town is the stuff they put in my cup at McDonald's."

"Trust me," he said, chuckling, "you're gonna see ice. Plenty of it, and sooner than you think."

"Hmm…I'm a 'warm and toasty' fan. Maybe I'm not made of hardy enough stuff to hack it after all."

He turned her so that they stood toe to toe. "Homesick?"

Sam shrugged. "I'd be lying if I said I didn't miss my family...even those rowdy brothers of mine. But I'd hardly call that 'homesick.'"

"Didn't they say you'd run home to mommy and daddy in less than a month?"

Sam couldn't be certain, but she would've sworn she'd shared that bit of information with Olive, not Bryce. Either way, some busy bees had been buzzing, and she'd been the main topic of conversation in the hive. She nodded, proud that she'd already lasted months longer than they'd expected her to.

"Winters are the toughest for newcomers," he said as his thumb drew slow circles on her jaw. "Twenty-plus hours of darkness is tough to cope with, even for those of us who've experienced it before. Add to that the unrelenting cold. If you can survive the first year..."

Sam nodded, understanding exactly what he meant. "I was talking with a woman just the other day who admitted that it takes her a couple of weeks to adjust, even though she was born and raised here." Grinning, she added, "I suppose the jigsaw company manufacturers love us Alaskans."

"Us?" he echoed.

"I like it here," she admitted. "I like it a lot, and I want to stay."

"Just to prove your brothers wrong?"

She studied the worry etched on his brow and wanted to kiss it away, along with his concern over the success of Rudolph's...and whatever else might be troubling him. "I've already done that." Shrugging again, she smiled. "I have plenty of other reasons for wanting to stay."

He smiled back and said, "Good."

As they walked hand in hand to the van, Bryce couldn't help but wonder if he'd made a big mistake by bringing her here. It had been one of his favorite places in the whole world—and thanks to the marines, he'd traveled the globe—yet he'd never shared the spot with anyone.

He'd been nine or ten when Olive had first brought *him* here. It had been during one of his parents' trips to DC to protest—he couldn't even remember what that particular "cause" had been—but he remembered Olive smoothing a blanket onto the ground and ordering him to sit beside her.

"This is where I come," she'd confessed, "when I'm feeling lonely and afraid, when I don't know how many more challenges I can handle before collapsing under their weight." Sliding her Bible from her bag, she'd told Bryce to find I Corinthians, chapter 10, verse 13.

"'There hath no temptation taken you but such as is common to man,'" he'd read haltingly, "'but God is faithful, who will not suffer you to be tempted above that ye are able; but will with the temptation also make a way to escape, that ye may be able to bear it.'" When he'd finished, Bryce admitted he hadn't understood a word of it.

"It means," Olive had said, "that the Father knows you better than anyone in your life, so He knows exactly how much pain and pressure you can handle. And because He knows there will be times when you *think* He's forgotten what your limits are, He gave you this verse, to remind you that no matter how tough life seems, He'll always, *always* provide the strength to cope…or a door to escape through."

He'd leaned on the advice—and the verse—more times than he could count. And returned to this *place* more times than he could count, to make tough decisions or escape bad memories.

"When's the best time to see the aurora borealis?" Sam asked, interrupting his thoughts.

"Couple of weeks, I guess."

"When was the last time you saw it?"

"Hard *not* to see it when you live here. It's up there, every night for months…when it isn't cloudy, that is." And then, without knowing why, Bryce launched into a mini-lecture, explaining that it's up there high in the atmosphere, a miraculous blend of oxygen and nitrogen, molecules, electrons, and protons that moves in a colorful curtain against a backdrop of inky sky.

He heard himself droning on and on, sharing every fact and bit of minutia he'd learned about it over the years, knowing that he sounded like a monotonous college professor, yet powerless to shut himself up. And God bless her, Sam sat in the passenger seat, nodding and smiling as if he'd woven a tale that ranked up there with *Gone with the Wind*.

"Still feel like it's a big deal?" she asked. "Or have you grown so accustomed to it, you sorta forget it's there?"

"Depends," he said with a grin, "on who's watching it with me." Hopefully, he could time it so she'd hear the distant, haunting notes of the train whistle while she watched them for the first time.

They drove in silence for a few miles—something Debbie had never been able to do—making Bryce acutely aware just how unlike other women Sam was. Man, but he wanted her to stay in North Pole, to learn to cope with the cold and nights of endless darkness and days that seemed to melt, one into the other. With her nearby, he might just learn to stomach the always-blinking Christmas lights and the maddening holiday music.

Sam exhaled a long sigh and then leaned against the headrest.

"Tired?"

"No, just drinking in that amazing view."

He glanced slightly right, toward the peaks of the Alaska Range visible in the distance. "Some days you can actually see Mount McKinley."

She sighed again. "Wow."

He remembered the time he'd brought Debbie up here on a night when the full moon lit the mountaintops like a spotlight. He'd pointed out a shooting star, told her to make a wish...and she'd responded with, "How do you expect me to see *anything* with those stupid mountains in the way?"

Yeah, Sam was different, all right.

"Maybe we'll bring your brother Bill up here, introduce him to Forever."

She shook her head.

Before he could ask why, she shrugged. "I'd just hate to stand there, looking out at that magnificent vista, beside somebody who might not get it, y'know?"

The corny line from some old black and white movie pinged in his memory, and it took all the willpower he could muster to keep from asking her where she'd been all his life.

Chapter Sixteen

Bill had decided not to rent a car after all, thinking he might get more out of the visit if he hiked, like Sam did, through town. He'd grown a strange little beard, and Sam did her best to pretend she liked it as much as he did. She generally disliked facial hair, with one rare exception in Johnny Depp's portrayal of Captain Jack Sparrow. Sam grinned at the comparison, because with the scruffy fuzz on his chin, Bill could have passed for Johnny's brother.

"Do you mind if we head into town," she asked as he loaded his bag into the back of Olive's car, "so I can shop for some wheels of my own?"

"Not at all. I think it's quite wise, little sister, to get some advice from a car guy."

She handed him the keys to the Jeep. "Better get used to it," Sam told him, "because you'll be drivin' it home."

He climbed in behind the wheel, and as he adjusted the seat and mirrors, said, "You're calling it 'home' already?" Bill chuckled. "Mom's not gonna be happy to hear that...."

"Then don't tell her." And regretting her terse tone, Sam grinned. "It's so great to see you."

"You, too, sissy."

No one on earth was allowed to call her that except Bill. "So how is everybody?"

"Fine, fine. Except that they miss you, of course."

"Good."

He gave her a quizzical look.

"Maybe that'll inspire them to come see me and get a taste of this amazing place for themselves. Those pictures I've emailed just don't do it justice." Sam pointed. "Take this exit and head north."

"Do you already know what kind of car you want?"

"I haven't the foggiest notion." Sam laughed. "Surprised?"

"Only that you've gone this long without one."

"Well, like I told you on the phone, North Pole is a great little town. Everything is just a short walk. But that won't be nearly as much fun once the cold weather sets in. Besides, Olive will want her car back when she gets home from her honeymoon."

"So you plan to sit out the winter here, do you?"

"Of course." She looked at him, hoping to discern his attitude about that. "Why wouldn't I?"

"You're as cold-blooded as an amphibian, for starters."

"Comedian."

"Well, it's true. I'll bet you say 'I'm freezing!' ten thousand times between October and April. And it's nowhere near as cold in Maryland as it is in Alaska."

Since she couldn't argue with that, Sam said, "We

have furnaces here, too, y'know. And fireplaces, and wood stoves and—"

"*We*?" Bill shook his head. "Hoo boy, Mom really *isn't* gonna be happy, is she?"

Sam winced. "I wish you'd quit saying that."

"Sorry. Guess it's true what they say."

"What?"

"The truth hurts."

On the heels of a deep breath, she asked, "Is that why you're here? To talk me into going back to Baltimore?"

Bill gave her shoulder a gentle brotherly punch. "No, I'm not here to drag you back to Baltimore." And shaking his head, he added, "I've been in Alaska—what, twenty minutes?—and already I can tell that'd be near impossible."

"So you admit you guys were wrong, then?"

"When we said you'd never last out here, you mean?"

Sam nodded.

"Maybe we should wait until you've survived your first winter to point fingers. *If* you survive your first winter."

"Silly me. I thought you'd be on my side."

"This isn't about 'sides,' Sam."

"I suppose not."

He gave her arm a playful jab. "Be fair. Would you have stood up to them if the shoe was on the other foot?"

He'd made an excellent point. Her brothers almost always formed a united front, and to disagree with one of them was tantamount to disagreeing with all of them, which amounted to an invitation to full-out verbal warfare. "Not on your life," she admitted, returning the gentle arm punch as they spotted a car dealership just inside the Fairbanks city limits.

Within minutes, Sam had spotted the perfect vehicle.

"Won't your friend think you're a copycat?" Bill asked as she inspected the Jeep.

"Olive's is maroon, and this one's red." But even as she said it, Sam knew that a degree or two in shade variation was nil in a guy's mind. "And hers is an older model," she added.

It took less than an hour to cut the deal that made the SUV her very own. "Let's celebrate," she said as they waited for the salesman to drive the car around front. "I'll buy you lunch at the best eatery in North Pole."

"Let me guess...the restaurant that gave your job to some wet-behind-the-ears teenager?"

"No way." She laughed. "Though it might be fun to introduce you to the guy who owns the place, watch him squirm when I introduce him to my overprotective big brother..."

"Oh fine. Get me beat up on my first day in Alaska...."

She dangled the keys to her new car in front of his face. "Just follow me. And don't worry. If anybody in town picks on you, I'll take care of 'em." Sam shook a fist in the air and laughed again.

In no time, it seemed, she found herself sitting across from her brother at a table at Dalman's, ordering coffee and burgers with fries.

The waitress delivered squatty glasses of water. "So who's this handsome fella?" Cora asked.

Sam didn't fail to notice that although the question was for her, Cora's eyes never left Bill's face. "My brother Bill," Sam said, "who's visiting from Maryland."

"Love the beard," Cora said, winking.

Sam couldn't wait to get him alone, so she could tease him for blushing like a schoolgirl.

"Back in a jiffy, *Bill*." Cora wiggled her eyebrows and gave a flirty little wave as she walked away.

"What's up with *that*?" he asked when she was out of earshot.

"What?"

He hadn't taken his eyes off Cora. "I thought men outnumbered women three to one in Alaska."

"So?"

"So with all those guys to choose from, why's a girl like that flirting with *me*?"

"Oh, I dunno…maybe because you're one of the best-looking guys in the restaurant?"

"Maybe I need to call the school," he said, laughing, "see if the principal will let me come back to work a few weeks late. Or not at all."

"I'd love that, but I don't think Susan would."

Bill's expression darkened. "Susan is one of the reasons I needed to get away." Eyes downcast, he fiddled with the napkin holder. "I saw her with a guy. She said he was just a friend, but I know better."

"How?"

Brows furrowed, he met her eyes. "Friends don't kiss like that, that's how."

Sam stopped his fidgeting by wrapping her hands around his. "Aw, Billy, I'm sorry."

"No biggie," he said, plucking a napkin from the

holder. "It was only a matter of time." And shrugging, he added, "Guess I wasn't the guy of her dreams."

Bill laughed good-naturedly, but Sam wasn't buying his upbeat attitude. Not for a minute, because he'd taken each of his three long-term relationships seriously. More seriously than his girlfriends had, and it had cost him, every time. "Have you told the family?"

"Do you see 'Idiot' stamped on my forehead?"

"Been there, done that," she said. "No way I'd want a repeat of their advice."

"If you wanna call it *advice*."

Their quiet laughter was interrupted by a deep voice. "Well, well, what have we here?"

Sam hoped her annoyance wasn't visible. "Dan. How have you been?"

"Good, good." He studied her face, then said, "Gonna introduce me to your new beau?"

Brother and sister shared a chuckle before Sam said, "Bill, meet Dan Brooks, the guy who fired me before I had a chance to show up for work in his hotel restaurant. Dan, my big brother, Bill." She grinned and added, "The prizefighter."

Dan's brows rose high on his forehead and the hand he'd extended in greeting froze in midair.

"My sister, the kidder." Bill shook Dan's hand. "Some might call what I do for a living 'fighting,' but I call it 'teaching.'" And after a hearty handshake, he went back to pressing accordion pleats into the paper napkin.

Cora showed up with their meals. "You wanna give a girl some room, Danny boy?" she said, frowning as she moved him aside with a well-placed hip bump. Flashing a bright smile at Bill, she added, "Some guys think 'cause they have a few bucks in the bank, they own the world."

"Spoken like the proverbial woman scorned," Dan countered.

The waitress dispensed the food and laid a hand on Sam's shoulder. "Looks to me like the good Lord was watchin' out for you the day this guy gave your job to his nephew."

As much as Sam agreed, she had no intention of getting involved in whatever dispute had inspired the angry interaction between Dan and Cora.

"Women," Dan said, grinning. "Can't live with 'em...and can't live with 'em." Then, "Good to meet you, Bill. And good to see you again, Sam. Say hey to Bryce for me."

"Looks like North Pole has all the relationship drama of the big city," Bill teased once Dan had left. "So how *is* Bryce?"

She felt the heat of a blush creep into her cheeks and hoped Bill was too busy putting catsup and mustard onto his burger to notice. "Fine."

"You always were a terrible liar."

"What!"

"Oh, give me a break, Miss Starry Eyes. If you like the guy, why deny it?"

"I'm not denying it. Or admitting it. I don't know what I feel about him, if you want the truth."

"Tell me about him."

If he was bored during her recitation of Bryce's finer qualities, Bill didn't let it show. Then, realizing how she must have sounded, going on and on about Bryce, Sam changed the subject. "I wish you could stay a month, so you could see the Yukon Quest sled dog race. I hear it's ten times more grueling than the Iditarod."

"Find me a job, and maybe I'll stay."

Sam remembered that before she left Baltimore, Susan had applied for a teaching job at Bill's school. If the principal had hired her, it was no wonder Bill had lost his enthusiasm for work.

"So how are things at that Christmas shop of yours?" he asked.

Sam blinked, uncertain what to make of the abrupt turn in the conversation. "I've accomplished a lot, but there's still more to be done."

"I think Cora hit the old nail on the head."

"When…".

"When she said the good Lord knew what He was doing, putting you in charge of Rudolph's instead of running Dan Brooks' restaurant. I haven't seen your eyes light up this way about anything in years."

She opened her mouth to ask "you think so?" when he added, "…except when you're talking about your boss, that is." And using a french fry as a pointer, Bill said, "And unless he wants a serious butt-kicking, he'd better treat you right."

"Love you, too, Billy."

"So when do I get to meet this marine of yours?"

"He's not *mine*," she reminded him. Then, "I'm making your favorite for supper—"

"Lasagna?" He rubbed his palms together. "I haven't had any decent Italian food since before you steered that big ugly RV west." He popped a fry into his mouth. "Is your, ah, *boss* going to join us?"

Sam shrugged. "He's invited. Hard to tell whether or not he'll show up." And giving in to impulse, she reached across the table and grabbed his hands. "You'll like him. You two have a lot in common...but I'll let you figure that out tonight."

"If he shows up, y'mean." Bill sat back. "I have to admit, kiddo...Alaska—or somebody who lives here—becomes you."

Chapter Seventeen

"So what's your brother up to this morning?"

"Adjusting to the four-hour time difference," Sam said. "It took me days to get used to it."

Bryce cringed as Sam stood atop the wobbly painter's ladder dusting Christmas ornaments. "So how long were you with the circus?"

Her hands froze, and frowning, she looked down at him. "Circus?"

Pencil poised above the ledger, he said, "Well, there you are, up there making like the tightrope walker. *Again.* I just naturally assumed…"

"Pshaw."

Who but Sam would say "pshaw," he wondered as she went back to dusting.

"I'm fine," she said. "Besides, I'm nearly finished with this shelf."

And then what, he wanted to say, *you'll do a swan dive as an encore…without a net?* But before he could form the words, Bryce realized she was cranking up to sneeze, and from the looks of things, it would be rafter-shaking. "Sam, be carefu—"

Too late. Just as he feared it might, the sneeze threw her off balance. Arms clawing the air as the dust rag dropped to the floor, she grabbed for the ladder's top rung, making it teeter from the top down.

Papers flew from the counter as Bryce leaped up to steady the ladder. Thankfully, she didn't fall, and he heaved a grateful sigh. Pressing his forehead to the ladder's side rail, he said, "Sam...*now* will you get down from there?"

Even terror-struck, her voice overflowed with music. "Okay. Just...just give me a minute to stop shaking."

"I'm right here," he promised, patting her jeans-clad calf. "If you fall, I'll catch you. You've got my word."

It seemed to take forever for her to descend the dilapidated old ladder, and even before both sneakered feet hit the floor, he gathered her close. Bryce could feel her heart beating hard against his chest, telling him her earlier bravado had died a quick death up there on that top rung. "You scared me to death. Don't let me catch you taking a chance like that again, you hear me?"

Sam took a tiny step back and looked up into his face with a trembly smile. "Yessir, boss." Then, "It's your fault, you know. You were supposed to replace that old thing."

Despite the teasing words, Sam's voice was still shaky, and Bryce frowned. She felt so tiny, so vulnerable, standing there in his arms, that he wanted to kiss the fear from her face. He might have done it, too, if the door hadn't burst open.

"Samantha Sinclair, I'm telling Mom!"

"Billy!" she said, leaving his arms to hug her brother. "I thought you were going to sleep till noon."

"I tried, but all this commotion down here woke me up." Grinning, he held out a hand to Bryce. "Name's Bill Sinclair."

"Good to finally meet you," Bryce said. "Sam's been talking about you pretty much nonstop."

The overhead music changed just then, from Elvis Presley's "White Christmas" to Gene Autry's famous recording of "Rudolph the Red-Nosed Reindeer." Bill shook his head. "You guys here in North Pole listen to that kinda stuff all day?"

"All day, every day," Bryce droned.

"Then maybe when you get a minute," Bill said, his thumb indicating the overhead speaker, "you'll tell me how you keep from going stark-raving mad."

It was immediately apparent that Sam's sense of humor ran in the family. "Oh, I think I'm gonna like your brother," he told Sam.

Propping one fist on her hip, she feigned shock. "Ack! I'm outnumbered by scrooges!"

"I'm not a scrooge," Bill said.

"It'd just be nice if every once in a while," Bryce added, "somebody would play a country tune or—"

"—or some jazz."

"Blues."

"Classical."

"I'd even settle for opera now and then!"

"Uncle," Sam interrupted, both hands up in mock surrender, "I get the picture!"

The threesome enjoyed a round of laughter. "I have a ton of stuff to do in the storeroom," Sam said, "but I'll have supper ready at five, sharp. That's seventeen hundred to you," she said, looking at Bryce. "Don't either of you show up late."

Grinning, Bryce said, "Yes, boss."

Bill looked from his sister to her employer and back again. "Maybe I'll mosey on over to the diner, find out if that cute little waitress flirts with all her customers, or if I was a special case." He was halfway out the door before he added, "I was only kidding earlier, by the way. I won't tell Mom what you were doing before I so rudely interrupted." Smirking, he walked out the door, letting it slam behind him.

If Sam's whole family was like Bill, Bryce thought he'd get along with them just fine.

Sam had loaded the CD player with non-Christmas disks, and the threesome played a rousing game of Name That Tune all through dinner. Not surprisingly, Bill the Karaoke King won hands down. And while he rifled through Sam's music collection for more songs, Bryce volunteered to help clear the dishes and get dessert on the table.

"I really like your brother," he said, stacking plates on the counter.

She took a half-gallon of vanilla ice cream from the freezer compartment. "He likes you, too. I can tell."

Bryce grabbed its door in time to keep her from thumping her forehead on it.

"Oh wow," she said, rubbing the spot it might have hit, "thanks."

Scooping up a handful of dirty silverware, Sam opened the dishwasher as Bryce slid out the lower rack.

They both bent at the same time, clunking heads in the process.

"Hard as a rock!" they said together. "Great minds think alike?" they recited simultaneously.

The laughter started slow and escalated until they found themselves leaning on one another, limp with glee.

She was about to tell him that the ice cream was probably soft enough to serve when his cell phone rang.

"It's Olive," he said, grinning as he read the caller ID.

"Tell her I said hello and to keep having a good time. And that we miss her."

Winking, Bryce disappeared into his apartment.

Fifteen minutes later, when he joined Bill and Sam in her living room, he seemed quiet and distant.

"Is everything okay?" she asked.

"I guess." He shook his head. "At least, that's what Olive says."

"So what makes you think she isn't?"

"Can't put my finger on it, but something seemed… off."

Bill cleared his throat then stood and stretched. "I hate to be a party pooper," he said, "but it's been a long day. I think I'll turn in, if you don't mind."

"Of course we don't mind." Sam gave him a hug and kissed his cheek. "Sleep tight, brother dear."

"Pancakes in the morning?" he asked, wiggling his eyebrows.

"You bet."

He crossed the room in three long strides, and in the bedroom doorway, said, "Have you shown your boss your new wheels yet?"

"Not yet. Tomorrow, maybe." She chanced a peek at Bryce and caught his wary expression. "Oh, don't be such a worrywart. It has four-wheel drive!"

Once Bill had closed the bedroom door, she sat beside Bryce on the couch. "Did Olive let you talk with Duke?"

He leaned forward, elbows balanced on his knees and hands clasped in the space between. "No. She said she'd sent him to the lobby for ice."

"Maybe they had their first marital spat," Sam suggested. "This is a big step for both of them, Olive, especially. I mean…she's lived alone most of her life, so naturally it'll be a challenge—and a major adjustment—learning to share her life with someone. Even someone she loves as much as Duke."

He nodded. "Yeah, I guess that could explain things…."

"But you think it's somehow connected with the way she behaved and looked before she left for the honeymoon."

Turning, he looked deep into her eyes. "How could you possibly know that?"

It wasn't much of a stretch, since she'd been the one to bring it to Bryce's attention. Right now, all Sam wanted was to ease his mind and erase that look of concern from his face! "Will you pray with me?"

He sucked in a huge gulp of air and let it go slowly. "Aw, Sam, I don't know. It's been a long, long time since I've talked to God, out loud, anyway," he admitted. "I'm pretty rusty…."

"You did a fine job the night Duke asked for your

blessing on their marriage, as I recall. But even if you are rusty, the Lord won't mind."

Silence was his answer.

"Do you mind if I pray, then?"

"Here?"

"Why not?"

"Now?"

"No time like the present." Sam bowed her head and closed her eyes and silently asked the Almighty's guidance, so that whatever words He put upon her heart to pray would be those Bryce most needed to hear. Then she grasped his hand and gave it a loving squeeze.

"Dear heavenly Father," she began, "we can't know what Olive is thinking or feeling while she's so many miles from home, but *You* know, because You can read her heart. Shower us with strength, Lord, so we might trust You to watch over her. Bless her and her new husband, and let them enjoy these last days of their honeymoon, then bring them safely back to the friends and family who miss them so much. And Lord, I ask that You shower Bryce with the peace and serenity that comes from knowing You are in control, always and forever. We ask these things in Your most holy name, amen."

A moment passed before he spoke, and when he did, Bryce's voice was deep and gravelly. "That was…that was perfect." Nothing could have surprised her more than when he hugged her tight and buried his face in the crook of her neck.

Chapter Eighteen

Sam tried to pretend she hadn't noticed that Bryce seemed to be avoiding her. At first, she told herself he was just giving her time to visit with Bill, but despite numerous invitations, Bryce hadn't shared a meal—or a moment, for that matter—with them since the night Olive had called from Florida.

Sam racked her brain, trying to remember what she might have said or done to cause his standoffish behavior, and couldn't think of a single thing. What choice did she have but to blame the prayer she'd foisted upon him after Bill went to bed that night? He'd made it clear that the whole idea made him uncomfortable, but as usual, Sam went right ahead and did what she wanted.

Olive had told her that Bryce had never been the most spiritual guy, and that numerous battles had only increased his scoffing attitude toward God. The accumulation of tragedies weighed heavily on him, Olive had explained, so heavily that he'd done everything possible to wall himself off from the rest of the world…and God

"All he really needed," his aunt had told Sam, "was a little tough love, and I was more than happy to dole it out!" And with time and prayer, she believed her nephew had healed, inside and out.

But Sam knew better. Oh, his physical injuries had healed, but emotionally and spiritually, Bryce was hurting, and rather than admit it, he'd learned how to hide his feelings. Something told her that his sometimes sullen behavior had been hard-earned on the battlefield—but that with the constant care and tender ministrations of someone he could trust, he'd heal on the *inside,* too.

Bryce's aunt wasn't here to dispense tough love this time, but if that's what he needed, Sam was more than happy to act as Olive's stand-in. And if she wasn't tough enough to endure a few retaliatory verbal jabs to the chin, then she wasn't cut out to share Forever with him, literally *or* figuratively.

Olive had said, time and again, that she believed the Lord had sent Sam to North Pole for reasons other than a chef's job. Sam had pooh-poohed the idea back then, but now? She believed Olive had been right. When it had happened, exactly, Sam couldn't say. But she'd stopped pretending that her feelings for Bryce were strictly business. She liked him. Liked him a lot.

Sam's favorite Bible verse came to mind, and as she mentally recited 1 Corinthians 10:13, she nodded as a sense of peace settled over her, knowing in her heart that the Father had, indeed, provided a means for her to escape hard times. How else could she explain the idea she'd come up with to help Bryce turn his dream of a carpentry shop into a reality?

Sam paid extra attention to her outfit that morning, choosing clothes and colors that had inspired compliments from him before. He seemed to prefer her curly hair long and loose, and so she didn't pull it into clips or a ponytail. She wore a pink sweater over her jeans and a tad more mascara and lipstick than usual because, as Bill astutely pointed out, "It's not easy for a guy to growl at a pretty girl."

She found Bryce in his workshop, bent over a tool bench. He barely looked up when she crossed from the big double doors to the table that held a dozen awls and chisels, saws and drills. "Brought you some coffee," she said, "just the way you like it." And holding up a brown paper bag, Sam added, "Made you a tuna sandwich, too. Where would you like me to—"

"Just leave it over there." Using a Phillips head screwdriver, he pointed at the one bare spot on the table.

She decided to ignore his rude response. Maybe, like her dad, he didn't appreciate being interrupted while he was working.

Sam spotted a battered clock radio on the shelf behind him and walked over to it. "Does this thing pull in any decent stations?" she asked, reaching for the On button.

"Yeah, it does. But I'd rather not listen right now... if you don't mind."

Was that his way of telling her he didn't intend to cave to her control, as he had the night she'd prayed for him and Olive? Sam inhaled, determined to give it one more shot. "I baked brownies this morning and wrapped a couple in foil for you." She shrugged. "Dessert, you could call it, for after you finish your—"

"Was that a delivery truck I saw out back this morning?"

"Yeah, bringing the Christmas cards Olive ordered right before she—"

"Have you unpacked them already?"

"Well, not entirely. I'm still trying to rearrange the stock, so I can group like items together. Customers have a much easier time finding what they're looking for if—"

"And the stuff that came yesterday? Is it all inventoried and labeled and ready for the shelves?"

Was Bryce deliberately testing the limits of her patience, or did it just seem like he wanted to get a rise out of her? She'd come in here with nothing but good intentions. If this was an example of how he'd treated Olive after he came home from the war, well, the woman had a stronger constitution than Sam had given her credit for. "'Love is patient, love is kind,'" she whispered through clenched teeth. "'Love is patient, love is kind…'"

The brow above his eye patch raised slightly as he asked, "What's that?"

"Oh, nothing." And in a brighter, louder voice, Sam added, "I'll be in the shop if you need me." She stomped to the door and resisted the urge to slam it. Thought about snarling, "You're welcome for lunch!" but bit her tongue. Felt like stomping right back up to him and planting a big juicy kiss on his lips.

Now *there* was an idea…

What started as a little smirk had grown into a full-blown smile by the time Sam stood directly in front of him. She paid no attention to his shocked expression. Instead, she pressed a palm to each of his cheeks and stood on tiptoe.

When Bryce realized what she aimed to do, he leaned backward. "But...but I had an onion bagel for breakfast," he said, "and haven't brushed my—"

She felt his shoulders tense as their lips met, heard a soft sigh escape his lungs. Slowly, one of his big hands moved to cup the back of her head as the other pressed gently into the small of her back. And, just as he started to really respond to the kiss...Sam stepped back and gave his broad chest a *pat-pat-pat*.

"There's more where that came from, if you can get over your grumpy self," she said. Then she turned on her heel and marched toward the exit, knowing she'd see his stunned expression every time she closed her eyes.

And the thought made her giggle all the way back to Rudolph's.

Bryce stared at the door for a full minute, wondering if Sam might come back and finish what she'd started. When she didn't, he figured he had nobody to blame but himself. How in the world she'd summoned the patience to put up with his little pity fest, he didn't know. But he couldn't help grinning and thanking the good Lord that she had.

He'd often imagined what it might be like...holding her close, kissing her...but the vision paled by comparison to the real thing. Bryce licked his lips, knowing he'd taste that kiss for hours. He'd no doubt hear her parting comment in his head a couple hundred times, too, and that made him smile even wider.

Show a little class, he told himself. *Go to the shop and apologize for acting like a jerk.*

He glanced at his workbench, where miscellaneous pegs and boards lay scattered among sawdust and shavings. Fortunately, Sam hadn't seemed to notice the well-sanded wood he'd turn into a gift, just for her. But even if she hadn't built up a solid head of steam after delivering his lunch, it wasn't likely she'd know what all the pieces and parts would become, once he'd sanded and polished them to perfection.

Eyeing the brown bag amid it all, Bryce shook his head. How like her to remember that he'd confessed how often he forgot to eat when a project was under way. If he knew Sam, she'd worked her special brand of kitchen magic on everything, from the sandwich to the brownies. It didn't surprise him, when he opened the rumpled sack, to find that she'd added potato chips, a pickle, and a juice box. Or that she'd scribbled a note on the neatly folded napkin. Something to keep the grumbling at bay. And she'd signed it with her by-now familiar smiley face.

Bryce shook his head, amazed that somebody as sweet and big-hearted, as smart and funny as Sam could be interested in a disfigured grump like himself. But he held in his hands proof-positive that she was. "Lord," he said out loud, "I don't know what I ever did in my miserable life to deserve her, but if You'll tell me what it was, I'll do it over and over, to guarantee I never lose her."

"That's about the smartest thing I've heard anybody say about my baby sister."

Bryce lurched slightly in response to Bill's voice.

"Sorry, man," he said, ambling up to the workbench, "didn't mean to startle you." Chuckling, he added, "But in all honesty, it would've been tough *not* to, deep as you were in la-la-land."

"Blame that sister of yours," Bryce said. "She's turned my brain to mush."

"Ha. Never thought I'd hear a big bad marine admit a thing like *that*."

Bryce chuckled. "Never thought I'd *say* a thing like that."

"Does she know yet?"

"Know what?"

"That you're nuts about her."

Bryce considered denying it. "If my idiotic behavior hasn't signaled her…"

"She's a lot of things, that kid sister of mine, but 'mind reader' isn't one of 'em."

"Tell you the truth, Bill, I was asking myself right before you walked in here what in the world the girl sees in me—"

"So I heard."

Another shrug, then, "—'cause I'm not exactly a prize."

It was Bill's turn to shrug. "So what are you working on there?"

Bryce told Bill what he'd planned for Sam's birthday, and since her brother seemed mildly interested in the shop, Bryce gave him a tour. He described each gizmo and gadget and listed the tools on his "wish list" that would help him turn his carpentry dream into reality. "Only way any of that can happen," he admitted, "is if I sell Rudolph's."

"If the market is as tight here as it is back East, I don't envy you."

Nodding, Bryce said, "I've had one decent offer, but I turned it down."

Bill didn't understand why, and said so.

"Because the offer came from Dan Brooks, that clown who gave your sister's job to his scrawny nephew, for one thing. I'm the first to admit the place isn't much, but God only knows what that greedy fool would do to it." He tucked his hands into his pockets. "Besides, where will Sam work if I sell it?"

"Hey, don't get me wrong…I admire your loyalty, but business is business. Sam would understand that. Did she tell you how she pretty much paid her own way through college, and how she worked her fingers to the bone to help that loser fiancé of hers build his construction company from the ground up?"

"No," he said. But the information didn't surprise him.

"We used to call her 'Jane of all trades, master of none' because she worked at so many jobs." The memory inspired a quiet chuckle. "That girl did everything from waiting tables to bagging groceries to managing a video store. There were times we only saw her on major holidays, and even then, just long enough to hug everybody and scarf down a quick meal."

"And I'll bet she managed to get straight A's the whole time."

Bill nodded. "Not only that, but she double-majored." On the heels of an admiring sigh, he added, "She's something else, that sister of mine."

Bryce couldn't have agreed more.

"So when will you tell her?"

"How I feel about her, y'mean?"

Another nod.

"Just between you and me, I don't know that I will." Bryce held up a hand to halt Bill's protest. "Because she deserves more than a one-eyed jarhead who can't get his mind out of Afghanistan."

"Can't," Bill said, "or won't?"

"Does it matter? Bottom line is...I'm not good enough for her."

Bill crossed both arms over his chest. "You sure you were a marine?"

Bryce didn't need to hear more to know what Sam's brother meant. Marines had a reputation for being tough and uncomplaining, and his confession sounded more like self-pity than a rational explanation for not telling Sam how he felt about her. "Sounds like whining, I know, but it isn't. Last thing I want to do is burden her with my—"

"She's not one of your recruits. If you respect her as much as you say you do, don't you think you owe it to her to let *her* make the choice?"

It was a good point. Still...

"You probably know this already, but Sam is never happier than when she's doing something for people she cares about."

Bryce emptied the contents of the lunch bag onto his workbench. "Don't I know it," he said. Then, "Had lunch?"

"Don't mind if I do," Bill said, scooting a stool closer to the table.

As they ate, the men swapped stories of Bill's days in Iraq and Bryce's tours of duty in Afghanistan. And by the time they divided up the brownies she'd baked, they realized they had far more in common than their fierce, protective love for Samantha Sinclair.

Chapter Nineteen

She'd left explicit instructions for every member of her family that they were not, under any circumstances, to tell Joey Michaels where she'd gone, lest he get the misguided notion she'd had to run all the way to Alaska to escape the hurt and humiliation of their breakup. "How did you find me?" Sam demanded.

"Your best friend Marsha told me," he said, "when she found out I broke it off with—"

"I'm working, Joe," she snapped. Maybe hearing her call him that, instead of the more affectionate "Joey," would send the clear message that she didn't want to hear the story of his heartbreak…and spare him from the "What goes around comes around" that was on the tip of her tongue.

"You never asked me where I'm calling from."

"Frankly, Joe, I don't care where you're calling from." She warned herself to be careful. Too much ire and he'd think she'd been pining away for him; too little and he'd get the idea their relationship could be repaired. And it most definitely could *not*.

"I'm in Anchorage."

"Hundreds of miles from where I am," she pointed out. But curiosity prompted her to ask, "On business, I hope?"

Joey explained how he'd sold his construction company to a high-profile developer with offices in almost every state in the union, and they'd asked him to spend a few months opening an office in Alaska. "I was hoping you'd let me buy you dinner, so I could at least try and show you how sorry I am for—"

"Listen, it's over and done with, okay? Forgiven and forgotten." And it was the truth. She'd never been happier, never felt more fulfilled, than since she'd moved to North Pole. Sam knew that if Joey hadn't left her when he did, she'd still be in Baltimore, catering to his every whim…and getting nothing but grief in return. "I absolutely love it here. The good Lord has blessed me in more ways than I can count."

"Are you, uh, seeing anyone?"

"As a matter of fact, I am." Not the whole truth, but not exactly a lie, either. She saw Bryce every day, didn't she?

"Is he treating you well?"

"You bet he is." Also true, too…if she didn't count these past few days.

"How's the family?"

"Great. Yours?" Their conversation made her feel increasingly uncomfortable, but two wrongs didn't make a right, and she simply couldn't bring herself to be cruel.

"Lost my grandmother last month."

"I'm sorry to hear that." And she was, too. Sam had always liked the Michaels family matriarch. "She was

such a lovely lady. I'm sure she'll be missed." But she'd
had enough of his small talk and prayed for the strength
to end the call gently and quickly. "Well, I'm not getting any work done standing here chatting," she said,
"so you take care, Joe." And with that, she hung up.

It surprised her, as the hours passed, that no negative emotions surfaced following Joey's call. As she
prepared supper for herself and Bill, Sam wondered
why the sound of his voice hadn't inspired feelings of
regret or sadness. Would it have been so easy to get on
with her life if her love for him had been genuine? Sam
didn't think so.

"Where's Bryce?" Bill asked when she called him
to the table.

"Still puttering in his shop, I expect. He's pretty concerned about his aunt, and I don't think he'll really calm
down until he can see with his own eyes that she's all
right."

"His own *eye*, you mean." Bill smiled at his own
cleverness. "I take it Olive raised Bryce?"

"Pretty much. From what I gather, his mom and dad
were hippy types who did a lot of traipsing around the
country, picketing against this and marching for that."

"And he enlisted in the marines?" Bill laughed.
"Guess *that* showed 'em!"

Though Sam had never given that a thought, she supposed it made sense. "Olive said they were so opposed
to his decision that they refused to write to him after
he was deployed, so it fell to her to send care packages
and letters." She heaved a sigh.

"Bummer." Then, "I stopped by his shop today, and

he shared his lunch with me." Bill winked. "That was nice of you, considering…"

Considering? Considering *what*? But wait…was that a smirk on Bill's face? "All right, out with it," she said, narrowing one eye.

"Out with what?"

"Oh, come on, don't play the innocent with me. I grew up looking at your 'I've got a secret' expression, and it's written all over your face right now."

Shoulders up and hands extended in supplication, he said, "I have no idea what you're talking about."

"Ri-i-i-ght," she replied. "Just remember what Granddad said about fibs…"

"…'Each one leaves a stain on your soul,'" they said in unison.

After a moment of warm sibling laughter, Sam said, "You'll never guess who called me today."

"Santa?"

"Always the comedian," she teased. "No…this guy doesn't deliver anything good."

His eyebrows shot up. "Not Joey…"

She nodded. "One and the same."

"What did *that* good-for-nothing lowlife cheating hunk of trash want?"

She laughed. "To tell me that he's in Anchorage on business. Thought he could talk me into having dinner with him, so he could apologize."

"The guy's got gall, all right. How'd he find out where you were?"

"Marsha."

"Ack. I should have known. I told you that big mouth of hers would bring you heartache some day."

"She's a jabberjaw, I'll give you that much, but I'm not upset with her about it. Because oddly enough, talking with Joey today confirmed what I knew in my heart long before he dumped me…and long before I saw Baltimore in my rearview mirror."

"That he's a good-for-nothing lowlife cheating hunk of trash?"

"No, silly," she said, giggling, "that I'm better off without him. That if he hadn't cheated when he did, I'd have gone ahead with the wedding plans. And then I'd have been his *wife* when he finally decided to cheat. And he would have. You know it as well as I do."

"Reminds me what Grandmom used to say…"

"'Once a cheat, always a cheat'?"

"You got it." He shoved back from the table. "Supper was great. What was that stuff, anyway?"

"Chicken and rice in cream sauce. I hate to admit it, but you were my guinea pig. I'm supposed to bring something to a covered-dish supper at church in a few weeks."

"It'll be a hit for sure." He smirked. "What's for dessert?"

"I'm afraid all I have is vanilla ice cream." She jumped up to poke around in the fridge. "There's some chocolate syrup in here, though, and a can of whipped cream." Straightening, Sam asked if he'd like a sundae.

"When have you ever known me to turn down anything sweet?"

"The day that happens," she said, "is the day I'll

pop a thermometer in your mouth to see how high your fever is."

After their sundaes, Bill cleared the table as she filled the dishwasher.

"So what are you doing this evening, sister dear?"

"Same thing I do most nights…I'm heading back downstairs," Sam answered, "to try and get the last of today's deliveries put away. If I make some headway tonight, I can probably start redistributing merchandise tomorrow. I figure it'll take a few more days before I have everything just so for Olive's homecoming."

"What's Bryce say about the magic you're working at the store?"

"Why would I ask *him*? He hired me to manage the place, so I'm managing."

Chuckling, Bill shared the story Bryce had told him, about his dream of selling Rudolph's so he could invest the proceeds in his carpentry shop. He ran down the short list of materials and machines Bryce thought he'd need, should the good Lord bless him with a sale. "I asked him what *you* were supposed to do if he managed to get rid of the place, and he said having you close was the only good thing about keeping it."

Sam's heartbeat quickened. "He said that?"

"He said that."

"How sweet," she cooed, laying a hand over her heart. "Makes me wish I *had* made dessert, so I could leave some out to surprise him when he finally finishes up for the day."

"Well, I won't be awake when he gets home. I'm hitting the hay early, 'cause I have a hot date tomorrow."

"With Cora?"

"Yep."

"Where's she taking you?"

"Panning for gold. Out to see the pipeline." He shrugged. "She rattled off so many things, I can't remember them all. And to be honest, it doesn't matter where we go or what we do. I'm just looking forward to finding out what she's like *without* a coffeepot in her hand." Pocketing both hands, he leaned his backside against the counter while Sam wiped the table. "What do you know about her?"

"Not much, I'm afraid. In fact, you've probably accumulated ten times more information, hanging out at Dalman's, than I could tell you."

"She makes me laugh till my sides ache, so as long as she isn't hiding an ex who's a big ugly lumberjack, that's all I need to know."

"Just don't go fallin' in love, bro."

"Said the pot to the kettle."

Sam widened her eyes and pretended his comment had offended her. "May I point out that it took me *months* to go ga-ga? You, on the other hand, have only been in North Pole a week!"

"Down, girl," he teased. "It's a date, not a lifetime commitment."

"I just don't want to see you get hurt again."

Bill hugged her. "I have no desire to *be* hurt." He popped a brotherly kiss to her forehead. "And by the way? Ditto, sissy, ditto."

Sam had no way of knowing why, but she felt certain that her heart was safe in Bryce's hands.

"See you in the morning, sis," he said, heading for the bedroom. "If I'm not up by six, shake my cage, will ya?"

"Will do," she promised.

Bill hadn't even rounded the corner before Sam started pulling together the ingredients for sticky buns, for no reason other than that they were Bryce's all-time favorite treat.

Chapter Twenty

The delectable aroma of fresh-baked pastry still filled the air when deep, quiet voices woke Sam. She recognized them instantly as belonging to Bill and Bryce. The soft blue green glow of her wristwatch told her it was shortly after midnight. She'd learned by living across the hall from him that Bryce often stayed up into the wee hours of the morning, but hadn't Bill said he wanted to be up early for his date with Cora?

"They melt in your mouth," she heard her brother say.

"Is there anything that sister of yours *can't* do?" A pause, and then Bryce added, "I've seen her sketchbooks and I've heard her sing. Every day, she puts a little more military precision into the chaos at Rudolph's." She could almost picture him licking sweet white glaze from his fingertips. "And man-oh-man, the girl can cook."

Grinning into her pillow, Sam wished she could see through the wall. How much better would the compliments sound if she could see his expression, too?

"She's awful at sports," Bill said. "And all she has to do is walk past a plant to kill it."

"I don't believe it."

"And here's something weirdly ironic: she's terrified of snakes but doesn't give a second thought to squashing a spider with her bare hands."

"Hey, even I get the heebie-jeebies at the sight of a snake."

"Same here. Even a garter snake can send me screaming indoors like a little girl!"

More quiet laughter preceded Bryce's "You still haven't told me something she *can't* do."

"Well…"

Don't try too *hard, Billy,* she thought, smiling.

"…she can't take a compliment."

"Man, are you ever right about *that*. She turns four shades of red every time I tell her she looks gorgeous."

Was playing possum on the living room couch akin to eavesdropping? But even if it was, what choice did she have? She'd given her room to Bill for the duration of his visit. To change her mind now just to have a place to go so she couldn't hear them talking would only invite Bill's all-too-familiar childhood taunt, "Indian giver!"

The memory required her to stifle a giggle.

"So did you get hold of that real estate agent?"

Groaning, Bryce said, "Yeah, for all it was worth. She said the market is sluggish and probably will be for years."

"That's rough, man." He paused, and then added, "But maybe that's a good thing, since Rudolph's is your only tie to your folks."

Sam could almost picture Bryce nodding his agreement.

"How'd you lose them, if you don't mind my asking?"

Every time Olive had started telling Sam the story, Bryce appeared from out of nowhere, forcing her to stop talking. Sam knew only the bare facts, so now she tensed, wondering if she'd finally hear the whole story.

"My parents were avid ice fishermen, and one year, they just up and disappeared."

Sam cringed, waiting for her brother to crack some sort of inappropriate joke. Much to her relief, he said nothing. Nothing at all. Obviously, the facts had stunned him, too.

"People said they saw their hut out there on the ice one minute, and it was gone the next."

The ensuing quiet was unbearable, and Sam said a quick prayer that the Lord would provide Bill with comforting words as the story unfolded.

Bryce's voice was low and gravelly when he said, "Some speculate they built the fire too hot in their potbellied stove, and that while they were sleeping, it melted the ice and…"

His voice trailed off, and Sam's heart ached for him. Faking slumber as he talked openly about this painful chapter in his past meant she couldn't comfort him. But if she'd been in the kitchen, Bryce probably wouldn't have discussed the subject at all. Talk about frustrating.

"Now, that just doesn't sound logical," Bill said. "I mean…isn't the ice, like, two feet thick on every body of water around here?"

"Yeah, that's true some winters, anyway."

"How long do you suppose it would take a fire, even one that was good and hot, to melt ice that thick?"

More silence.

"That's rough, man. Really rough." Then, "How long ago did it happen?"

"Long, long time."

Sam couldn't decide if Bryce's answer sounded sad… or disgusted.

"Well, for what it's worth," Bill said, "I'm sorry, man, truly sorry."

A heavy sigh permeated the air. "Thanks."

"And they never found 'em?"

"Nope."

"Whew, that's rough," Bill said again. "As the shrinks would say, 'no closure.'"

"Yep."

"Any idea what happened to—"

"The search teams found stuff that had been in their hut—like the wood stove and coffeepot, a frying pan, a cot—downstream. Near as anybody can tell, their bodies floated under the ice, and before they could be identi—"

"Holy moley, Bryce," Bill interrupted, "that's…that's just…. I don't know *what* to call it, except awful!"

"The Alaskan version of 'ashes to ashes, dust to dust.'" Another brittle pause, and then, "Things went full circle, as I see it, so at least their deaths weren't totally useless…."

For the first time in her life, Sam understood the term "dead silence." The utter stillness seemed oppressive, burdensome, and Sam wanted to hug both men…Bill, for having to listen to the heartrending story, and Bryce for having to tell it.

"Don't know how you survived it."

"Same way anybody survives a thing like that…"

Sam half-expected him to say that prayer, or faith, or his church family had helped him get through those tough times. But it didn't really surprise her when instead he said, "…put one foot in front of the other, and throw yourself into your work."

"So *that's* why you re-upped so many times."

"Yep."

She could hardly believe how much information Bill had managed to get out of the closemouthed marine in such a short time. Bryce might have shared so much based on the camaraderie borne of their similar military backgrounds, or because they'd each survived recent heartbreak. But Sam had grown up with Bill and remembered the many times he'd comforted *her* when life had treated her unfairly. She hadn't been the only one to lovingly tease him by saying his heart was as big as his head. Maybe, she thought, Bryce simply found her brother as easy to talk to as she did.

Later, when they were alone, she'd make a point of thanking Bill, of stressing how blessed she was to have him for a brother and that working as a guidance counselor and athletic coach had no doubt been smart, God-willed choices.

"Well, I'd better turn in," she heard Bill say. "Cora's taking me sightseeing in a couple of hours."

Bryce laughed. "Watch your wallet, man. And your back."

If she knew Bill, the comment had inspired him to thrust his head forward, like a turtle, and open his eyes as wide as the lids would allow. "Whoa. No way. Aw, man…leave it to me to attract a pickpocket."

"And here I figured you'd been out long enough to lose the 'dumb army' patch. Boy, was I wrong!"

Sam heard the smile in Bill's voice when he said, "Spoken like a true marine."

Bryce laughed harder. "I'm just messin' with you. Seriously? Cora's good people, and she'll take good care of you."

"Uh, how would you know *that*?"

"Don't worry," Bryce said, "she isn't my type."

"Good answer. Now I won't have to kick your marine butt."

"In your dreams, *army*."

Sam joined their laughter—though hers was stifled by the pillow—as their chairs squealed on the linoleum. A moment later, Bill's silhouette filled the living room doorway. "But I think I'll put a padlock on my wallet, just to be safe...."

Bryce's good-natured chuckle sounded farther away, and Sam guessed he stood at the opposite end of the kitchen to say, "Lookin' forward to hearing all about your Cora-venture over supper."

She waited for the telltale sound of his door clicking closed and said, "If there's such a thing as a schmoozing trophy, you earned it tonight."

"Jiminy Cricket, Sam, you scared me half to death!" Perching on the sofa arm, he turned on the lamp. "I guess it's true what they say..."

She levered herself up on one elbow. "What do 'they' say?"

"'The more things change, the more they stay the same.'"

Yawning, she patted her mouth. "I'm sleep deprived, so you'll pardon me if I don't get it."

"You always were a nosy little busybody."

Sitting up, she tossed her pillow at him. "What!"

He caught it neatly. "Please. You think we didn't know you were always close by, listening in when we had team sleepovers and stuff?" Bill threw the pillow back, and it hit her square in the face. "Bull's-eye!" Then, "So you've been lying here eavesdropping the whole time?"

"Pretty much, I guess, though I didn't really *mean* to." She hugged the pillow. "So what do you think of him?"

Grinning, Bill shook his head. "Seems like a nice enough guy."

"Oh, come on, you can do better than that."

"He sure does talk a lot…"

"Because of you, Father Confessor."

"Hey, what I have is a gift, I'll have you know."

"Gift of *gab*, you mean."

"Call it what you will," he said, shrugging, "it's magic."

"You know, I have to agree. It's why you're so good with kids. It's the reason you've always been my favorite brother…and if you tell the rest of them I said that," she said, using her bare foot to nudge his knee, "I'll deny it."

Bill grabbed her big toe and pinched. "I love you, too, sissy." And standing, he stretched. "Better grab a few winks," he said from the bedroom doorway, "or Cora will have to drag me from pillar to post." The door swung shut, jerked open again. "And those sticky buns you made?" He blew her a kiss. "'Fraid all we left for you was the sticky *plate*. I tried to talk the guy into saving one for you, but he's a marine, and as anybody in the *army* can tell you, they're all pigs." He chuckled good-naturedly. "Sorry, kiddo."

"G'night, Billy," she said, giggling.

Sam snuggled into her pillow and flapped the covers back into place, smiling into the darkness. Eyes closed, she counted her many blessings and thanked God for every one. Drowsiness settled over her as she listened to the quiet ticking of the kitchen clock, counting out the seconds until she'd see Bryce again.

Chapter Twenty-One

The next days passed in a flurry of activity, with Sam working overtime in the shop and in her apartment to get things ready for the newlyweds' homecoming. The table set and dinner in the oven, she dressed for the drive to the Fairbanks airport.

To save Olive and Duke the bother of renting a cart, Bryce had suggested the newlyweds grab their luggage and meet the threesome at the curb. "Won't they be surprised," Sam said as they circled the arrival lanes, "when they see how much work you and Bryce did at the B and B."

Bill displayed his blistered palms. "Just in case there's any doubt about my contributions..."

"There they are!" Bryce all but shouted. And in a more subdued voice, he added, "Sam, what do you make of that?"

Olive's wan complexion was hard to miss, but her smile seemed as bright and cheery as ever. "Oh, don't be such a worrywart," she said, squeezing his hand. "It's a long flight from the Keys to Fairbanks."

"Not to mention that nasty recycled air on the plane," Bill put in. "Maybe she picked up a bug."

"Maybe," Bryce said none too convincingly. But he was smiling when he got out of the car and headed for his aunt and her new husband.

"I've never even met the woman," Bill whispered, "but she looks pretty green around the gills to me, too."

"Well, thanks for being here for Bryce," she said, patting his hand. "You haven't known him long, but already you're behaving like a good friend."

Bill squeezed her shoulder before they stepped onto the pavement.

"Sam!" Olive said, disengaging from Bryce's hug. "I'm so glad you're here!"

The instant the woman's arms went around her, Sam knew something was wrong. Terribly wrong. Because Olive's zest for life showed in everything she did—her big bear hugs in particular—and this one was anything but hearty. "I hope you guys took lots of pictures," Sam said, forcing a joy that she didn't feel, "so you can tell us all about the trip after supper."

"Who's this handsome young fella?" Olive asked as she grabbed Bill's hand.

"My brother, Bill."

"Her *favorite* brother," he said, "but that's our little secret."

When the introductory hugs and handshakes ended, Bryce grabbed the couple's suitcases. "Sam made your favorite for supper, Olive," Bryce said, sliding them onto his pickup's bed.

"Fried chicken with mashed potatoes and gravy? Sammie-girl, you're a peach!"

Duke pulled her into a hug, "She's right. You *are* a peach, girl!" And then he whispered, "Something's bad-wrong with my sweet Olive, and she refuses to let me take her to the hospital. I'm hoping you and Bryce will help me talk some sense into her...."

Sam peered over his shoulder at Olive, who was struggling to buckle her seat belt. "How long has she been like this?"

"The better part of a week. She barely ate, kept getting weaker and paler, but every time I suggested we see a doctor, she got all riled up, which only made matters worse."

Sam thanked God when Olive leaned against the headrest and closed her eyes, and she took advantage of the moment to signal her brother. "Help Duke distract her, will you, while I have a quick word with Bryce?"

She thanked God for Bill, too, because instead of asking for an explanation, he read the urgency in her tone and said, "You got it, kiddo."

Even before she joined Bryce at the back bumper, Sam could hear Bill cracking jokes that inspired tired laughter from Olive and Duke. She positioned herself in a way that forced Bryce to stand with his back to the truck.

"What's with the 'cat that ate the canary' smile?" he asked, slamming the tailgate.

"Duke just asked me to help him talk Olive into going straight to the hospital."

Bryce started for the driver's door, but she grabbed his arm, stopping him. "She might be able to see your face in one of the side mirrors," Sam explained, silly smile still in place, "so bear with me a minute, okay?"

Nodding, unspoken pain etched his handsome features as he crossed both arms over his chest.

On the heels of a deep breath, Sam said, "It makes no sense to drive all the way back to North Pole, just to appease her, when we're already so close to the hospital." She swallowed, hard, and prayed that the Almighty would give her the strength to continue the façade, for Olive's sake as well as Bryce's.

"I know her, Sam. If she doesn't want to go to the ER, she won't go, period."

She gripped his forearms and gave a gentle shake. "We can't give in to her. Not this time. It's probably like Bill said, just an ordinary virus or something. But if it's more serious than that, we can't afford to waste precious time."

"You have something in mind. I can tell…"

Sam looked toward heaven and closed her eyes, then ran both hands through her hair. "I don't know what, exactly, but I'll think of some reason for you to drive to the hospital. I'll fake a pain in my side or—"

"You'd lie for Olive?"

She hadn't thought of it in terms of truth versus lie, and his question shook her to her core. Chin up and back straight, she said, "If it's a choice between telling the truth and risking Olive's health, and asking God's forgiveness for being *un*truthful? What choice do I have?"

He pulled her to him in a fierce hug. "I don't know what I'd do without you, Sam."

"Better get a move on," she said, "before Olive gets suspicious."

"If I know her, she's *already* suspicious." Then, "So what's it gonna be? Migraine? Appendicitis?"

"Now there's an idea! My brother Scott had an emergency appendectomy a few years ago. I think I remember enough about it to fake the symptoms…."

"Your ambulance awaits," he said somberly.

And as Sam climbed into the passenger seat, she hoped the Father would forgive her for the boldfaced lies she was about to tell.

"I don't think I'll ever forget the look on her face," Sam said, sobbing into Bill's collar, "when she realized I'd betrayed her."

"She's sick, not stupid," he said, patting her back. "She knows you only did it to help her. Down deep, Olive realizes she needed to have herself checked out." He plucked a tissue from the box on a nearby table. "She's got more to live for now than ever before," he said, handing it to Sam. "I think once the docs figure out what's wrong and she's home again, safe and sound, you'll be forgiven."

Dabbing her eyes, Sam nodded and slumped onto the seat of a chrome-and-orange chair. "I pray you're right," she said as Bill sat beside her.

Bryce entered the waiting room and flopped onto the chair on Sam's other side. "Believe it or not, she hardly fussed at all." Leaning forward, he knuckled his eyes. "Too weak to protest, I guess."

"It's been almost three hours," Sam said. "Do they have any idea what's wrong?"

Shoulders slumped, he shook his head. "They're still running tests, so we probably won't know anything for a while yet."

She rubbed his back. "Well, I'm not going any-where."

"Me, either," Bill chimed in.

A sad, slanted grin on his face, Bryce said, "Thanks, guys."

Sam grabbed Bryce's left hand and Bill's right and squeezed. "I think we need to pray."

"Have at it," Bryce said.

She hardly gave a thought to the way he'd reacted the first time she suggested that they pray together. Instead, Sam turned to her brother. "Bill?"

He gave one nod of his head and closed his eyes. "Dear heavenly Father," he began, "we come to You this evening with heavy hearts and worried minds as Your beloved daughter Olive awaits the doctors' prognosis. We ask that You bless the medical team, Father, that they might know how to heal her. Bless Olive, too, Lord, with complete trust in You and Your will for her life. Watch over Duke as he stands beside his new bride, and bolster him with the strength to be a supportive, loving husband.

"Cloak us now, O God, with abundant and abiding faith, so that we can remain steady in our trust in You, so we will believe with every fiber in our beings that You will answer the prayers said here on Olive's behalf. Lord, we implore You to help us comprehend and comply with Your will, and grant us the wisdom to know what You would have us do—for Olive and for one another—until she is home again, safe from all harm and pain, from all fear and illness. We ask these things in Your most holy name, amen."

Sam wasn't the slightest bit surprised at her own

tears or at the glisten in her brother's eyes, for heart-to-hearts with the Lord often invited a bit of dampness, but the damp streaks coursing down Bryce's face rocked her to her core. If not for Bill's firm grasp on her hand, she might have lost it completely. "That was beautiful, Billy," she said softly.

"Yeah," Bryce agreed, "it was." Lips taut and brow furrowed, he ground out a quiet "Thanks."

"Mr. Stone?"

Bryce stood ramrod straight as Bill and Sam flanked him.

"I'm Doctor Eversly," he announced, extending his right hand. "I've been overseeing your aunt's case. Her husband asked me to update you." Eversly fidgeted with the black tubing of his stethoscope and said, "We're re-running the tests, to be sure our initial diagnosis is correct, but I'm afraid it's serious."

Sam glanced up in time to see Bryce's Adam's apple bob up and down. "How serious?"

"Looks like cancer." He held up a hand to add, "But Fairbanks is home to one of the country's best cancer centers, and their top expert is on his way here now, so there's no need for immediate alarm."

"What kind of cancer?" Bryce ventured.

Everybody tensed when the doctor's jaw muscles bulged. "I think I'll let Dr. Dugas provide the specific details once he's had a chance to study your aunt's file."

"You're saying you don't know what kind?"

The doctor removed his glasses and ran a hand through his hair. "Mr. Stone, I—"

"Either you know or you don't." Bryce stared him down. "And if you know, I'd appreciate your honesty."

Quiet *pings* overhead prefaced a nasal female voice that droned from the overhead speakers. "Paging Doctor Marcus…"

A nurse hurried by, clipboard in hand and crepe-soled shoes squeaking on the highly polished linoleum floor.

A door slammed in the distance.

The elevator doors across the hall hissed open with a *ding*.

Dr. Eversly swallowed as Bryce cleared his throat and Bill coughed, and Sam thought surely all three men could hear the hard beating of her heart. Finally, the doctor's voice cracked the quiet. "The tests are only preliminary, understand, which is why we ran them more than once." Staring at the pale blue-and-green flecks in the tile beneath his wingtips, he continued. "Looks like it might be pancreatic cancer."

Sam stifled a gasp. Wasn't that one of the worst kinds? *Lord Jesus*, she prayed, *let the tests be wrong.…*

Dr. Eversly opened his mouth to say more when the voice floated from the speakers yet again. "Doctor Eversly," she said this time, "paging Doctor Eversly. Please report to the ER…"

"Sorry," he said, looking almost relieved that an emergency required his attention. "A nurse will be out soon as your aunt is settled into her room." And with that, he hurried through the double doors leading into the emergency room, white coat flapping as he disappeared around the corner.

Bryce took a step back and all but fell into the seat he'd been occupying when Dr. Eversly had made his appearance. "Pancreatic cancer," he breathed. And balancing elbows on his knees, he buried his face in his hands. "Isn't that the one that kills within months of a diagnosis?"

Sam sat beside him and rubbed his back. "Not always," she said, resting her head on his shoulder. "We've got to keep the faith, believe the doctors have caught it in time."

"She's right, man," Bill added, taking the chair on Bryce's other side. "You heard Eversly...the tests could be wrong, or maybe some newbie in the lab read the results incorrectly. Either way, this Dugas expert will have answers."

"She's all I've got," Bryce grated.

"You're wrong about that," Bill said, one hand on Bryce's shoulder.

"You'll never be alone," she whispered, "as long as I draw breath."

Nodding, Bryce whipped off the eye patch and tossed it to the floor. And as his friends sat helpless, the big, no-nonsense ex-marine broke down and sobbed.

Chapter Twenty-Two

Since there wasn't much he could do for her, Bryce took Olive up on her suggestion to go home for some much-needed food and rest.

"Besides," she'd said as the foursome stood around her hospital bed, "Bill needs to pack so he can get back to Baltimore. School starts soon, and I know from past experience how important it is to get into the classroom early. Isn't that right, Bill?"

Sam's brother had grinned and, firing off a few wise-cracks, agreed. But his red-rimmed eyes were a dead giveaway that Olive's quickly failing health had impacted him, too. And though Bryce had only known Bill for a few weeks, the man had earned his respect and friendship, and Bryce hated to see him go.

To give her her due, Sam held up well through all the hospital mumbo jumbo, the farewell supper with Bill, and the uncomfortably quiet ride to the airport. Somehow, she'd managed not to get more than a little damp-eyed bidding him goodbye at the curb outside the airline terminal, and she probably would have made it all the way back to North Pole without blubbering if Bryce hadn't insisted on stopping to visit Forever.

Side by side, they'd stared in respectful silence at the vast expanse of evergreens, at the steel blue sky and looming thunderclouds that blocked the noonday sun. And with no warning whatever, she'd thrown herself into his arms, her lurching shoulders his only clue that she was crying.

Bryce hadn't known what to say or do to comfort her, and the powerlessness threatened his own precarious hold on self-control. He wanted to be her rock, to shield her from every sadness the world might throw at her. Wanted to protect her from fear and loneliness and despair. But how could he be the man she needed—the man she so richly deserved—when it was all he could do to hold it together himself?

He'd considered prayer but then decided against it. Why bother? There was too precious little time, in his opinion, to waste even a minute of it, voicing some futile plea to a God who had obviously turned a deaf ear to him. He'd more or less believed it for decades, because any time he'd turned to the Almighty, Bryce had gotten nothing in return. He'd never expected to have *every* prayer answered; he was too practical for that. But none of them? Even a war-hardened jarhead like himself knew to quit while he was ahead!

God hadn't turned his cause-loving parents into people he could look up to, people who could help mold and guide him. He hadn't stopped the bleeding when his comrades lay dying on the battlefields. Hadn't helped the search party find his mom and dad after they went missing. Hadn't changed Debbie's mind when she decided that being a career marine was more important than Bryce's heart.

By the time that land mine detonated, taking out a young soldier and wounding half a dozen others, he'd given up all hope of capturing the Almighty's attention. Other people promised to pray for him as he lay alone and in agony at the VA hospital, and for a while, he allowed himself to hope that maybe the Lord would answer *their* prayers. But the sight never returned to his left eye, and the kids who'd been hit by the same flying shrapnel that had blinded him went home in far worse shape than Bryce. When *he* got home and entertained the idea of selling Rudolph's, the place had fallen into such disrepair that no one in his right mind would fork over hard-earned cash for it. What else was he to think but that God was the product of overactive imaginations, like Santa and the Easter Bunny and the Tooth Fairy.

He'd never voice his bitter opinions, because why wake the believers from their happy dreams? If leaning on a Being who promised to move mountains if His followers had faith as minuscule as a mustard seed could help them cope with the ugly things of the world, who was he to take that from them?

Sam, he realized as he sat at his computer keyboard, had more faith than any ten people he could name. If she ever came to her senses and walked away from him, he'd need strength like he never needed it before. And surely that would happen when she figured out what a heathen she'd fallen for, because didn't her beloved Bible say she wasn't supposed to yoke herself to an unbeliever?

Staring at the glowing monitor, he scrolled through page after page, searching for the latest facts and figures on pancreatic cancer. The more he knew, the better he could help Olive. After a lifetime of uncomplainingly caring for others—her parents, her students, his parents, him*self*—Olive had earned the best, and he intended to see to it she got it, or he'd die trying.

Her uncomplaining attitude, as it turned out, was partly to blame for her condition. If she'd said something sooner about the pains in her gut, about her exhaustion and insomnia, about the aches in her muscles and joints, maybe the experts could have diagnosed the cancer in time to remove the tumor surgically, put one of the newfangled drugs to the test.

Tonight, when nothing new showed up on his screen, Bryce rolled back from his desk and slammed a fist into the nearby wall. "In God's hands," he muttered. "What a lot of—"

A soft knock kept him from finishing his sentence. "What?" he barked.

"It's just me," Sam said, walking toward him, a piled-high plate of who-knows-what in her dainty hands. "I thought you might be hungry...."

Might as well get the wheels turning, he thought, because putting off the inevitable would only make things harder for both of them. She needed to go back to Baltimore, where a loving family would help her get back to her life as it was before North Pole. Then he'd sell the shop, even if it didn't make a profit, and take that boring desk job in Quantico. In time, maybe he could parlay it into a special ops assignment.

"Just put it over there," he snarled, pointing at a bare

spot on his desk. Bryce glanced at the plate and noted that, as usual, Sam had thought of everything, from a big white paper napkin to a tall glass of fresh-squeezed lemonade. Oh, how he wanted to show her, to tell her how much he appreciated her thoughtful, loving gestures! But because he genuinely believed she deserved better than the likes of him, he sat, silent as a statue, staring at the glare of the computer monitor.

"Find anything?" she asked, setting up the corner of his desk like a table in some fancy restaurant.

"Nah." He hit a button, putting the computer into hibernation.

"Better eat while it's hot…"

He got to his feet and started pacing between the door and the desk. It didn't really surprise him when Sam got up, too, and walked beside him.

"Good exercise," she kidded. "But you keep this up, you'll wear a path in the carpet."

Just look at her, he thought, *all tiny and cute, all loving and kind…and completely unaware that I'm about to turn her world upside-down.*

On more than one occasion, she'd accused him of being able to read her mind. He thought maybe the condition was catching, because she said, "If you think for one minute you can get rid of me, you're sadly mistaken, marine." Then she planted herself in his path and, hands on hips, glared up at him.

He couldn't afford to let her get to him. Couldn't afford to let her niceness soften the hard decision he'd made. Didn't she realize he was doing it to protect her? Bryce did his best to scowl. Standing taller, he crossed his arms over his chest, fully prepared to tell her to take a hike. To get lost, bug off, leave him be…

But before he could formulate a stern lecture in his head, before he could summon the ire required to convince her that he meant what he said, Sam wrapped her arms around him and leaned her curly-haired head on his chest.

"You're not fooling me, you know."

He stared at the ceiling, wondering what to say next.

"I know exactly what you're up to."

"Oh, you think so, do you?"

Nodding, she hugged him tighter. "You think if you act all big and bad and mean, I'll scurry off like a scared little rabbit and drive back to Baltimore where my folks and my brothers will surround me and say silly things like 'there, there' and 'poor baby' until I'm over you."

Pressing both hands into his chest, she took half a step back, and when he refused to look at her, she grabbed his ears and gently tugged, forcing him to meet her eyes. "So *that's* why they call you guys 'jarheads,'" she said, grinning. "These things are *handles*!"

Bryce felt his resolve weaken as he stared into flashing blue eyes that brimmed with affection.

"So admit it. I hit the old nail on the head, didn't I?"

"Close, but no cigar."

"Lucky for us both, I don't smoke." And standing on tiptoe, she kissed his chin. "This is all your own fault, you know."

"What's my fault?"

"The fact that I'm madly, crazy, out-of-my-head in love with you, that's what."

He'd known for some time that she cared for him, but

love? How in the big bloody world was he supposed to send her packing, now that the words were out?

"You can't get rid of me," she said, snuggling closer.

The supposedly impenetrable wall he'd built to protect her from him crumbled further. He watched as she shook her head and smirked. *Smirked*! It was all he could do to keep from smothering her gorgeous face with kisses. "Oh, I can't, huh?"

"Of course not, silly."

"Why not?"

"Because I said so, for starters. And because you pull this goofy stunt every time you're up against—"

"Stunt? *What* stunt?"

"I've heard all about the way you go off by yourself, like a wounded animal, whenever you think you can't control your life. Haven't you lived long enough yet to have figured out you can't control *anything*?"

Well, he was having a dickens of a time controlling *her*; that much was certain.

She wriggled close again, squeezed him so tightly that he wondered if she had it in her to crack a rib. Then again, he'd known her for months. Of *course* she had it in her. The idea inspired a grin that grew into a slow, grating chuckle. Oh, but it felt good, borderline miraculous, to laugh. If Sam could pull off a thing like that, in the middle of all this death-and-dying stuff no less, what other miracles might she perform?

She touched a finger to the tip of his nose. "Don't you *ever* shut me out again." She laid a hand on each of his cheeks and, frowning, added, "You hear?"

He hadn't slept or eaten a proper meal in days, and simply didn't have the strength to fight—whatever this was—any longer. Maybe after he devoured whatever delicious thing she'd piled on that plate and got a couple hours of sleep, he'd pick up the gauntlet again, but for now...

"I just have one more thing to say, and then I'd like very much for you to eat your supper."

"Just one?" He chuckled. "Now, why am I having trouble believing that?"

Smiling, she said, "And here I thought my brother Bill was the only comedian in my life."

"All right, I'll play along, since you've piqued my curiosity." Bryce tucked a tendril of dark wavy hair behind her ear. "What one thing do you have to say before I eat my supper?"

"I'm only gonna say it once, so pay attention, okay?"

"Okay."

"You're listening, right?"

"Listening..."

"Because if you're not..."

"I give you my word, I'm listening."

"Are you sure?"

"Positive."

"Okay..."

"Okay what?"

"Okay, here goes..."

"Oh for the love of—"

"Kiss me," she said.

He'd expected a "you shouldn't skip meals" lecture, or even advice on why he needed to get more sleep. But this? "'Kiss me'?" he quoted. "*That's* the all-important thing you were gonna—"

Lips pressed to his, she mumbled, "I'm not kidding, marine."

"Yes, ma'am," he muttered against her mouth...and then he surrendered to the wonderful warmth of her love.

Chapter Twenty-Three

"Now then," she whispered when she finally came up for air, "let's get some nutritious food into you." Grabbing the plate, she headed for the kitchen. And over her shoulder, Sam added, "You coming?"

That was way *too close for comfort*, she thought, sliding his plate into the microwave. He'd almost succeeded in climbing into a hole so deep and dark, she may never have reached him. *Thank You, Jesus*, she prayed, *for getting me there just in the nick of time.*

The microwave beeped as she arranged his napkin and silverware at the narrow end of the table. Laying the plate beside them, she put his lemonade at two o'clock. "Dinner is served, mon-sewer," she said, deliberately mispronouncing the word.

Bryce sat and said, "And a sincere 'mercybuckets' to you."

Sam flopped onto the chair nearest his and sat on her foot. Propping her chin on a fist, she said, "I finally finished inventorying all the stock, so now the only thing left to do is—"

His ringing cell phone silenced her, and she did her

best to hide the first frightening thought that entered her head: who'd call at this hour except the hospital staff? And why would they, unless...

Bryce was on his feet, a hand to the back of his neck, pacing as he nodded. "We'll be right over," he said before snapping the phone shut. "Duke," he explained. He took a swallow of the lemonade. "Olive is...she's...she wants to see us."

Sam hoped that didn't mean what she *thought* it meant. "Want me to drive?"

He palmed his keys. "But you'd better grab your purse. And a jacket, because..."

Because there's no telling how long we might be, she thought, finishing his sentence.

Half an hour later, they stood side by side at Olive's hospital bed. Though Sam had seen patients in her condition before, she didn't think she'd ever get used to the piercing beep of the monitor or the tangle of tubes jutting from the back of Olive's hands.

"How 'bout if you men go down to the cafeteria, have a cup of coffee or something," Olive suggested.

Duke started to protest, but she held a finger aloft in true schoolteacher fashion, effectively silencing him. "Just give us a few minutes, okay?" She winked and then added, "I promise not to die while you're gone."

"For the love of Pete, Olive," Duke said, "what a thing to say."

"Can't help it if I'm the type who calls a spade a spade, now can I?"

"Well, it wouldn't *kill* you to consider a slightly gentler approach now and then," he countered.

"Touché!" she said, returning his grin. She waved

them away and added, "Say your prayers while you're down there, nephew, 'cause you're next." And once they were gone, Olive told Sam to close the door and pull the guest chair closer to her bed.

Lord be with me, Sam prayed, following the woman's instructions.

"I've never been one to mince words, Sam…"

Smiling, she slid her hand beneath Olive's. "So I've heard."

"…so I'm not going to waste time with nonsense, now."

Oh, please, Jesus…strengthen me for what's about to come.

"All my years as a teacher taught me a thing or two about sizing people up. And I know a good and decent person when I see one." She squeezed Sam's hand. "You're perfect for that thick-skulled nephew of mine, so I want your promise that you won't let him drive you away."

"I promise."

"He'll try, you know…and sometimes it won't be easy, breaking through the barriers he builds around himself."

"Tell me about it," Sam said, grinning as she rolled her eyes.

"Ah, so he's started already, has he?"

"I'm at least as stubborn as he is, so don't worry."

Tears welled in her dark eyes. "He and I…we're the only blood kin the other has in the world. I'd hate to think nobody would be around to fight for him, to fight *him*, if need be, after I'm gone."

"You've got my word, I'm not going anywhere."

"So you love my nephew?"

"With all my heart."

A wan smile brightened her face. "I know. Just needed to hear you say it."

"Then you'll be happy to know, *he's* heard me say it."

Eyes closed, Olive shook her head. "Let me guess… he didn't say it back, did he?"

"Not yet. But I have it on good authority that he will."

The woman's lids snapped open and she zeroed in on Sam's face. "Who told you that?"

Thumb aiming at the ceiling, Sam said, "I've spent hours on my knees, pleading for a sign…if Bryce and I are wrong for one another."

"And?"

"Not a heavenly peep."

Olive's relieved sigh echoed in the small room. "Praise the Lord."

Her breaths came more quickly as she said, "Now, this is gonna sound weird, even from me, but I want you to do me a favor…"

"Anything," Sam said, meaning it.

"I want to be cremated in my red dress."

"In your…you want…*what*?"

A grin played at the corners of her mouth. "You heard right. My red dress. With my red earrings and bracelet, and my red shoes, too. You'll find them all in my closet." Olive sandwiched Sam's hands between her own. "And I want you to have my pearl necklace. I don't much care what happens to the other stuff, but the pearls belonged to my mother."

Sam didn't know when anything had touched her

more deeply. *Sweet Lord,* Sam prayed, *please,* please *don't let me cry.*

"I'm really gonna miss you, Sammie-girl."

Sam wanted to be strong, for Olive, Duke, and Bryce, but God help her, the woman wasn't making it easy! She bit her lower lip to still its trembling. "Can I...can I get you anything? One of your romance novels? A fudge brownie? A big stick to hit me with, so I'll shut up?"

Olive snickered. "Ice chips would be nice...."

She'd seen the plastic cup on the tray, already filled to the brim with crushed ice, and understood that sending her on this mission of mercy was Olive's way of giving Sam time to recover. She'd barely rounded the corner before the enormity of the situation engulfed her. The tears came hot and hard, and she did her best to hide them by pressing herself into the corner near the pay phones. If losing Olive was this tough for her, how much harder for Duke? And for Bryce, who loved her like a mother?

Sam slid to the floor, and on her knees, she quietly prayed. "Let her last hours go easy, Lord, so that her beloved husband and nephew won't have to watch her suffer, so that their final moments with her will leave them with memories of the strong, capable, funny woman who loves them more than life itself instead of..." She couldn't bear to make herself say, "instead of a pain-wracked dying woman," not even in private prayer. "Make me strong, Father, so I can provide the care and support Duke and Bryce will need after—"

"You're something else, you know that?"

Bryce...

She didn't want him to see her this way! *Please, Lord, dry my tears*!

He helped her to her feet and drew her close. "I don't know what I ever did to deserve you, but whatever it was—"

Sniffing, she placed a finger over his lips, silencing him.

"I'm glad you're here."

"Me, too," she managed to say.

"Will you do something for me?"

Sam looked up into his handsome, haggard face. She didn't dare say "sure, anything, just name it," because what if what he wanted to ask her was to go away, out of some ridiculous notion he was protecting her from the anguish and turmoil that lay ahead? "What?" she said, choosing the word carefully.

"Say it again."

"Say what again?"

"That thing you said, earlier, in my apartment."

"Good grief, I said a hundred things!" And then she knew. Knew *exactly* what he needed to hear. "You mean that thing about how I'm crazily, madly in love with you?"

"Yeah," he said on a sigh, "that."

"If I say it again—and I'm sure I needn't remind you that 'if' is the biggest little word in the English language—what will *you* say in response?"

He tucked in one corner of his mouth. "I'm not sure, exactly."

She racked her brain, searching for the scripture that said something like, "if you ask this mountain to move, and believe I can move it, it will move." Would God help her move this mountainous marine who'd stolen her heart?

Sam closed her eyes and placed her fear and frustration at the foot of the Cross. "I love you, Bryce Stone, you stubborn, thick-headed, eye-patch-wearing ex-marine, you. I have, almost from the moment we met, and—"

"I think you're out of your ever-loving mind, but it's your life."

That was her reward for putting her heart on the chopping block? A paltry little "it's your life"? If he wasn't about to lose the only family he'd ever known, she'd let him have it, with both barrels, because—

"I love you, too, you know."

Sam blinked up at him, wondering if he'd really said the words or if she'd merely heard what she wanted to hear. "What?"

"You know, you're gorgeous even when you're mad as a wet hen."

"What!"

Duke poked his head out of Olive's hospital room. "Bryce? She wants to see you."

The furrow between his eyebrows deepened as he said, "Be right there." And to Sam, "You okay now?"

Guilt and self-recrimination coursed through her as she considered how selfish her thoughts had been. Nodding dumbly, she gave him a gentle shove. "I'm fine. Go. She needs you." Then, "Take your time. I'm not going anywhere."

Bryce kissed the tip of her nose. "If I didn't believe that, no way I could walk down that hall without blubbering like a baby."

She watched him stride toward Olive's room, every bit the straight-backed, take-it-on-the-chin marine. At the door, he stopped and faced her and, smiling sadly, mouthed, "I love you," sending her heart and her spirit soaring.

"She asked me to dim the lights," Duke whispered as Bryce walked into the room.

"Just as well," he whispered back. "Harder for her to see the proof that I've been bawling like a baby."

"Duke, darlin'," Olive said sweetly, "please get your ornery Texas bee-hind out of here so I can talk to my mule-headed nephew, will you?"

Jaw trembling, he sent her a three-fingered salute and stepped into the hall.

"Shut that door," his aunt ordered, "and sit yourself down here beside me."

"Yes ma'am."

"You look tired," she said when he kissed her forehead.

"Too much TV, not enough shut-eye."

"You can't fool an old fool."

Even now, she could make him smile. Oh, how he loved this crazy old woman! "So what can I get you? Ice? Something to read?"

She waved the offers away. "All I need from you is a promise."

He'd walk into hell and back if she asked it of him. "You name it," he said, "and it's yours."

"Tell Sam that you love her."

"Too late for that."

It pleased him that his simple admission brightened

her face. "Good. I was beginning to think you'd lost all your marbles." She chuckled softly. "Well, since you can't promise me that, I have another request."

"Uh-oh. Do I really want to hear this?" He would put on this brave front as long as she needed him to.

"Ask her to marry you."

He laughed, too long and too loud, but honestly, what did she expect, springing a thing like that on him?

"I'm dead serious."

"Humor me, will you, and dispense with the dead jokes, okay?"

"Sorry," she said. "Okay, let me rephrase that. I wasn't kidding just now when I said I want you to ask Sam to marry you."

"What makes you think she'd want to spend the rest of her life with a guy like me?"

"What's that mean…'a guy like you'?"

This was neither the time nor the place to burden her with his self-pitying reasons, so Bryce flicked on the TV and started scrolling through the channels.

"Give me that thing," she said, snatching the remote from his hand. And hitting the Off button, Olive snapped, "Show an old dying woman some respect, will you?" Then, "Oops, sorry. Nix the word 'dying.'"

"Thanks."

"Remember that movie where the guy said, 'If you build it, they will come'?"

Bryce nodded, though he had no idea where she might go with this line of thought.

"If you ask her," Olive said, "she'll say yes."

He leaned the back of the chair against the bed rail and then straddled its seat. "Yeah, I know," he admitted, laying one arm atop the other on its top rung. "I guess maybe she's not as smart as we thought, is she."

"I see only one dummy in this room, and he's wearing an eye patch."

"Always was my own worst enemy. How many times have you told me that?"

"Hundreds. Thousands, even." Olive grimaced, clutching the sheets so tightly her knuckles whitened.

"What...what's wrong? Want me to get the nurse? Is it time for your pain medi—"

"You just sit right back down there, nephew," she husked. "I don't want the meds. They make me groggy and fog my brain. I want to be wide awake and alert when...." Her voice trailed off and she bit her lower lip. And on the heels of a short, shuddering breath, she added, "There are things I need to say, and things I want to hear before Jesus comes to take me home. Can't do that if I'm all doped up, now can I?"

"When was your doctor last in to see you?"

"Couple of hours ago."

"And what did he say?"

She frowned. "Nothing I care to repeat." Then, "I'm only interested in hearing what *you* have to say."

"Olive..."

"Can I be perfectly honest with you, Bryce?"

He could probably count on both hands the number of times she'd called him anything but "nephew" and have fingers left over. "'Course you can."

"I don't have much time left."

He looked down and nodded in acknowledgment.

"And you know better than most how I feel about wasting time."

Smiling sadly, he nodded again.

"I need to say a proper good-bye to my husband, but I can't, I *won't*, until you promise me you'll ask her to marry you."

Just because he asked didn't mean Sam would say yes, so what could it hurt, making the promise that seemed so important to Olive.

"Oh, who are you kidding? Of *course* she'll say yes. She's in love with you!" A shuddering sigh escaped her lungs before Olive said, "Let me rephrase it for your thick-headed benefit. I want you to promise *you'll* marry *her.*"

He noticed a strange sparkle in her eyes. Having seen it before—on the battlefield—Bryce knew Olive hadn't been exaggerating when she'd said the end was near. "I promise." Life would be bleak enough without her in it. But facing the future without Sam, too? He didn't even want to think about it.

"Go on, then, skedaddle. And send Duke in here, will you?"

Every muscle in him tensed. Was she…was she saying good-bye…right here and now?

"Don't worry, nephew," Olive said, smiling weakly, "I'll hang on a little longer."

"Promise?"

"Aw, wipe that sad grin off your one-eyed face, will you? I don't want to meet my Maker until everybody I love is right here beside me."

As he made his way from her bed to the door—a distance of perhaps six feet—it felt as though someone had filled his shoes with lead. And in the hall, when he waved Duke closer, it seemed his arms were made of wood.

Duke paused for a long moment, one hand on Bryce's shoulder, as if hoping to sap strength from the younger man. He gave a squeeze, and without looking up, entered Olive's room.

If he was a praying man, Bryce might have asked God to deliver Duke a huge portion of strength and peace. Might have asked the same for himself, too, if he thought for a minute He'd answer. He spotted Sam just then, walking toward him with a little smile on her face even as her big eyes brimmed with concern and love…for *him*. In the short time it took her to get from the water fountain to where he stood, a sense of calm settled over him, and for the first time since he was a boy, Bryce thought maybe, just maybe, God *had* heard his prayer.

And when she came to him and settled into his arms, he knew without a doubt that God had, indeed, answered.

Chapter Twenty-Four

"What? You're joking!" Bryce said, faking a smile for Olive's benefit. "Christians don't get cremated." He glanced at Sam, standing on the other side of his aunt's hospital bed. "Do they?"

Olive gave a helpless shrug. "Some do. This one *will*. And I want my ashes scattered at Forever."

"But…isn't that against some sort of rule? What's the Bible say about it?"

"It says we're to look forward to joining the Lord our God." Olive tried to lever herself up on one elbow to emphasize her point. "This old shell of a body is of no use to Him. It's my *soul* He wants." She lay back, spent and gasping before adding, "Besides, I don't want my flesh and bones becoming worm food."

"Olive, darlin'," Duke said, blue eyes wide in his suntanned face, "please…don't say things like that!"

Despite her weakened condition, she cut him a flirty, mischievous grin. "Sorry, darlin', guess I'm doomed to tell it like it is, right to the bitter end."

Brow furrowed, he shook his salt-and-pepper-haired

head. "How am I supposed to visit you and remember you if—"

"Duke, sweetheart, if you need a tombstone and a grave to remember me," she said, laughing softly, "maybe I didn't make a very big impact on your world after all."

"Aw, Olive," he countered, kissing her forehead, "that isn't what I meant at all. I'll never forget you!" He slumped onto the seat of the chair beside her bed as tears flowed from his eyes. "But where will I lay roses, darlin'?" he all but sobbed. "And where will I go to talk to you when I get to missin' you like I know I will?"

Olive wiggled a finger, beckoning him near. "I'll always be here," she said, touching a fingertip to his chest, "and here," she added, pressing it to his forehead. "And—"

Pain choked off the rest of her words. Grimacing, Olive held her breath, making the seconds that ticked by seem like an hour.

When finally Olive opened her eyes, she grinned. "Scared you, didn't I?" A low, playful chuckle emanated from her as she said, "Don't worry. I'm not leavin' you just yet. I have a few more loose ends to tie up before I meet my Maker." She aimed a forefinger at each of them in turn. "'Ashes to ashes, dust to dust,'" she quoted, "scattered across Forever."

Duke heaved a sad sigh. "So you won't change your mind?"

She shook her head. "Nope. No way."

The increased *beeps* from her heart monitor made it clear the subject had agitated her. It took just one quick glance at the bright green numerals skittering across the screen to inspire Duke's defeated, "I declare, woman, you are the most stubborn female I've ever run across, and I've raised Brahma bulls for half of my life!" Smiling sadly, he patted her hand. "All right then, if that's what you want, that's what you'll get."

He looked to Bryce for approval and agreement. Sam watched an array of emotions flicker across his tortured face before he said, "Well, after all the time and effort she put into that little church of hers over the years, I guess the good Lord won't bar her from Paradise just because she doesn't want a typical burial."

With a sideways nod, Sam invited him to follow her into the hall. "I'm going to the cafeteria for some coffee. Care to join me, Bryce?"

"Sure. I guess."

"Can we get you anything, Duke?"

When his puffy, red-rimmed eyes met hers, Sam could have cried. But the newlyweds needed strength surrounding them, not weakness, and so she smiled.

"No, I'm fine," the big man said. Then he pulled the chair closer to Olive's bed and sandwiched her hand between his own, kissing her knuckles and whispering sweet, soft words.

"What about you, Olive?"

"Cheesecake," she said, licking her lips, "if they have it."

"And if they don't?"

"I'll settle for a big wedge of chocolate cake."

She wouldn't eat it, because the cancer had weakened Olive beyond the capacity to chew and swallow, but Sam aimed to deliver both, anyway. "We won't be long."

"Take your time," Olive called after them. "Duke and I need some cuddle time, anyway."

Sam didn't dare look back, for fear the sight of Duke's agonized expression would cause her to lose her precarious hold on self-control. Besides, Bryce needed her strength every bit as much as the newlyweds did. Neither Sam nor Bryce spoke as they walked toward the elevators. Didn't speak as they waited for the doors to hiss open, either. But once the rumbling car headed for the first floor, he pulled her close and rested his chin on her head.

"Thanks for being here with me," he said, his voice thick with a pent-up sob.

"Can't think of any place I'd rather be." Easy to say, since it was the truth, pure and simple. She loved him, and he loved her. *Here* is where she belonged.

"You want to take a walk?" he said when the doors opened. "I'm not really in the mood for more coffee…"

"That sounds great, because neither am I." It had been nearly two days since either of them had set foot outside. Perhaps some fresh air and sunshine would help him cope with what would happen, possibly very soon.

The hospital grounds seemed serene and beautiful… in direct contradiction to the shape Olive was in. Sam slipped her hand into his and they slowly made their way to a bench.

"I feel so helpless," he said. "She's always done so much for me, and I can't even *think* of something to do for her."

"You're doing the most important thing of all, just being available when she wants to talk to you."

Nodding, Bryce breathed a long heavy sigh. "I have

to admit, Sam, I can't wrap my mind around this crazy cremation idea of hers."

"If it's any comfort," Sam said, "I saw an interview with Billy Graham years ago. When he was asked about it, he quoted 2 Corinthians 5 verse 1, where Paul says that our bodies are like tents that can be taken from place to place, while our resurrected bodies are our permanent homes."

He pressed a kiss to her temple. "Are you always this sane and rational?"

"Absolutely!"

Chuckling, he got to his feet and held out a hand. "Guess we'd better get to the cafeteria, see if there's any cheesecake on the menu."

They headed back inside as the piercing wail of sirens announced the arrival of a new patient in the ER. Sam said a silent prayer for the person in the ambulance, because one thing the world didn't need right now was another family preparing for the death of a loved one.

While he'd served overseas, it had been Olive who'd mailed boxes stuffed with enough shampoo and soap, toilet paper and other hard-to-come-by items to supply Bryce and every soldier in his barracks. At Christmastime, she'd sent decorated sugar cookies, and during the Easter holidays, baskets of candy. The guys came to count on her regular supply of hunting and fishing magazines, John Grisham and Tom Clancy novels, and prepaid calling cards that allowed them to phone their families back home. *She would have been a terrific mother*, Bryce thought. Immediately he corrected himself, because she'd *been* a great mother!

How would he say goodbye to the woman who'd taken a neglected, lonely young boy under her wing and made him feel wanted and loved, unconditionally? How would he face every day, knowing he'd never hear her mellow laughter or look into those sparkling eyes so filled with love…for *him*?

Bryce didn't think he could…without Sam to bolster him. He glanced down at her curly-haired head, amazed that he felt he could lean on someone so small. But he could, and knowing it filled his heart to overflowing with a peculiar mix of love and guilt, because how could he feel joy of *any* kind in light of Olive's ever-failing health?

"I still can't believe it," he said, holding the door for her. "I mean, what's it been, three weeks, and already she's at Death's door? How can that be?"

"I don't know," was her quiet response.

"The doctors said 'months,' not weeks."

Sam's expression said what words needn't: *The doctor said* maybe *she had months…if she was lucky.* Bryce fought the urge to slam his fist into the wall or kick the elevator door—*something* that would help vent his pent-up frustration.

"Better not cry," she advised.

"Why? You think my eye patch will fill up with tears and make weird bubbling noises as they ooze out?"

Passersby wouldn't have thought twice about a couple hugging and crying in the middle of a hospital hallway. But hugging, crying, and *laughing*? That inspired more than a few quizzical stares, which only made them laugh harder. If there was any truth to the theory that laughter alleviated stress, they'd surely eased some in those moments.

"Looks like we're in luck," she said as they entered the cafeteria. "They have cheesecake *and* chocolate cake."

Moments later, they tiptoed into Olive's room.

"It's about time you two got back," she said, opening one eye as a corner of her mouth lifted in a wry grin. "Is that cheesecake you're holding?"

Bryce nodded.

"Somebody get me a fork!"

Duke plucked one from his shirt pocket, and as he peeled away its protective sleeve, Bryce couldn't help thinking what a perfect match Duke and his aunt made, because until now, he'd never met a person who carried disposable flatware and paper napkins "just in case."

He hid a smile as Sam helped Olive shove the fork through the thick, gooey cheesecake, her own mouth opening slightly as she watched Olive bring it to her lips.

"Would you like a sip of water to wash it down?" Sam asked.

"Wash it down? Are you nuts! I want to relish the flavor." And winking, Olive added, "Somethin' tells me I ain't gonna get either of these in heaven!"

Though Duke had put his back to Olive, his lurching shoulders made it obvious that her comment had broken him. Sam's eyes filled with tears, too, and much to his surprise, so did Olive's.

Bryce went to her bedside and kissed her cheek. "I love you, Aunt Olive."

"I know you do, nephew, and I love you, too. Now

step back so I can look into your eyes." With a weak smile, she added, "Correction…your *eye*."

He did as she asked as she added, "You've meant the world to me, and I couldn't have loved you more if you'd been my own flesh-and-blood son." Squeezing his hand, Olive added, "I sure am gonna miss my big tough marine."

"Gonna miss you, too," he choked out.

"Duke, honey," Olive said, "come close, will you, so I don't have to shout?"

Immediately he did as she'd asked.

"You've made me so happy," she said, "marrying me in the autumn of my life. I never thought the good Lord would send me a husband to love, but He did. He *did*!"

"If only we'd had more time."

"We had exactly enough time, darling man. Just exactly enough." Olive glanced around the room, at her husband, at Bryce, at Sam. "I couldn't have asked for more in the last moments of my life than to be surrounded by the people I love most in the world." Reaching for Sam's hand, she said, "Promise me you'll take good care of my nephew?"

"You know I will!"

"It won't always be easy, but I have a feeling you can handle anything that stubborn man dishes out, because you're special, Sammie-girl." Olive paused, closed her eyes, and took a deep shuddering breath. "You know what makes me a little sad?"

"No," Sam admitted as tears streamed down her cheeks.

"That I won't be here to help you get ready for your

wedding. You know, to fuss with your hair and fluff up your veil."

Now Olive met Bryce's eyes. "And you!" she said. "Oh, how I regret not being here to pin a boutonniere on your lapel!"

"Knowing you, you'd stick me with the pin and tell me there'd be worse in store for me if I didn't pay attention during the ceremony."

Her weak, quiet cough punctuated his statement. Bryce wanted to wrap his arms around her and hold her tight, so that maybe some of his own strength would seep into her, give them a few minutes more.

True to form, she read his heart. "No, darlin' boy," she said, "it's time, and it's for the best that I let go now." In a gentle, motherly voice, she added, "I know it doesn't seem like it now, but you're gonna be fine, just fine, because I'm leaving you in very good, very loving hands." Olive punctuated the comment with a slow wink aimed at Sam. "Name one of your kids after me, why don't you...."

Before Sam or Bryce could respond, Olive turned to Duke and said, "Thank you, you big sweet Texan, for making all my dreams come true by loving me."

A serene smile brightened her face. "See you all in Paradise!"

Chapter Twenty-Five

Sam had hardly left Bryce's side since the moments following Olive's death. When she'd finally breathed her last, Sam had been beside him in a heartbeat, arms around him, pressing sweet kisses to his tear-dampened cheek. Her outpouring of love and affection reminded him of the last thing his aunt had said to him. How like Olive, he thought, to reserve her quickly waning strength to make sure he understood that he'd survive this…that he wouldn't be alone once she'd gone.

When Bryce hadn't been able to tell his own tears from Sam's, his sobs had finally abated. She'd helped him to his feet and gently removed his eye patch. "Wow," she'd said, grinning a bit, "it really *does* fill up with tears!"

The quiet chuckle her remark inspired had surprised him. Life would be different without his beloved Olive, but it wouldn't be boring, thanks to Sam.

Bryce had watched as she tenderly led Duke from the room, listened as she promised to help with the arrangements and as she told the older man there was no shame in his tears.

In some of her last words to him, Olive had told
Bryce that she was leaving him in good hands. Now, as
Sam looked up into his face, her blue eyes alight with
love, Bryce realized Olive hadn't just left him in good
hands, she'd left him in *the best* hands.

Sam's hands.

Duke stood between Sam and Bryce at Forever, head
bowed and eyes closed. "Oh, how I wish she hadn't
asked us to do this…"

"I hear ya," Bryce said, "but she didn't leave us much
choice, did she?"

"Just remember what peace it gave her, hearing you
both agree to grant her last wish," Sam said, hoping to
ease any second thoughts they might be having.

Nodding, Duke heaved a shaky sigh. "Well, then,"
he said, removing the lid from the cardboard box con-
taining Olive's remains, "I can only hope St. Paul was
right when he said these bodies of ours are little more
than temporary dwellings where we reside until God
calls us home."

"Like eggshells," Bryce added.

The wind whistled around them, bending the pines
and making it appear they'd bowed in memory of Olive.
An eagle screeched overhead, its dark wide-winged
shadow blanking out the bright sunlight for a blink
in time. A wolf howl was answered by another in the
distance.

"That's odd," Bryce said. "They don't normally do
that at this time of day…."

As if to prove him wrong, a third haunting *ow-
oooooo* pierced the air. Chalky white clouds rolled
through a barely blue sky as the breeze rustled knee-

high grasses that ringed the overlook. Finally, the robust trumpeting of a bull moose completed the wild symphony.

"If she told me once," Duke said, "she told me a dozen times what that sound could do to a man, and by golly, she was right. Every hair on my head is bristlin'!"

The next sound didn't come from nature, but from Sam, rifling through her pocket to find the envelope Olive had given her just days before her death. Bryce looked over her shoulder and read the familiar script: *To be read atop Forever.*

It was a balmy September day, and even Sam, who hadn't yet experienced a North Pole winter, understood they should be grateful that they hadn't needed to tramp through a foot of snow to reach this amazing place. A puff of air riffled the page, almost stealing it from her fingers as she slid it from its matching envelope. Heart pounding, Sam thanked God it hadn't blown away and squeezed it tighter between her thumbs and forefingers. *Lord, let me get through this without choking up.* She cleared her throat and began:

"'So there you stand, the three of you, side by side in my favorite place, where the human voice is a strange and unwelcome sound. You can't hear a radio there, can't get a cell phone call or television reception, praise the Lord!

"'I can think of no better way to experience heaven than to know that my soul and body will both rest for eternity in Paradise—one with our heavenly Father, and the other right here in His heavenly creation.

"'When you miss me, my loves, just come here and fill your lungs with clean air and feast your eyes on wild rivers and rugged mountains, on creatures most folks only see at the zoo, and remember how at peace I am to be a part of it all.

"'I will love you all more than words could express… forever. Olive.'"

Sam finished on a deep, ragged breath, and then she folded the note and returned it to its envelope. Strange, she thought, that while tears shimmered in Duke and Bryce's eyes, neither felt a need to cry or sob as they had in Olive's hospital room on the day she died. Instead, a quietude settled upon them. Indeed, the entire area Olive had named Forever had gone utterly still and silent.

Bryce and Duke took turns flicking the box that bore her remains, and then the trio stared in stunned awe as the silvery dust cloud mingled with a whiff of wind before vanishing into a small puff.

"Goodbye, sweet Olive," Duke said, putting his back to the beautiful vista as he trudged toward the car.

Nodding, Bryce followed, glancing once over his shoulder.

Only Sam remained, still clutching the envelope that held Olive's last words.

"Rest in peace, Olive Stone," she whispered, "with the Almighty and His angels."

"Amen," Bryce said, hugging her from behind. "Amen."

Chapter Twenty-Six

"Hard to believe it's been three months since Olive died," Bryce said, slipping an arm around Sam's waist. "I don't think she'd recognize the place."

"I hope she'd be proud," Sam said, smiling. "What the store looks like now is all thanks to that crazy list of hers."

Chuckling, Bryce kissed the top of her head. "She was a list-making nut, wasn't she?"

"I'll say! I'll bet I found a couple hundred of them while going through the desk and file cabinets."

"God rest her beautiful soul. She was great at writing lists, but not too great with the follow-through. It took you to make it all happen, you little dynamo."

"I'm just happy the place is turning a profit now." She faced him and added, "Think maybe now it'll sell, so you can open your carpentry shop?"

A quiet grunt was her answer, and Sam didn't quite know what to make of it. She kept her questions to herself, though, because it was obvious that he'd made a concerted effort not to wallow in grief or self-pity. Quite the contrary, in fact… "So how'd you and Duke make out at the B and B today?"

"It's finished, finally."

"So he can open for business in the spring, just as he and Olive planned?"

Bryce groaned quietly. "I don't know. Something tells me he'll pack up and head back to Texas soon."

"Oh, that'd be a shame!" Sam said. "But…I can't blame him, really. He doesn't know us all that well, and we're all the family he has here. And besides, everywhere he turns, there are reminders of Olive and the life they might have had together." She sighed. "It just breaks my heart, watching him wander around like a lost lamb."

Bryce nodded.

"So," she began, changing the subject, "when are you planning to make good on your promise?"

"Which one?" he asked, his heart suddenly pounding.

"You said you'd show me the aurora borealis in September, if the weather cooperated." Arms akimbo, she added, "And it's November already!"

Bryce chuckled. "So it is." And glancing at his watch, he said, "What are you doing tonight?"

"Oh, please. You know better than anyone what I'm doing tonight."

The brow above his eye patch rose slightly as he considered her comment. "I do?"

"I'll be with you, of course, somewhere north of town, watching the aurora!"

And hours later, at two in the morning and bundled in a thick quilt on the hood of his car, Sam and Bryce leaned on the windshield and stared into a sky that seemed to throb and pulse with life.

"I don't know if I've ever seen anything as beautiful!"

"That's what you said when I showed you Forever."

"Well, that's a whole different kind of beautiful. This," she said, pointing to the waving, undulating green lights above, "this is just...well, it's a miracle is what it is!"

"I've seen it hundreds of times, and I have to admit, it never gets old." He gave her a quick, sideways hug. "You ought to feel really special."

"I always feel special when I'm with you."

Laughing, he mussed her hair. "No, goofy girl, I mean because the skies are putting on such a great show for you. September really *is* the best time to see it, so we lucked out big time, catching a display like this in November. We couldn't have picked a more perfect night... clear and dark, with a full bright moon."

"I'll admit, I hoped we'd see more colors."

"We might have...in September. But shades of green and gold are the norm. Once in a while, if you're lucky, you'll get a glimpse of red and yellow or purple and blue."

"Well, it's amazing, positively amazing!" She sighed. "I hate to admit it, but I'm cold."

"So I noticed, icy nose," he said, kissing her. "Want to head back?"

"Guess we'd better. I have a group of schoolkids coming to the shop tomorrow. Field trip of sorts, so they can buy ornaments and whatnot as Christmas gifts."

"Did you hear there's gonna be a TV crew in town tomorrow?"

"Yeah" she said. "They're supposed to film the field trip. And when I was at Dalman's the other day, having coffee with Cora, I heard they're filming the Santa Claus House and the Christmas museum, and if there's time, they'll even take a trip on the train. Exciting, huh?"

Bryce held open his pickup's passenger door. "Um, I guess."

"Not everybody in town shares your attitude, Mr. Scrooge." With that, she closed the door.

And as he slid in behind the wheel, he said, "Pardon me if my enthusiasm doesn't runneth over."

"To each his own," she said, giving him a playful jab to the shoulder. "You leave me no choice but to enjoy all these Christmas festivities enough for both of us."

They were home before she knew it, and Sam wondered aloud how productive she'd be in a few hours, with so little sleep.

"You're a buzzing ball of energy," he told her. "If the electricity goes out tomorrow, the film crew can always plug into you and run their cameras for hours."

"Always the comedian." Then, as an afterthought, Sam said, "Pity you can't conjure a little of that attitude about Christmas."

He opened his mouth to protest, but Sam laid a finger over his lips, preventing it. "See you in the morning," she said, popping a quick kiss to his lips. And hurrying into her own apartment, she waved over her shoulder. "Sweet dreams, Bryce!"

"Oh, they'll be sweet, all right, but only because you're bound to be in them."

Sam handed the TV host a steaming mug of home-made cocoa topped off with whipped cream and a cherry. "You look frozen to the bone," she told her. "Hopefully, this'll warm you up."

Grinning, Melody Malone wrapped her mittened hands around it. "What are you, a mind reader?" she teased.

Laughing, Sam handed a second mug to the cameraman.

"John O'Toole," he said. "Happy to meet you. And thanks for the cup o' heat."

Sam grinned. "There's plenty more where that came from. Think the rest of the crew might like a cup?"

"No question in my mind. We're Californians," John said, "totally unaccustomed to this kind of cold."

Laughing, Sam said, "I'm from Maryland myself. This is my first winter here, and so far, it's been a doozy."

"I assumed the place was covered in ice and snow pretty much all year."

"That's what most people think. I got here in May, and believe it or not, by the middle of June, I was wishing my apartment had air conditioning."

"Maryland, eh," John said. "So what brought you to North Pole?"

The memory of her breakup with Joey flashed in her head, followed by her brothers and parents chorusing, "You're going *where*?"

"Work *brought* me here, but the place and the people

are magnetic. I can't seem to tear myself away. I manage Rudolph's Christmas Emporium," she said, pointing at the storefront. "That guy over there, chatting with Melody in front of the Santa Claus House, is Bryce Stone, the owner."

John chuckled. "Is that patch for real?"

"It is. Earned in Afghanistan."

"Well, if Tinsel Town ever revives cowboy westerns, he's in like Flynn with an eye patch and a name like Bryce Stone!"

It *was* a powerful name, Sam thought, watching him. But why not? He was a powerful man, and—

"So do you think you'll stay in North Pole?"

Sam nodded. "Definitely."

"That's no surprise. I heard how you turned that little store into a thriving business in just a couple of months."

"Who spilled the beans?"

"Curt, the barber. Amazing how much that guy knows about this town…and everybody in it." John stood and handed Sam his empty mug. "Well, I'd better get back over there," he said. "Looks like Melody's ready to start. What time does your field trip begin?"

She glanced at the nearest clock…a red-and-green elf whose hammer moved up and down in time with the second hand. "Fifteen, twenty minutes. But I'm sure they won't mind waiting. It isn't every day they get a chance to be on a national TV show."

"Don't worry," John said, waving as his boots hit the snow-covered walk, "we'll be on time. I'll make sure of it."

As it turned out, John was a man of his word. Melody and the crew squeezed into Rudolph's to film the kids as they shopped for their families' Christmas gifts. Sam couldn't help but wonder, as John's camera panned the shelves, how *her* family would feel, finding out this way that she managed the place. Maybe Bill had let it slip, once he got back home, that she'd been passed over for the chef's job and taken this one to keep the wolf from the door. *And maybe you should make a phone call, today, so they won't be shocked when friends and neighbors call to say, 'Hey, I saw your daughter on that house and garden channel!'"*

"That's a wrap," the director announced. "Have you lined things up with that guy at the Santa Claus House?" he asked Melody.

"Only thing missing is you," she said, grinning. Grabbing her fur parka, the host shrugged one arm into it, then the other. "I don't know how you manage it, day after day, year after year," she said to Sam. "Being Alaskan is…well, it's *cold,* that's what!"

"I can't say yet that I 'manage it.' This is my first winter here. I might not be cut out for it."

Melody gave Sam a quick once-over. "Oh, something tells me you're gonna do just fine. In fact—"

"She's more than cut out for this life."

Everyone turned toward the deep, resonant voice. "Bryce," Sam said, smiling. "How long have you been standing there?"

"Long enough." And as the TV crew and schoolkids filed out of the shop, he slipped his arms around her waist. "Promise me somethin', will ya?"

"Depends…"

"Don't ever go all Hollywood on me, okay?"

Giggling, she said, "But I thought you liked your girls tall and willowy, blond and green-eyed."

His brow furrowed. "She has green eyes?"

Sam gave his shoulder a playful slap. "Oh, please. The way you were staring at her during the interview, I'd think you could tell me how many eyelashes there are on each lid!"

Bryce kissed her forehead, a long, lingering kiss that sent Sam's heart into overdrive.

"I guess she's okay…in a too much makeup and hair-spray kinda way." And holding her at arm's length, he added, "But she's nowhere near as gorgeous as you."

"Aw, I bet you say that to all the—"

A scream, followed closely by a ruckus outside, interrupted them, and they raced to the door. "Holy moley," Bryce said, "somebody let the reindeer loose!"

They ran to the Santa Claus House, where a small crowd had gathered around Melody, who lay flat on her back in the snow.

"What happened?" Bryce asked.

"She thought it would be cool to 'interview' the reindeer," the shopkeeper explained. "I warned her they didn't much cotton to all this noise and activity, but she said something about Snow White genes."

"Snow White—"

"All animals love her," Paul explained, rolling his eyes.

The host scrambled to her feet and, giggling, asked Sam, "Any idea how to get reindeer poo out of fur?" But before Sam could answer, she said to John, "You got that on film, I hope…."

"Does Santa wear a red hat?"

"Whew," she said, fanning her face. "We'll need to do a voice-over, but that's gonna be a hoot for our viewers!"

"Have the reindeer escaped before?" Sam asked Paul.

"Couple times, but they'll make their way back. They always do…eventually."

She glanced down the street, where a couple of them pawed the snowy ground in search of grass. Grinning, she nudged him with an elbow. "And if they don't, will you have to round up a posse to herd 'em home?"

"What bus did this tenderfooted Easterner ride into town?"

he asked Bryce.

"It wasn't a bus," Sam corrected, "it was a—"

Thankfully, Paul and the others were too preoccupied with herding the animals back into their pen to notice when Bryce planted a big juicy kiss on her lips. "Promise me something else?" he asked.

"What…?"

"That you'll never *ever* aim that big ugly RV of yours east again."

"If I survive the rest of the winter, you're stuck with me."

Chapter Twenty-Seven

"Oh, Bryce, it's absolutely beautiful!" Sam sat on the glossy seat of the rocking chair he'd made her.

"There's a message for you, burned into the underside of the seat."

Hopping up, she tilted the chair on its side and read aloud, "'To Sam, my one and only, now and forever, Bryce.'" After returning the rocker to its upright position, she said, "It's one of the best birthday gifts I've ever received." Hugging him, she added, "Thanks, Bryce."

"Well, I had to do something extra special, considering I missed your actual birthday by a couple of months."

"You were a little preoccupied," she admitted, "with Olive in the hospital and all."

"Still, I—"

"Still nothing!" she interrupted. "What's that old saying? 'Better late than never'?" If only she could convince herself to adopt that viewpoint about his so-far-non-existent marriage proposal... "*Your* birthday is right around the corner, and we'll get to celebrate that right on time."

His grin reminded her of the little boys who'd traipsed through Rudolph's last week, eyes wide with wonderment as they chose gifts for their parents and siblings. "You're okay with a triple-layer chocolate cake, aren't you?" she asked.

"Well, sure. Who wouldn't be?" He hesitated and then added, "You're not planning a whole big thing, I hope, 'cause I hate a fuss."

"Guess you'll just have to wait until tonight," she told him, grinning, "to find out just how big—or little—a fuss I've made."

"Not a party," he said, slapping a hand over his eyes. "Please tell me it isn't a party."

"Patience," she said, "because in just a few hours, you'll know for sure."

Wincing, he shook his head. "Samantha Sinclair, what am I gonna do with you?"

Ask me to marry you, you big oaf, she thought, *that's what!*

"You'd better get baking," he said, kissing each corner of her mouth, "because you woke a sleeping monster with all your chocolate cake talk."

When she didn't react, Bryce turned her around, lifted her off her feet, and deposited her on the next step up from the landing. "I wasn't kidding, woman," he added, his voice deepening an octave. "Go. Now. Kitchen."

He clapped his hands as she raced up the stairs, giggling like a giddy child. Oh, she'd bake him a cake, all right. And wouldn't he be surprised when he bit into her very special present to him!

As the cake baked, Sam tidied her apartment, showered, and spent far more time than normal trying to figure out what to wear to their private birthday dinner.

She did her best to set a pretty table, considering how few of the dishes matched, but Sam wasn't worried about his reaction to it. One of the best things about growing up in a houseful of boys was knowing they didn't give a whit about things like that...if they noticed them at all.

It was far more important to take care while frosting the cake, so she'd know which slice held his special surprise. Every time she imagined how he'd look once his fork poked into the plastic bag, it was all she could do to keep from squealing. Part of her wished she'd prepared a simpler supper, one that would be over quickly, instead of soup and salad and rolls, all made from scratch, that would precede her Italian specialty, stuffed shells. He'd promised to knock off work by five so that he'd have time to shower and change for their dinner at six. In an hour, two at most, he'd have tangible proof of how much she loved him and what she was willing to sacrifice to prove it. Maybe with that knowledge tucked into his thick marine skull, he'd be inspired to pop the question.

She looked at the cake. At the perfectly set table. At the coffeepot, all set and ready to go. "Well, a girl can dream," she whispered. But rather than take chances, Sam headed for the living room and grabbed her Bible. What better way to pass these remaining minutes than by reading God's word?

Just as she'd expected, spending time with the Lord calmed her and hurried the hands of time. When at last she heard Bryce's gentle knock on the other side of the kitchen door, her heart leaped into her throat. "Help me, Father," she said, "not to spoil everything by blurting out his surprise...."

Two hours later, when Bryce shoved himself away from the table, she nearly cried when he patted his belly and said, "I'm just way too full for dessert."

"But it's your birthday," she protested. "You have to at least have a *bite* of cake." She didn't wait for him to agree or disagree. Instead, Sam gathered up the supper dishes and stacked them in the sink. And because the kitchen hadn't come equipped with dessert plates, she used saucers.

"If I didn't know better," he said, chuckling as he watched her distribute them, "I'd say you were a dealer in Vegas in a former life."

Sam put the cake on the table and lit the fat candle in the middle of it. And with no fanfare, she launched into a super-speedy rendition of the birthday song. "Now make a wish," she instructed.

"I'm a little old for stuff like that, don't you think?"

"Humor me."

While he closed his eyes, Sam tapped a foot.

"Happy now?" he asked.

"I will be, soon as you blow out the candle—"

"Sam..."

"—so your wish will come true."

And even before the wisp of smoke curled toward the ceiling, she'd carved off an enormous wedge of cake and plopped it onto his plate.

"Good grief," he sputtered, opening them, "have you mistaken me for the Jolly Green Giant?" Pointing, he said, "Surely you don't think I can eat that whole—"

"Humor me," she said again.

He picked up his fork and used it as a pointer. "You're behaving mighty strangely tonight. More so than usual. It had better not mean there's a crowd of well-wishers on their way over here to sing 'Happy Birthday' *slowly…*"

"You said no fanfare, so you have my word. No party."

"Well, good," he said, slicing into the wedge, "because I—"

Sam held her breath.

"Hey…there's something…there's *plastic* in my cake!" Bryce speared it with the tines of his fork. "What…? Did you put this in there?" he asked, holding it above the plate.

Sam nodded.

"Why in the world would you shove a sandwich bag into the middle of my birthday cake?" he asked, snickering.

"You'll see."

He gave it a closer look. "Hey, wait a minute. There's something in it.…"

Sam's heart was pounding so hard, she thought surely it would explode. How long did it take a guy to open a zipper bag and withdraw a little envelope? she wondered, grabbing a wet dishcloth so he could wipe fudge icing from his fingers. Would he hate the gift? Love it? Think it was too much, too soon in their relationship? A ghastly thought made the breath catch in her throat. What if he saw it as an insult…like she thought he wasn't capable of—

"Samantha Sinclair!" he blurted, interrupting her worries, "is this what I think it is?"

She gulped. "What do you think it is?"

"A check." He looked from the slip of paper to her face and back again. "A big *fat* check." Without wiping his fingers, he grabbed her hand. "Sam, I don't get it. What's it—"

"It's so you can buy all the machines and tools you'll need to open your furniture shop." She reached behind her and gave him the file folder where she'd stored orders for end tables, rocking chairs, chifforobes, taken while waiting on customers at Rudolph's.

He looked inside and figured out instantly what it held. He picked up the check again, and this time looked from it to the thin stack of orders. "Where did you get this much money?"

Shrugging, she smiled. "I sold the RV."

"But…I thought you had plans for that money…to open a little catering business…"

"My goodness, that aunt of yours had a memory like an elephant! I only mentioned in passing, while we were unpacking a shipment, that someday I'd like to put my cooking skills to use. You know, just for side money." She shrugged again. "I can't believe she remembered it, let alone that she shared it with you!"

"So why am *I* holding this check, if that was supposed to fund *your* dream?"

Sam got to her feet, waved both hands as a signal for him to scoot his chair back, and when he did, she plopped onto his lap. "It wasn't a dream, I was just, you know, thinking out loud. Olive had just finished telling me about Duke and all their plans, and then she asked me if *I* had any silly dreams like that."

He put his forefinger on the check. "But now that you have the money…"

"I don't *want* a catering business, silly, I want you to have your carpentry shop. Don't you get it?"

Frowning and smiling at the same time, Bryce said, "No, I guess I don't. Why would you sacrifice your dream to give me mine?"

She bracketed his face with both hands. "Maybe," she said, kissing his right cheek, then his left, "because I know your dream means a whole lot more to you than mine ever did to me." She kissed his forehead, his chin, his lips. "And maybe, because I love you that much."

He looked at the check again. "Sam, I can't let you—"

"You aren't *letting* me, mister. These aren't the dark ages. Even married women get to decide a few things for themselves nowadays!"

One corner of his mouth lifted in a slow grin. "Married women?"

She heaved a huge sigh. "Lord, give me strength," she said, staring at the ceiling. She removed his eye patch and tossed it onto the table. "You love me, right?"

"More than life itself."

"And you know that I love you, right?"

Bryce nodded. "Hard not to, when you're always doing stuff like this for me."

"So the money isn't really mine, then, is it? It's *ours*. And I happen to think a carpentry shop will bring in just enough extra cash to help us afford, oh…." She looked left and right, as if trying to find what they'd be able to afford written on a wall. And pressing her forehead to his, Sam finished with, "We'll be able to afford diapers, and a high chair, a crib and changing table.... I don't want to wait years and years to have a baby. I want to start a family right away. Just as soon as we're..."

It dawned on her, suddenly, that Bryce still hadn't asked her to marry him, and the fact, like a cold slap to the face, silenced her. The heat of embarrassment flooded her cheeks, and she hid them behind both hands.

"On your feet, elf," he barked.

The instant she stood, he did, too. "Now, sit down, and for the love of Pete, please be quiet for five minutes, will you?"

Sam did as he asked, her heart nearly bursting with joy when he got down onto one knee and sandwiched her left hand between both of his.

"I don't know why I've been putting this off," he admitted, kissing her knuckles. "Guess I was waiting for just the right moment." He looked deep into her eyes and said, "I think maybe this is that moment." After kissing the tip of her nose, he added, "There's a little something for you in my shirt pocket."

Too flat, she thought, to hold one of those little velvet ring boxes, so it couldn't be an engagement ring.

"Go on," he urged. "I don't want to turn loose of your hand to fish it out of there myself."

A tiny gasp popped from her lips when she withdrew a diamond-encrusted gold band.

"I didn't figure you for the big rock type, so I got this

instead." Bryce took it from her and started sliding it over her left ring finger, stopping at the first knuckle. "Samantha Sinclair, will you do me the great honor of becoming my wife?"

Tears welled up in her eyes and rolled down her cheeks as she threw her arms around his neck. "Hooboy," she said past the sob in her throat, "you sure do know how to scare a girl."

Hands on her shoulders, he held her at arm's distance. "Scare a girl?"

"I didn't think you were *ever* going to ask me to marry you!" She kissed him. Hard. Then held out her hand so he could finish sliding the ring onto her finger.

"Not so fast, missy," he said, slipping it off and dropping it back into his pocket. "That's a *wedding band*, not an engagement ring." He gave the pocket two quick pats. "You want that baby," he said, choking back tears, "you'll have to marry me first."

"There's a calendar in that drawer behind you," she said, pointing over his shoulder.

"Who needs a calendar? Marry me on Saturday."

"*This* Saturday?"

"Sure, why not?"

"It's the big ice-sculpting competition in town. Nobody will be available to perform the ceremony!"

Bryce nodded. "Good point. So…Sunday then?"

Her heart did a flip-flop in her chest. "Sunday it is."

"Does that give you time to round up a poufy white dress and tiny satin shoes and a gauzy veil that I can lift before we seal the deal?"

"Good thing for you I'm not the big rock type *or* the poufy dress type, because there's no way I could do all that in just a few days." She winked. "But I do have time to call my folks, so let's just pray these crazy plans of ours aren't too last-minute for them to fly in for the wedding."

"It won't be."

She narrowed both eyes. "You seem awfully sure of yourself...."

"They'll be here on Thursday. It's all arranged."

"But...*tomorrow* is Thursday!"

"Hmm, so it is."

"But...how'd you know I'd say yes?"

Bryce kissed her, and she put everything she had into it. "*That's* how."

Epilogue

Bryce and Sam stood toe to toe at the entrance of the Santa Claus House amid the fresh blanket of snow God had delivered the night before. Her parents and brothers and most citizens of North Pole—wearing down-filled parkas, fat mittens, and fur-lined boots—formed a tight circle around the soon-to-be bride and groom.

Breath-smoke puffed from Pastor Davidson's mouth as he said, "Repeat after me. 'I, Samantha Sinclair, do solemnly vow....'"

"I, Thamantha Thinclair, do tholemnly vow..."

Curt the barber leaned toward the pastor's wife. "Why's she lisping?" he whispered. "I never noticed before that Sam had a lisp...."

"Because," the woman said, "that silly girl took a dare."

"A dare?" He glanced at Sam, who'd just tugged her fur-trimmed hood farther to the front of her head. "What sort of dare?"

"Well," she began, "she and Bryce were working on the reindeer sculpture they entered in the Christmas in Ice contest, you see, and they got to joking about that movie…you know the one, where the little boy gets his tongue stuck on a frozen flagpole?"

"No, but go on."

"You're joking. I thought *everyone* had seen that one. It's one of the funniest, cutest—"

"Carol," Curt reminded gently, "the dare?"

"Oh. Yes." She snickered behind one leather-gloved hand. "Well, you see—and who knew Bryce could be such a card!—he told Sam it wasn't just a movie trick, that tongues really could get stuck to flagpoles. But Sam said it had to be a Hollywood stunt of some kind. So he dared her to stick her tongue on one of their ice-reindeer's antlers, to see for herself."

Curt gawked at Sam again. "Don't tell me she actually *did* it?"

"Yes, she actually *did* it!" she said, hiding again behind her gloved hand.

"Aw, just my bad luck…I was in the shop and missed all the fun!"

"Oh, don't worry, you'll see it in living color. It was all captured on film, don't you know. The newspapers were here covering the event, just like they do every year. Along with a film crew from that decorating show." Her giggle was muffled by the mitten. "The director told me the show will air tomorrow."

"But tomorrow is Christmas Day!"

"Exactly."

"Seems to me they should have won first prize for that alone."

Carol laughed as Pastor Davidson quirked a brow in his wife's direction. "Goodness," she whispered, "I've been caught jabbering during a church service again!"

She and Curt faced the makeshift altar of polished ice that had been carved by the pastor himself in preparation for the ceremony.

"I now pronounce you man and wife," he said. "Bryce, you may kiss your bride."

Cheers rose from the small crowd as one voice called out, "Don't kiss her too long in this weather, marine, or you'll stick to her like she stuck to that reindeer!"

Laughter echoed up and down the street as Gene Autry sang "Rudolph the Red-Nosed Reindeer," right on cue.

* * * * *

REQUEST YOUR FREE BOOKS!

2 FREE RIVETING INSPIRATIONAL NOVELS
PLUS 2 FREE MYSTERY GIFTS

Love Inspired®
SUSPENSE

REQUEST YOUR FREE BOOKS!

2 FREE INSPIRATIONAL NOVELS
PLUS 2
FREE
MYSTERY GIFTS

Love Inspired

HISTORICAL
INSPIRATIONAL HISTORICAL ROMANCE

YES! Please send me 2 FREE Love Inspired® Historical novels and my 2 FREE mystery gifts (gifts are worth about $10). After receiving them, if I don't wish to receive any more books, I can return the shipping statement marked "cancel." If I don't cancel, I will receive 4 brand-new novels every month and be billed just $4.74 per book in the U.S. or $5.24 per book in Canada. That's a savings of at least 21% off the cover price. It's quite a bargain! Shipping and handling is just 50¢ per book in the U.S. and 75¢ per book in Canada.* I understand that accepting the 2 free books and gifts places me under no obligation to buy anything. I can always return a shipment and cancel at any time. Even if I never buy another book, the two free books and gifts are mine to keep forever.

102/302 IDN F5CY

Name	(PLEASE PRINT)
Address	Apt. #
City	State/Prov.	Zip/Postal Code

Signature (if under 18, a parent or guardian must sign)

Mail to the **Harlequin® Reader Service:**
IN U.S.A.: P.O. Box 1867, Buffalo, NY 14240-1867
IN CANADA: P.O. Box 609, Fort Erie, Ontario L2A 5X3

Want to try two free books from another series?
Call 1-800-873-8635 or visit www.ReaderService.com.

* Terms and prices subject to change without notice. Prices do not include applicable taxes. Sales tax applicable in N.Y. Canadian residents will be charged applicable taxes. Offer not valid in Quebec. This offer is limited to one order per household. Not valid for current subscribers to Love Inspired Historical books. All orders subject to credit approval. Credit or debit balances in a customer's account(s) may be offset by any other outstanding balance owed by or to the customer. Please allow 4 to 6 weeks for delivery. Offer available while quantities last.

Your Privacy—The Harlequin® Reader Service is committed to protecting your privacy. Our Privacy Policy is available online at www.ReaderService.com or upon request from the Harlequin Reader Service.

We make a portion of our mailing list available to reputable third parties that offer products we believe may interest you. If you prefer that we not exchange your name with third parties, or if you wish to clarify or modify your communication preferences, please visit us at www.ReaderService.com/consumerschoice or write to us at Harlequin Reader Service Preference Service, P.O. Box 9062, Buffalo, NY 14269. Include your complete name and address.

LIHDIR13R

REQUEST YOUR FREE BOOKS!

2 FREE WHOLESOME ROMANCE NOVELS IN LARGER PRINT

PLUS 2 FREE MYSTERY GIFTS

HEARTWARMING™

Wholesome, tender romances

YES! Please send me 2 FREE Harlequin® Heartwarming Larger-Print novels and my 2 FREE mystery gifts (gifts worth about $10). After receiving them, if I don't wish to receive any more books, I can return the shipping statement marked "cancel." If I don't cancel, I will receive 4 brand-new larger-print novels every month and be billed just $4.99 per book in the U.S. or $5.74 per book in Canada. That's a savings of at least 23% off the cover price. It's quite a bargain! Shipping and handling is just 50¢ per book in the U.S. and 75¢ per book in Canada.* I understand that accepting the 2 free books and gifts places me under no obligation to buy anything. I can always return a shipment and cancel at any time. Even if I never buy another book, the two free books and gifts are mine to keep forever.

161/361 IDN F47N

Name	(PLEASE PRINT)	
Address		Apt. #
City	State/Prov.	Zip/Postal Code

Signature (if under 18, a parent or guardian must sign)

Mail to the **Harlequin® Reader Service:**
IN U.S.A.: P.O. Box 1867, Buffalo, NY 14240-1867
IN CANADA: P.O. Box 609, Fort Erie, Ontario L2A 5X3

* Terms and prices subject to change without notice. Prices do not include applicable taxes. Sales tax applicable in N.Y. Canadian residents will be charged applicable taxes. Offer not valid in Quebec. This offer is limited to one order per household. Not valid for current subscribers to Harlequin Heartwarming larger-print books. All orders subject to credit approval. Credit or debit balances in a customer's account(s) may be offset by any other outstanding balance owed by or to the customer. Please allow 4 to 6 weeks for delivery. Offer available while quantities last.

Your Privacy—The Harlequin® Reader Service is committed to protecting your privacy. Our Privacy Policy is available online at www.ReaderService.com or upon request from the Harlequin Reader Service.

We make a portion of our mailing list available to reputable third parties that offer products we believe may interest you. If you prefer that we not exchange your name with third parties, or if you wish to clarify or modify your communication preferences, please visit us at www.ReaderService.com/consumerchoice or write to us at Harlequin Reader Service Preference Service, P.O. Box 9062, Buffalo, NY 14269. Include your complete name and address.

HWDIR13

REQUEST YOUR FREE BOOKS!

2 FREE CHRISTIAN NOVELS
PLUS 2
FREE
MYSTERY GIFTS

HEARTSONG

PRESENTS

ReaderService.com

Manage your account online!

- Review your order history
- Manage your payments
- Update your address

---

*We've designed
the Harlequin® Reader Service
website just for you.*

Enjoy all the features!

- Reader excerpts from any series
- Respond to mailings and special monthly offers
- Discover new series available to you
- Browse the Bonus Bucks catalog
- Share your feedback

Visit us at:
ReaderService.com

RS1